COLCHICUM- a cure fc

DEDICATION

To my lovely husband

To Alice,
with love
from
Glenis
xx

INTRODUCTION

My intention was to write a book which gives insight into the way medical research sometimes works, whilst telling a love story, in fact several stories of different kinds of love.

Many readers will empathise with the situation in which Lila finds herself and her mother, but will be out of sympathy with animal experimentation. I understand, being an animal lover myself. However without the highly-regulated and careful use of animals only when there is no good alternative medical research would find it hard to progress. One day it will be anachronistic- the sooner the better.

The experience of dementia, either personally or in a loved one, can be horrendous. One would do anything, or almost anything, to make it go away.

To those of you who are carers for a demented loved one I have to state that the subject matter of this novel is wish - fulfilment for me. Colchicum and its product colchicine are not cures for dementia. However old drugs can sometimes find new uses: for example the trials of hydroxychloroquine in COVID-19. Here's hoping that someone will stumble upon one useful in neurodegeneration.

CHAPTER 1

London, 2017.

She let the sensations take her: the long downhill swoop, the wind chilling her face, no need to do anything but balance and enjoy the ride. Then, as the gradient levelled out, the bike slowed, reality returned and she had to pedal to keep moving. Moments of freedom like that, she thought, were rare now. Her life had become so circumscribed by her mother's illness, the need to succeed at work, to earn enough to support them both, that pleasure was an alien concept. She pushed harder and faster, determined to clear enough distance between her and a following car so that she could get to the road centre and turn right. Pressing the small switch in her right glove made the chain of outdoor lights sewn onto the back of her waterproof jacket illuminate, giving an arrow pointing right. Lila was proud of her invention, made from her mother's Christmas gift. It was so much safer than shoving out her right arm. The car driver was not impressed, he accelerated to catch up and overtake Lila. Infuriated she swung in front of him and leaned into a sharp right turn, just clearing his bonnet. Brakes screeched and Lila could imagine, but not actually discern, what he was shouting at her. An alleyway on the left allowed her escape from any pursuit and acted as a short cut to her hospital. She arrived panting, sweaty and shaking, but less angry than when she had left home.

Later that morning her phone vibrated again, the third time. Lila knew she ought to answer, it was almost certainly Mum. She had ignored the first two calls whilst pipetting out her reagents and was now in the process of drawing up the first syringe.

"Shannon," the young blonde seated on a stool beside her failed to respond, still gazing at her own mobile.

"Shannon, please answer my phone." Lila spoke more loudly. Shannon jumped.

"Sorry, I was miles away."

She picked up Lila's phone, swiped the face and held it close to Lila's ear.

It was Mary Dewhurst.

"Hello Mary"

"Oh Lila! I am so sorry to bother you at work, but Grace is insisting on speaking to you. She says she hasn't seen you today and she is worried. Is it OK if I put her on?"

"Of course... Hello Mum."

The well-loved, but quavery voice came faintly through the device:

"Oh! my darling, I was so worried about you. Are you all right?"

"Yes Mum, I'm fine. I had to get in early this morning as I have a very busy day, so I didn't bring you your cuppa in bed or make you breakfast. I'm sorry. I'm sure Mrs. Dewhurst is looking after though."

"Oh yes, she has been very good to me. I think that she made me breakfast"

"I'm sure she did, and you'll have your lunch soon. I'll be home in time to do supper and we can watch TV together then."

"That'll be nice."

"It will, Mum. I'll see you later then, got to go now. Lots of love. Bye."

"Bye sweetheart."

Lila nodded to Shannon to put the phone down, then asked her to switch it off. She could not afford further interruptions which were likely if it was one of her Mum's bad days. Lila settled back on her stool, picked up the syringe from the beaker and started methodically giving injections one by one into the abdomen of each of six mice from the cage in front of her, transferring each mouse to an adjacent empty cage once treated.

"Do you understand what I am doing?" she asked. Shannon, known as Shan to her friends, nodded.

"You are trying out the stuff that worked in test tubes in real mice now."

"Yes. The initial data in tissue sections suggests that this molecule might work in dementia- so now we move on to work in animals. If that is successful there will be trials in man. I am using the new molecule from

Immunogenomics at several different doses, plus control molecules, six mice treated with each one. In any experiment there must be appropriate controls: one will be a placebo, others might be a verum, that is molecules that are known to work in that system."

"What's a placebo?"

"It is a substance which has no therapeutic effect, used so any natural variation in symptoms can be assessed and subtracted from the benefit given by the test medicine."

"Oh, thanks." Shan returned to the intensive study of her mobile phone. Lila sighed inwardly. Why did she get given the new technicians to teach? It slowed her down and irritated her, especially when they were like Shan, more concerned with Instagram than the progress of science.

Then her thoughts turned to the message from her own phone. When did Mum started to show signs of dementia? With hindsight, Lila realised the early signs were there, perhaps as long as 5 years ago. Over that winter, Grace had taken to drinking a little more, though still only at dinner, and her palate had changed - she wouldn't finish her main course, but would never forego dessert, often followed by a chocolate from the cupboard above the fridge. She'd put on weight for the first time, though not a great deal. But of course, this didn't ring any alarm bells at the time, particularly as Grace had only retired early in July that same year and might just have been letting-go and indulging a little, or perhaps she was just a bit bored.

But by the following spring there was undeniably a problem. Grace became increasingly anxious about money, not something that had troubled her much in life. Not that she'd been rich - though equally she'd never been very poor – but she'd never had much affinity for numbers, unlike Lila, and had seemed to maintain an almost child-like innocence of financial matters. She'd always worked, teaching English and history, never had extravagant tastes, and, as with many of her generation, had been lucky with bricks and mortar. But now Grace had taken to withdrawing money from the bank ATM on an almost daily basis, albeit not in large amounts, just ten, twenty or thirty pounds at a time. Lila noticed this after calling round for tea with Grace on a Sunday afternoon.

Grace insisted they go out to withdraw some money as soon as Lila arrived, but they'd been and done just that after meeting on Kilburn High Road the previous morning. Grace was unable to say what the money had been spent on, and even became uncharacteristically defensive and agitated when Lila questioned her.

Not long after this, Lila had to accompany Grace to the bank to discuss with the manager why Grace had been refused a new debit card. It turned out she'd already been issued two replacement cards in the past 6 weeks. Lila had taken Grace to the GP who had administered some brief test of knowledge, which Grace passed easily. They had been dismissed with a prescription for an anti- anxiety drug. They colluded in burning it in the fireplace.

It took months for Lila to get sufficient courage to return with Grace to the same surgery. By then Grace was now wearing her house key on a ribbon around her neck, having become locked out one afternoon, requiring Lila to come and let her in after work with her spare key. She couldn't explain where or how she'd lost her key, so Lila had to have the lock changed. A different doctor had seen Grace, had listened carefully and had promised to refer Grace to the hospital to see a neurologist. The appointment was a long time coming- and when it did it was for a year's time. There was no money for Grace to see someone privately so they'd had to wait.

The sixth and last mouse was done so Lila placed it and the other five back into their original cage, ready to take back to the animal house. It was then that she realized her error. She had picked up the wrong syringe. The syringe she had carefully filled with the new molecule to test, IG0047F, was still there, lying on top of the test tube rack; she had just injected the 6 mice with colchicine. The colchicine should not have been on the bench at all. It was left over from the previous day's cellular work in the sterile hood, why hadn't she taken it out? And now the lid was off outside the hood it was no longer sterile anyway, so she would have to throw it away.

"Shit! Shit, shit, shit."

Shannon looked up, surprised.

"What's wrong?"

"I've made a mistake. I 've given these mice the wrong stuff- colchicine, an old drug used for gout, instead of the new molecule."

Lila felt an unpleasant mix of nausea and remorse. Bad Lila briefly toyed with the idea of pressing on regardless, injecting the same mice with IG0047F and pretending nothing untoward had happened. Shannon was probably too naive to give her away. But Good Lila was an honest woman and an honest scientist, and quickly decided that there was nothing for it but to put the error down in her laboratory book and own up to her boss. She would need another six mice too. And what would she do with this lot? Lila could morally justify animal experimentation by virtue of the potential benefits of the work on human disease, alongside the assurance that every effort was made to reduce the discomfort of the animals, but clearly these six had suffered in vain at her hands. Mice weren't kept as pets - unless they could be used for alternative work they would be destroyed. Lila decided they could be an extra control group, in addition to the dose ranging groups on the active substance and the sham group. Hadn't her old supervisor said you could never have enough controls?

But she still needed another six of the special strain of mice, bred to develop brain plaques. That would mean going cap in hand to Terry, the animal house technician; fortunately, he seemed to like her. She laid out the new plan in her lab book, then took the colchicine-injected mice back to the animal house and fetched out the next group in their cage. To this group she administered the IG0047F. She worked steadily through the morning, completing the remaining groups. The Shan remained immobile beside her, but later helped in returning the mice to the animal house. They seemed untroubled by the process, nor by the little notches in their ears denoting their group membership nor, indeed, by Lila's error.

Before seeking out Terry, she made a cup of instant coffee and drank it in the break-out area. Her mind wandered back to her mother. Grace's decline had been gradual, but undeniable. Initially, along with the money worries, she had become generally more anxious, typically calling Lila four or five times each morning, more if some organisational matter had arisen, such as a friend planning a visit, or an arrangement to meet at a certain time and place. One Friday, Lila had arranged to meet Grace at

Paddington Station at 4pm for the two of them to catch the 16.15 train to Oxford together, to stay with Grace's friend Sarah and her husband for the weekend. Lila had first received a call from an agitated Grace at 10.30am, whilst Lila was in the darkened microscope room at the university. Grace wanted to leave home and head to Paddington right away, just to make sure she wasn't late; this was despite Paddington being just four stops away from home on the tube. Lila managed to talk her down on this and two subsequent calls, but the next time Grace called, Lila was in an inter-departmental meeting involving the Immunologists and her own Neurobiology lab, with the imposing Professor Susan Armstrong chairing, meaning she fumbled for the silent button as soon as her phone bleeped. Half an hour after the meeting her phone rang again, and she answered, except this time there was a stranger's voice on the other end, another Susan, a paramedic. Grace was being tended to by Susan and a colleague in Paddington Station, having been found in a confused state by a passer-by. They were considering taking Grace to St Mary's A&E around the corner, but Lila implored them to hang on and give her a chance to race over and save everyone a lot of trouble. Very reasonably Susan agreed, and before long Lila and Grace were having a leisurely lunch by the canal behind the station, with time to kill before the 4.15 train.

After this, Lila had moved back in with Grace, back into the bedroom she had grown up in, and had managed to sublet her own tiny flat, unbeknown to the landlord, for more than the rent which she paid. Good Lila felt guilty about this but could not afford to do anything else as she could not afford to pay a carer. So now they would breakfast together before Lila left for work, and Grace was left to potter, watch television and read the newspaper. (This last matter was something that bugged Lila disproportionately. Her mother had taken to reading Daily Chronicle! Lila had to do a quick search of the house before either of them had visitors to make sure any copies were hidden). In the evenings, in a role reversal from former days, Lila would cook for them both and they would listen to the Archers on the radio, then watch something on TV before an early bed. This became more and more necessary since Grace was liable to wake in the night once or twice, occasionally getting up in the early hours as if it were morning. For the last couple of weeks Lila had asked a neighbour, Mrs Dewhurst, to look in on Grace for an hour or two over lunchtime to check she was OK and to make sure she ate and drank something. That day Mrs D, as they called her, had been asked to come in and do breakfast as well.

Lila's PhD had been on Multiple Sclerosis, looking at the inflammatory basis of demyelination, the loss of the sheath that surrounds nerve cells within the brain and spinal cord and which appears so essential to their function. Professor Susan Armstrong had been one of her examiners when she defended her thesis. She headed the Neurobiology group at the university and worked predominantly on mouse models of dementia, with a back catalogue of several prestigious Nature papers. When she offered Lila a post-doctoral position in her lab, Lila felt compelled to accept, notwithstanding the potential conflicts and soul-searching that living with and working on the same currently untreatable condition might produce.

Six months into the job, Lila was juggling two projects: the first an industry-sponsored collaboration with the firm Immunogenomics. This was a pharmaceutical firm of less than 10 years standing which had grown by swallowing up a series of single-drug start-ups - mostly academia-based - with venture capitalist funding. Immunogenomics manufactured and marketed monoclonal antibody drugs – mAbs – antibodies generated in animals, usually mice, against a target molecule, typically with the aim of blocking or downregulating its activity. Successful antibodies were then structurally altered, making them more 'human' - typically, by keeping the portions of the antibody that bound the desired molecule and attaching these to the main body of a human antibody as a scaffold, in the process making the antibodies less likely to be recognised as 'foreign' and consequently rejected when finally trialled in human subjects. But first they had to go back into mice, to see if they could effectively bind their target molecule and alter the disease process. That was what Lila was doing, testing IG0047F, a monoclonal antibody against human Alzheimer's precursor protein, APP, to see if it would offer protection to mice genetically engineered to produce APP. These mice were predisposed to amyloid plaque formation as seen in the brains of patients with Alzheimer's disease. It wasn't her own work, rather she was doing it on behalf of Immunogenomics, but that brought in significant funding for the department (from which the university as a whole took its cut) and kept most of its junior staff employed. A bigger pharmaceuticals firm – one that the man on the Clapham omnibus would have heard of – would do all this sort of work in-house, in their own labs, by their own scientists; but Immunogenomics had grown so fast it was in no position to do this, and instead of cementing the status of the drugs it already had on its own books – only one of which was actually on the market, with approval from the European Medicines Agency and its US equivalent, the FDA – the board viewed continued expansion and gobbling up of smaller, embryonic firms as the best way of hedging its bets for at least one blockbuster drug.

The second project was her own intellectual work. But she had precious little funding, so most of the work was performed using waste-materials from the Immunogenomics project. Lila had read about the anti-inflammatory properties of an old drug, colchicine - in clinical practice used to treat gout and a few other, rarer conditions - when tested *in vitro* on explanted brain tissue in a mouse model of auto-immune encephalitis (brain inflammation). It had been a chance finding, whilst searching PubMed, the on-line library of listings for medical and biomedical science publications, appearing in a minor journal – so minor that she had needed to order a scanned photocopy of the relevant pages of the journal from the British Library as the University did not hold a subscription. Since then she had done something similar on spare pieces of tissue from the mice used in the Immunogenomics project. To her surprise, the colchicine appeared to reduce the density of the plaques in brain explants compared to buffer solution alone and, notably, also in comparison to IG0047F. But these experiments were kept under the radar; Professor Armstrong was, as yet, unaware of any of this, and of course, this was not something Immunogenomics would be pleased to hear.

Following on from the results in brain tissues, the next step would have been to test the effects of colchicine in the mice specially bred to develop plaques. Unfortunately, Lila had no funding to pay for mice for this, so had put these findings to one side, unwilling to disclose them lest she be either reprimanded or scooped. She mulled this over now, looking into her empty coffee mug, and wondered if she had made an honest mistake, or whether it was, at best, a Freudian slip.

She found Terry drinking a cup of tea in his office near the animal house. It was a small room, too warm, and had the feeling of an incubator. Lila confessed to having given a set of mice the wrong dose in the Immunogenomics project, but did not say what of, and asked as politely as she could for a further 6 mice, explaining that the previous set would simply make up an extra set at an intermediate dose. She also asked if he would mind not mentioning this to Prof Armstrong, at least for now. Terry sighed and finally gave a nod of assent.

"Thank you, Terry, I'll buy you a drink!"

He laughed and said he'd remember that promise at Christmas.

Back in the lab, Lila took the additional group of mice back to the bench and administered each in turn with the final, top dose of IG0047F. The Shan was nowhere to be seen. Just as she was finishing, Professor Armstrong put her head round the door into Lila's small shared lab space.

"Lila, could you come and talk to me for a minute?"

Lila shuddered. Had Terry already snitched on her? She nodded meekly and emerged from the lab to follow the Professor, elegant as always in designer suit and heels, to her spacious windowed room.

"Thank you, Lila. I hope you realise how important your work is to our department. Funding for dementia studies is getting harder and harder to access since so many promising lines of treatment have failed to deliver in clinical trials. How are you getting on?"

Should she confess now? Did the Prof know? Bad Lila stumbled on.

"Er, OK, thank you. I've just finished the first round of injections to all the groups of mice. "

"Good. Now I want to ask you something. Do you think you will have enough data for an abstract at the World Neurodegeneration meeting in October? You'll have to check the late-breaking abstract deadline, it'll be May at the latest.

"Oh, yes, I think so. There's the in vitro data, and we should have preliminary in vivo data in time for the submission too. Shall I make a start on what we've got so far and show it to you?"

"Yes please. And I'd be grateful if you would be quick about it - why not e-mail a draft to me in a day or two? It may be possible for me to find some funding for your fares, accommodation et cetera. I'm meeting the head of Immunogenomics at the end of the week. He wants a progress report, so it'll tie-in nicely."

"Thank you. I'll make a start tonight."

"Good".

Prof Armstrong looked down dismissively at papers on her desk and Lila backed out of the office, then scooted back to her own cubbyhole. There had been no indication that Terry had let her mistake slip out, and she was grateful for that, but she also had a sense of foreboding, a feeling that it was bound to come out in the end, and only be worse for the delay. She picked up her laptop and her notebooks, put them into her rucksack and left for home. Lila's salary was not large and carers were expensive, so she organized her day in a way that let her do most of her computer work at home rather than in the lab. That meant mornings at work, no lunch, then leaving for home at 3pm. With luck Grace would be happy with daytime TV for an hour or three and Lila could concentrate hard in her bedroom until time to prepare supper.

Lila avoided the Underground unless her bike had a puncture or it was pouring with rain. Out of rush hour the tube was bearable, during it the experience was horrible: crowded, claustrophobic and smelly and she preferred biking, though that was no picnic either going home as it was mostly uphill. Luck was with her today, with green traffic lights and she was home in just over half an hour.

"Hi Mum", she called as she turned her key in the new lock and opened the front door, "it's only me."

"Who's that?"

"Me, Mum - Lila."

"Hope? is that you?"

Hope was Grace's older sister. They had always been close, though Hope lived with her family in Northumberland, so was not a frequent visitor these days.

"No Mum, it's me, Lila," giving her Mum a kiss on the forehead as she sat on the couch staring at the TV. "Do you want a cup of tea?"

Oh yes please, Hope darlin', that would be lovely."

That's the first time that she has failed to recognise me, thought Lila, resignedly.

CHAPTER 2.

Oxford, next day.

Dermot Banks sat behind a large, completely clear desk in his spacious, uncluttered room at Immunogenomics HQ just north of the Oxford University science campus. He was glancing at an email advertising the next World Neurodegeneration Conference in Boston.

"With a focus on neurodegenerative research and its translation into patient benefit, the World Neurodegeneration Conference is the major meeting to empower drug development."

That sounded just right for him and for the company, he thought. Immunogenomics needed to show the data on IG0047F soon to the circling sharks of the big pharma companies in the hope that one of them would bite, make a bid for the molecule and take it into trials in man. His company did not have the capital, nor the personnel to undertake such expensive research as things stood. It depended on capturing innovative ideas and creating putative new drugs from these, before selling them on to truly big pharma – at the best price – and letting them take the big financial risk of clinical trials. Banks had had his fingers burnt 10 years previously in a phase 1 – first use in man – study of an older generation monoclonal drug. Having tested the supposedly immune-suppressant drug in primates without so much as a minor glitch, his previous firm hadn't foreseen any problems when administering just a tenth of that dose to 8 healthy young men – so much so that they'd simply given each of them their first dose one after then other, on the same day. But he had been called back from his office less than an hour later by an ashen faced nurse to find that two of the volunteers had already lost consciousness and the rest were looking distinctly uneasy. Fortunately, the NHS had stepped in to save the lives of those two, both requiring intensive care prior to long in-patient rehabilitation. Neither would ever return to normal life. The company folded, but Banks landed on his feet, receiving a call with a job offer from Immunogenomics, an Oxford-based start-up firm developed by a couple of scientifically gifted, but financially naïve young post-graduates. Before the year was out, he was effectively running the show and had found that bright-young scientists weren't as rare as all that, particularly if you could tempt them over from Europe and beyond.

He read on,

"Combining presentations from biopharma and academia, the meeting aims to widen thought in the development of efficacious neurodegeneration treatments and gives an opportunity to engage with the leading minds in the field.

Including:

Alternative aetiologies of disease, including neuroinflammation, microglial activation and lysosomal dysfunction

R&D technologies to effectively identify novel targets and candidate therapeutics

Preclinical case studies exploring means to improve the translatability of pre-clinical models

Clinically relevant biomarkers to inform translational research programmes and improve the success of clinical studies."

Banks sighed. The field was plagued by an inability to translate successful work in mice into drugs that had any meaningful impact in patients with dementia. Chasing the hallmark Alzheimer's brain abnormalities - aggregates of beta-amyloid plaques and tau protein tangles, assumed to be crucial to the pathogenesis of the disease - had led to promising studies in animals, but no effects in human patients, possibly because the disease was too advanced by the time of diagnosis, or simply because the obvious targets were the wrong targets. Currently used treatments like donepezil, which could help with daily life in some patients for a while, all relied on improving communication between brain cells, replacing lost neurotransmitters in a pretty blunt manner. But they did not alter the course of disease, which remained uniformly fatal in the long term. The new antibody, IG0047F, was an attempt at a different target, a protein causing inflammation. He knew that he would have to get some positive data soon, or the field would move on and leave him with an expensively manufactured molecule destined only for the dustbin of scientific failures. Some encouraging data just might get a firm from the big league interested enough to buy out his patent and take the drug off his hands, thereby keeping Immunogenomics afloat. Equally, he could not be seen to be trying to flog IG0047F - that was part of the reason for outsourcing the mouse work to an academic institution, leaving them to present the data like a ripe fruit, rather than risk the clumsy salesmanship of a pharma-pitch. He also knew just the person to do it. For a moment he allowed himself to remember her as she was when they first met at Oxford - long-haired, slim, clever and confident – a grown woman amongst boys and girls. Like several of his contemporaries he had invited her out but got nowhere. She had been polite, cool and distant and he hadn't found a way through the screen she projected around herself. He sighed, picked up his mobile and chose the number.

"Susan Armstrong speaking"

"Good morning, Susan. It's Dermot Banks. I'm sorry to disturb you. I know we are meeting for a catch up in a couple of days, but I wanted to ask you a question. Are you intending to go to the World Neurodegeneration Conference?"

"Probably not, I thought I'd send the post doc who is doing the work on your antibody. It would be good experience for her. Would your firm consider supporting her trip?"

"We'd much rather have you there to present the data. Of course, we could fund your trip and pay for your post doc to go too."

"Let me think about it. I've a lot on, but I might be able to free up enough time. It's in October isn't it?

"Yes, 22nd to 27th in Boston."

"OK let's discuss it on Friday. Goodbye."

Banks returned to his computer screen and reminded himself that he was a successful and rich man and that Susan Armstrong would one day be a stooped spinster with only a back catalogue of outdated research papers for company.

***

Lila meanwhile was hurrying to the local tube station at Queen's Park, having done a better job with her mother that morning, but having found a flat rear bicycle tyre. She walked through the Park, enjoying the sunlight filtering through new bright green leaves and the antics of the squirrels, searching for their buried treasure. She felt inexplicably happy. Perhaps it was because she had recovered from her stupid mistake of yesterday and succeeded in doing some more of her very own research. She failed to notice the young man whose path intersected with hers near the exit gate and nearly bumped into him.

"Sorry, I was miles away. "

"No problem, you go first." He smiled, a lovely bright smile- and indicated the gateway with his hand.

"Thank you. "

Lila walked on fast, intending to catch the Euston train, due to leave in 4 minutes.

At the station Lila picked up the free copy of Metro before tapping through the barriers and managing to slip onto the train just before the doors closed. She leafed through Brexit headlines, warnings of a looming financial crisis and celebrity tittle-tattle, and decided she was probably a little hypocritical for making such a fuss over her mother's choice of newspaper (not to mention the Shan's Instagram affliction), when she noticed a minor article about a potential breakthrough treatment for Huntington's disease. She had read the scientific paper produced by the scientists and doctors involved. The article was not, strictly-speaking, inaccurate, but it was sketchy on details and suitably hyperbolic for the tabloid press. The approach used by the scientists was interesting. They had administered a constructed chain of mRNA - messenger ribonucleic acid, the intermediate step between genes and their protein products - designed to be complementary to and therefore bind the mRNA produced by the abnormal Huntingtin gene. Binding should prevent the disease mRNA from being translated into the abnormal protein that accumulates in the brain in this devastating, fatal disease. Lila had already heard whispers that a group in the US were using a similar approach in the hope of treating, or at least stalling, Alzheimer's – if that worked, the putative drug from Immunogenomics that she was working on could be made redundant before it even got close to clinical use. She read on and noticed another commentary from a UK based researcher she knew.

"Urea is a natural chemical produced by the body that is normally cleared away in our urine, but this study suggests a build-up of urea in the brain could be involved in the development of Huntington's disease. This could be because the use of energy is compromised in the brains of people with Huntington's and urea is produced as the damaged brain tries to find alternative energy sources.

Previous research has hinted that urea might also accumulate in the Alzheimer's brain, which also experiences problems using energy. However, more research is required to understand if a build-up of urea is the cause, or the result, of brain cells dying so this study doesn't substantiate the researcher's claim that urea is a "pivotal" cause of dementia."

The word urea got Lila thinking about a different molecule, uric acid, the build-up of which is prevented by colchicine.

"Colchicine was used for gout – which is caused by a build-up of uric acid - so perhaps that explains its actions in my mouse experiments," Lila speculated. She was too involved with these ideas to notice the young man from the park, who was carefully observing her from behind his unread copy of Metro.

Her first task on arrival at the lab was to check on the mice injected the day before. She was pleased to find that they all seemed to be behaving normally. Then she repaired to her cubby hole and began collating the data from the in vitro experiments with IG0047F. By mid-morning she had analysed the results, which showed binding of IG0047F to brain cross-sections from the plaque-forming mice, with no binding of a control solution of antibodies. Homogenised brain tissue samples run on a gel column had located the binding to a protein of equal size to the amyloid precursor protein, APP, a large membrane protein that plays an essential role in nerve cell growth and repair, but a corrupted form of which can destroy nerve cells, presumably leading to the loss of brain function and memory in Alzheimer's disease.

All good so far, but no suggestion that it was actually doing anything beneficial. This was to be found in the last of the experiments, also the most controversial. Explants of brain tissue incubated in vitro over 7 days, treated with IG0047F or control antibody solution. Here, Lila again found a difference, reduced expression of APP in the treated mice when the sections were homogenised and run on a gel. This difference was modest, but just made statistical significance.

Lila took a coffee break, her head a little sore from staring at the screen and inputting data. She still had to write the abstract and was keen to have it done with before she left for the day. But she had not yet analysed the colchicine-treated explants and was dying to do so, even though she had no intention of adding this to the abstract. She stared out the window and let her mind drift for a while, then decided that she couldn't put off the analysis. She returned to her desk and began the task of collating the colchicine data then inputting it into the computer programme alongside the IG0047F and control data, taking care to duplicate the file first, so that a set of data remained without the colchicine – you never knew when Prof A was going to want to have a look at the raw data.

She could see the results looked good when the histograms popped up on the graphing option. The colchicine-treated explants had less than half the APP content of the IG0047F-treated sections and even less than the control-treated tissue. The statistical t-test showed clear significance too. Lila was both thrilled and felt distinctly uneasy. Life would have been easier if the colchicine had been a bust. She could have put it aside and simply got on with her day job. But what the hell was she to do now? Like most people, her initial response was to ignore the result and pretend it had not happened. She settled back into the immediate task of producing an abstract on the IG0047F data to send to Prof A that afternoon. In the end, it took the rest of the day to finish, in part because of the strict 250-word limit, but also because she felt there was something slightly dishonest about it, and the words just wouldn't fall into place in the way they usually did. At last she felt it was good enough to satisfy the prof without risk of it being returned to her for an extensive redraft. She emailed it and didn't wait for a reply before setting off home.

Susan Armstrong was online and heard the e-mail ping into her inbox. She was reading through it for the second time, making minor amendments when another e-mail appeared.

This was headed "World Neurodegeneration Conference Speaker Invitation".

"It never rains but it pours", thought Susan.

The sender was one Sarah Lincoln, a representative from Gentronic, another pharma company with an interest in dementia in its various forms. The e-mail invited her to speak in their company symposium on the subject of 'inflammation in neurodegeneration'.

Susan pondered the invitation. She felt obliged to help Dermot, whom she liked in a mildly pitying way; she had, more or less, decided to talk at the meeting for Immunogenomics. That would necessarily involve the topic of neuroinflammation as a background to IG0047F. She could speak for two different companies on pretty much the same subject, with some variation in emphasis, but preferred not to do so. She thought of Tom Jayne. Dr Tom Jayne was a clinician – a doctor in the ordinary sense – undertaking a PhD in her lab in an attempt to boost his academic credentials and thereby improve his chances of obtaining a consultant post in London, after he finished his training in neurology. Like most clinicians he was cack-handed in the lab, however nice he was to patients. He couldn't even use a pipette properly. Kate, Susan's redoubtable technician had found him using the waste material from the RNA extractor machine for his PCR experiments, throwing away the actual nucleic acid. Apparently, he'd been doing this for the best part of a month before Kate spotted his error. Tom was pretty clueless when it came to basic science, but he had the halo effect when he spoke – he looked good and sounded like he knew what he was talking about – so the audience always believed what he said. Susan replied to the email from Sarah Lincoln, offering up Tom as an excellent alternative, stressing that she would have loved to speak for Gentronic, but was conflicted given commitments with Immunogenomics.

At the back of her mind, though she would not have admitted this to anyone else, was the thought that Tom and Lila would make an excellent couple. Lila deserved a nice-looking fellow, and she was probably his only hope of coming up with a thesis worthy of the name.

 Susan returned to Lila's abstract.

CHAPTER 3

Two days later, Lila was still at home at 9.30am. Grace was breakfasted, up and dressed both were waiting for their doorbell to ring. The long-awaited home-visit from the old age psychiatrist was set for today.

"Are you OK, Mum?" asked Lila, "do you need the loo again before he comes?"

"No, darling, I'm just fine."

Grace settled back into her armchair, where she spent so much time these days, seemingly without needing anything to occupy her. This was such a change, thought Lila, from the busy, intelligent, interesting and interested Mum she used to know. She could not bear to see it.

"Here's the paper", Mum, she said, handing Grace yesterday's Evening Standard.

Grace smiled, took the paper and began to flick through it, looking at the photos.

Lila paced up and down the small room, wiped dust from the table, went to the sink to put away the breakfast things, until finally, ten minutes later the bell rang, and she raced to the door, heart pounding.

This meeting was so important. The outpatient appointments in the Neurology Department had been frightening for them both - even though it was part of the University and close to where Lila worked. There had been numerous investigations for Grace: brain scans, lumbar puncture, psychological assessment. The outcome had been terrifying, confirming Lila's fears: a diagnosis of probable Alzheimer's disease, with no prospect of curative treatment. Apart from the suggestion that cholinesterase inhibitors should be tried, there had been little practical advice and support. Grace had improved somewhat on the cholinesterase inhibitor donepezil, going back to where she'd been mentally about 6 months before. That improvement was now wearing off and the constant need for repetition, reassurance and care was getting Lila down. The broken nights were the worst part. Lila felt she could cope if only she could be assured of a regular night's sleep. She needed practical help and she hoped that this doctor would be able to provide it – or at least give her details of how to access it.

"Good morning. I'm Dr. Cartwright, here to see Grace Maraj."

"Hello," Lila put out her hand and shook that of the woman in the doorway, "I'm Lila, Grace's daughter. Please come in, she's in here."

Dr. Cartwright was what medical students were once taught was a typical candidate for gallstones - fair, fat and about forty; she also had a kind face and a warm manner. Grace was soon smiling and chatting away about her past as though they had been friends for years. Lila produced cups of tea and biscuits and listened carefully, adding details where they had slipped her mother's memory.

Grace had been born in Trinidad to an Indian family whose surname Maraj was a shortened form of Maharaj, meaning "great king." She thought she was related to Onika Maraj, known by her stage name Nicki Minaj, a Trinidadian-American singer. Grace's parents were converts to Christianity and had called their daughters Grace, Hope and Charity.

It was amazing, thought Lila, what you learnt listening to a relative – even your own mother - talking about themselves to someone else. For the first time Lila found out that her mother had been a twin whose sibling, Faith, had died within a few hours of birth. Grace, though tiny, was tough and had survived. She had been a highly intelligent girl, who did very well at school and who had gone on to become a teacher. She had met Gordon, Lila's father when he came to Trinidad as a medical student on his elective period just prior to qualification as a doctor. It was love at first sight for both and, despite opposition from both families (Gordon's were insular Scottish Presbyterians who would have preferred a local lass and Grace's thought she was too young), they insisted on marrying within 6 months of their first meeting. Her mother's strength of character, Lila thought, was also evident in the way she had insisted on keeping her maiden surname.

Lila arrived a few years later, by which time they were housed in lodgings in the UK with a variety of other young people, mostly medics. Apparently, this had been a wonderful time in Grace's life - they were poor, but very happy, and had a great social life - with babysitters on tap.

The crash came when Gordon, having qualified, done his initial few years in surgery and medicine and was well on his way to becoming a Consultant in Neurology, was killed one evening by a hit and run driver when he was pushing his punctured bike home. Lila was six and the memory of her mother's anguished scream when she heard the news had never left her. She had been in bed, almost asleep when the sound woke her. Lying there, terrified, she had not known what to do. Was there a monster in the house attacking her mother? At first, she hid beneath the bedclothes, but when she heard sobbing, and knew it was her mother, she had crept to the top of the stairs and peered down through the banisters. She stayed there for a long time, too scared to go down, but unwilling to creep back into bed until she knew what was happening. There were voices she did not recognise and a helmet on the table by the front door. It seemed like a good idea to check this out so, cautiously shifting from stair to stair, she descended. The helmet was blue with a big silver badge on the front saying ER. Lila knew that ER meant the Queen and that meant they were goodies in the sitting room with her Mum. She was still debating what to do when a goody came up and found her.

Since then it had just been the two of them against the world: Grace had gone back to teaching and coped with lonely single parenthood. For 4 years Lila was a pupil at the junior school where Grace taught, which made the daily routine easy, but also provided ammunition for bullies.

"Teacher's pet; cheat; mummy's little favourite," and similar complaints surfaced whenever Lila came top in a test, as she often did. She had learnt to shrug and walk away, but it meant that she was not popular and had few close friends.

Lila came out of her reverie to find that she was being asked a question.

"Night-time? Yes, Grace wakes in the night sometimes, two to three nights a week. Sometimes she thinks it is morning and gets out of bed."

The doctor went through a long checklist of questions and then asked that they go elsewhere so she could speak to Lila alone. They walked into the kitchen, ostensibly to clear the tea things. Grace was still sitting quietly in her chair, holding the open paper on her lap and looking dreamy. Remembering Gordon, Lila thought.

"Is there anything that you are particularly worried about, Lila?" asked Dr Cartwright.

"Oh, two things, I suppose. First, what will I do if she becomes incontinent? Second, how I would cope if she ever became violent? Not that she's ever acted in that way, but I know it can happen, personalities can change, especially with frontal lobe disease", Lila replied.

"OK," said Dr Cartwright, "let's deal with the second issue first. I think it's very unlikely that your mother will become aggressive or violent. So far as I have understood, she's not displayed any such tendency during her illness and it would also be very uncharacteristic given her premorbid personality. But if she were to become aggressive, it's usually a sign of confusion or fear on her part. The way to deal with it is to redouble your efforts to soothe and support her; any form of physical restraint is counterproductive and often frankly abusive, and pharmacological sedation is the last thing she needs. "

"Unfortunately, incontinence becomes almost an inevitability as the disease progresses, but in some patients that can be a very late development. Looking after an incontinent, potentially doubly incontinent, relative is very tough. For many carers that becomes the time to consider nurse-led care, usually in residential care. But others do manage at home."

"I want to look after my Mum for as long as it takes, I don't want her to go into a home. But I don't know how I'll manage it alongside my own career if she gets worse. At the moment a neighbour pops in to help, but Grace is here alone a lot. I don't know how long that will be safe."

Dr Cartwright looked at her sympathetically. "I quite understand. Unfortunately, dementia sufferers have been looked on as a social problem rather than a medical one by successive governments. Whether as a consequence of this or not, we are now in a situation where the support on offer is simply overwhelmed by the need. Acute support doesn't really exist, unless Grace has a concurrent physical problem, and patients with dementia do very badly in general hospital wards. There is some provision for help in the home and I can show you how to access this. You are also eligible for some monetary support, it used to be called Attendance Allowance, but it does not by any means cover the cost of having someone else look after Grace during working hours, particularly if nursing support is required. "

"Does Grace own this house?" she asked.

"Yes", said Lila.

"She said that Dad was keen that they buy their own place rather than paying rent right from the start - so they busted a gut to get a mortgage and to pay it - and now of course that has paid off handsomely. These houses have gone up in value massively."

"Of course. I would advise you to obtain Power of Attorney very soon, while your Mum is still capable of signing such a document. Unfortunately, the house's value will mean Grace is ineligible for some aspects of care and would have to pay the full amount for any care home, should you ever change your mind. However, it does mean that you have a source of money should you need it in the future."

"Oh, I don't want to sell this house, it's our home!"

"I don't necessarily mean selling it - one possibility would be to rent it out and live somewhere smaller and cheaper. It is just an option. Alternatively, you could also offer accommodation for someone who acts as carer whilst you are at work. Now, I have to visit another patient. Here are the various leaflets and applications that you may find helpful. I will ask a local social worker to contact you. I am very sorry about your mother's illness, I know that it must be very distressing for you. However, it seems to me that she is not unhappy, and you are clearly doing a fantastic job of looking after her."

Lila looked back at Grace who was sitting, smiling to herself, rocking a little to a tune on the radio, perhaps one she remembered from her dancing days. She thanked the doctor, saw her out and went back to her Mum.

"She was a nice lady," said Grace.

"Yes Mum, she was," sighed Lila, "but I wish she'd had a magic wand."

When she finally got to work late that morning Lila was greeted by an excited Ann, the Professor's secretary.

"Hello, Lila. Prof wants to see you in her office ASAP."

The meeting was, as usual, brief and to the point. Lila's abstract, as amended by Professor Armstrong, was suitable for submission. This should be done today, and Lila should organize her travel and accommodation as cheaply as possible in association with Tom Jayne, who was also going. All receipts to be kept and reimbursed from departmental funds.

"Thank you," said Lila, wondering how on earth she was going to arrange for someone to look after Grace while she was in Boston.

When she left the office, Ann was waiting for her, brandishing a newspaper.

"Lila, have you seen the Metro today?"

"No, why?"

"Look at this."

She pointed to a small section across from the letters page entitled Tube Crush, where she had circled one of the entries.

"Dark haired beauty in green parka on the Bakerloo line. You were so engrossed in your thoughts we nearly bumped into each other in the park. I'd love to know what you were thinking about. Coffee sometime?

"I think that's you, Lila. You told me that you were so worried about your Mum that you nearly knocked into someone at the park gate. What do you think?"

Lila smiled, "Ha, ha. Oh, I suppose it could be me – I doubt he had enough time to get a proper look at me though, or he wouldn't have written in."

"Well, aren't you going to answer it?" said Ann.

"Absolutely not! I know nothing about him, he might be dangerous, or just plain dull. It's a bit of an odd thing to do, don't you think?"

"Oh, Lila, where's your sense of romance? He might be just the man for you. I'd give it a go."

"Ann, you are so much better than me at getting on with people, I'd be terrified to meet a stranger in a bar, or even in a café. I wouldn't know what to say, and that's assuming he's not a nut anyway."

"You'd be fine, just be your natural self."

"I'll think about it."

"OK, you do that. "

Ann put the paper down on her desk, but Lila did not pick it up. Instead she said, "I have to find Tom. Is he around?"

"I think he has clinical duties this morning, a ward round, apparently, but should be finished by lunchtime. I'll let him know you want to see him if he comes in here, or you could phone him, but I'd leave it until after about 1pm, he always seems a bit stressed when he's at the hospital."

"Thanks Ann, see you later."

Lila went to check on the mice and then to find more details of the Boston meeting. She wanted to have a plan of the cheapest possible flights and hotels ready to show Tom so that he did not choose more expensive options. She knew Tom was used to the good things in life and was naturally generous, with no idea of economical living; and funding for research should not be used for expensive trips. She soon found that any hotel close to the Congress centre was likely to be too expensive and started to explore others, further away but with reasonable transport links.

Tom knocked on her door at midday.

"Hi, Lila."

"Oh, I thought you'd still be on the ward round," said Lila, surprised, turning to face the door.

"It finished early as Prof. Ferguson had to get away. I hear that we need to talk about Boston. I'm pleased you're going too. Prof Armstrong has passed on one of her lectures to me – no pressure then! Ha, ha. I'm not used to that sort of thing - half an hour amusing medical students is more up my street."

"Oh, you'll be fine, Tom. You're a confident speaker," replied Lila. "And it looks like a good programme, although there are always too many different sessions going on at once, and the Americans insist on having the morning talks start at 7am, though the time difference makes it easier to get up, I suppose."

She turned her computer screen so Tom could see the programme.

"Oh yes", he responded, "I want to hear Li Chung, the Shanghai group have some interesting ideas."

They discussed the meeting for a while, then Lila said,

"Prof. told me we have to do this cheaply, so I've been looking at flights and where to stay. There's a Canadian budget airline that does transatlantic flights, so that might be the best one to go for. With regards to accommodation, the conference centre hotels are pretty pricey, but some a little further away, including some in the town centre, aren't so bad."

"What about Airbnb?" interrupted Tom.

"Oh, I hadn't thought of that," Lila was surprised that Tom would consider Airbnb, and a little put out that the idea had not occurred to her. She accessed the site.

"Do you have an Airbnb ID? She asked.

"Yes, I've used it twice now, good both times," Tom replied. "Here let me sign in."

He leaned across her and she was uncomfortably aware of his smell - undefinable, not unpleasant, but undoubtedly male. She blushed, and hoped her own body odour wasn't too crippling, she'd run out of deodorant last week and hadn't got around to buying any more.

He leaned back, allowing her to enter the details of the trip. There were several possibilities, mostly better value than any hotel and one or two within walking distance of the Conference centre according to the Google map. After some discussion they put in a bid for a two-bed flat half a mile away.

"Great. Thanks for helping with that, Tom".

"Oh, no problem. Thanks for looking at flights and setting the ball rolling, I'd have left it to the last minute otherwise. I also owe you after the number of times you've saved me in the lab".

Lila smiled. Tom was pretty clueless in the lab and was forever seeking her out to ask for help. He had helped her too though, by obtaining an intravenous preparation of colchicine for her from the hospital with no questions asked. That reminded her about her error. Like most people the weight of carrying a secret was becoming too heavy, Lila needed to confess to someone. Tom would be a good person to tell, to sound out how it was likely to go down with Susan.

"Oh Tom, did I tell you about the mice?"

"No, what?"

"I made a mistake. "

"No way Lila, that's not like you! What happened?"

She confessed all - the mice wrongly injected with colchicine, the decision to include them in the series as a further control and the kindness of Terry in giving her more mice.

"Wow, Lisa. Does Prof. know?"

"Not yet. I was going to tell her that day, but, as usual, she was very busy, and I didn't feel that I could take up her time to explain it all. Now I think I'll wait until I see the outcome."

"Well, I hope they do well. Wouldn't it be funny if colchicine outperformed the monoclonal?"

"Yes, but there's little hope of that. Even something which makes a little improvement would be good. My Mum is getting worse, Tom, and I feel so helpless."

"You could give her some colchicine too," joked Tom.

"Do you know, I hadn't thought of that?"

"Hmm, steady on. I'm not sure it would not be legal or ethical," Tom was suddenly quite serious. "Lila you should try to get your Mum into a clinical trial. Have you spoken to Prof. Fergusson? I could introduce you if you like."

"Yes, I did. I spoke to him a few months ago when Mum was formally diagnosed. He didn't have anything to offer but suggested I looked at the Alzheimer's UK website. There was nothing local enough for me to take Mum to. Perhaps that's changed, I'll check again."

"You do that. Let me know what you find. Now, I have to go back to the ward to finish off all the things that came out of the round. See you later, Lila."

Tom turned and hurried away from Lila's desk, leaving her in a very thoughtful mood.

She looked up colchicine on-line. The only sides effect listed as 'common' were abdominal pain, nausea, vomiting and diarrhoea. Unpleasant, but not alarming. On the other hand, she could not ignore the warning that colchicine could also cause bone marrow suppression, including aplastic anaemia which was described as having a particularly high mortality rate. Also, there was the potential that colchicine toxicity itself could cause both peripheral nerve damage and, potentially, central nervous system problems including seizures, confusion and delirium, the last things Grace needed. The risk of toxicity could be increased if the patient was taking certain drugs that reduced metabolism of colchicine by the liver. These included several common drugs, such as certain antibiotics and blood pressure medications, and, most strikingly, grapefruit juice.

Having read this, she felt she needed to review the original information that had made her think of colchicine as a possible therapy for Alzheimer's disease. She had forgotten that it was a natural product from the autumn crocus, *Colchicum autumnale*, which she could see in Queen's Park at the right season. That made it seem more innocuous, although Lila well knew that, historically, most drugs, or at least the prototype for each major drug class, was derived from a plant or fungus, and many of these were spectacularly toxic in excess. *Colchicum autumnale* had apparently been used for the treatment of rheumatism and joint swelling, as detailed in an Egyptian medical papyrus, from around 1500 BC, and Benjamin Franklin, who suffered from gout, brought crocuses to North America. She again noted that it had anti-inflammatory properties used in various conditions which she had vaguely heard of, including Behcet's disease, relapsing polychondritis and familial Mediterranean fever (FMF). It was the latter that had sparked her interest. Colchicine appeared to reduce the risk of the development of amyloidosis, a condition involving deposition of abnormal proteins in tissues. Alzheimer's disease involves the build-up of beta amyloid protein plaques, derived from a precursor protein, termed Alzheimer's precursor protein or APP. So far so good with regards to similarities. On the other hand, the protein deposits seen in FMF were thought to be derived from a protein produced by the liver in response to inflammation, serum amyloid A (SAA), and the resultant amyloidosis could affect just about any tissue, with the exception of the brain - the reverse of Alzheimer's, at least with regards to where plaques became deposited.

Lila read on, recalling that colchicine inhibited the function of a protein called tubulin which was essential in the copying of chromosomes as part of the process of mitosis which occurs during cell division. Lila had come across colchicine while studying chromosomes during the genetics part of her undergraduate degree. It had been used to arrest cells during mitosis to allow the chromosomes to be easily visualised when lined up along the middle of the cell nucleus. The anti-inflammatory effects were presumably the result of inhibition of rapidly dividing and migrating white blood cells during inflammation. Grace was always significantly worse – more confused – when she was unwell, such as with a cold or urine infection. Lila wondered how the inflammatory response affected her brain function.

Interesting, but she knew Tom really had just been joking when he suggested she might consider giving the drug to her mother. On the other hand, there was nothing to hope for in terms of treatment following Dr Cartwright's visit, and she knew that, even in the unlikely event that IG0047F and similar prototype drugs proved successful in mouse models, it would be years before they were available to patients. At the rate Grace was declining she didn't have years to wait.

CHAPTER 4. London- a week later.

Lila was lost in thought as she caught the tube train home and again failed to notice the young man with a dark coat and a red scarf in the same carriage. He watched her carefully, following her out of the train and up the stairs at Queen's Park. He stayed behind her along Harvist Road, turned up Kingswood behind her and then, with a quick burst of speed was beside her as she walked up beside the park railings.

"Hello", he said, "did you see my message in the Metro?"

Lila stopped and turned to face him. He was slight, dark haired with a narrow face and deep set eyes.

"Look", she said, "I find this a bit unsettling. I don't mean to be rude, but please just leave me alone."

He backed off, holding up both hands. "No problem, I'll go if you want me to. I didn't mean to upset you, I'm very sorry." He walked backwards.

"Stop," shouted Lila, "there's a car coming."

He glanced behind him, "Oops," and with a wiggle managed to get himself back onto the path and out of danger.

"I'm not doing this very well am I?" He laughed, his face was so comical that Lila laughed too.

"I don't do this often", he said, "just once in a lifetime, I hope."

Lila remembered her mother's story of her first meeting with her father, Gordon, he told her he was in love with her straight off the bat, before he'd even managed to properly introduce himself.

She said, "OK, OK, you'd better tell me your name at least and what the hell you want from me." She stood still, not wanting to let him know where she lived.

He stood still too.

"I'm Dragan, I live over past the other side of the park. I'm trying to be a journalist, but not doing very well at it. I saw you the other day and just knew that I had to talk to you. I guess now isn't a great time, you must want to get home, and I need to get back home too. Do you think we could meet for a coffee? Perhaps this weekend, somewhere on the high street?

"Salusbury Road, you mean?" replied Lila, thinking it would be safe enough. Dragan nodded.

"OK. How about the deli at 11am on Saturday?"

"Yes", he said," perfect, thank you. Yes, yes. I'll leave you in peace now. See you on Saturday! Good bye!"

He hurried on up the path and turned into the park side entrance, leaving Lila watching him.

****

Friday came and the need to test her mice. The idea for this had come from her Dad's work years before. He had made a mouse model of a neurological disease called myasthenia gravis which caused rapid weakness after muscle use. Needing to quantify this, he'd used a large bowl filled with warm water and timed the mice for their ability to swim. The myasthenic ones had tired early and he'd fished them out after they went under twice; the controls could go on swimming for several minutes longer. Lila remembered him talking to her about his work; indeed, she'd told her friends that her Dad was a mouse doctor. She had only vague recollections of his explanation of the swim test but was able to check out the method since it was written up in full in his papers.

For her mice though, the test needed to be more complex - she was interested in mental ability, not muscle strength - so she devised a mouse pool with a way out which was hidden just under the water and led to the surface via a pipe. She put each mouse in turn in the pool and showed them the exit, encouraging them to swim up it to dry land. Then they went back into the pool and the time they took to reach dry land was recorded. If this took more than 5 minutes the test was ended and recorded as a failure. It was not ideal, but there was a clear difference between the control, wild-type mice, and those bred to develop the cerebral plaques. What she wanted to know was whether any of the putative dementia treatments would make any difference. Ideally someone else, with no preconceptions, would be doing this test, but there was no-one available. The Shan was off at her weekly training day of lectures. Lila did the next best thing - she put the mouse cages in random order without reading their labels and tested the mice, each individually earmarked, from each cage, meaning she was blinded with regards to which group was being tested, at least while the test was going on. The cages were returned to the bench in the order tested and, only after recording the results, would she note the treatment group status and align this with her results.

The testing took her all morning since only one mouse could be tested at a time. Once finished she checked the cage identification letters and added them to the results. Then she returned the mice to the Animal House, washed her hands well and went to the coffee room. Selecting her own mug, with poppies on it, she made a cup of what they all called Nesmess (something her dad used to say, passed on via her mum), added milk and sat down for a brief rest.

 "Hi Lila, how did it go?" asked Terry.

 "OK, I think", said Lila. "They all survived, some seemed much smarter than others, but I haven't analysed the results yet."

"How much longer will you be treating them?"

"Four weeks in all, so another three to go. Thanks so much for letting me have the extra mice."

"No problem, many of the great discoveries in science have been by serendipity - did you know that penicillin probably landed on Fleming's culture plates because the laboratory above was looking at fungal allergy? So, let's be hopeful."

Lila laughed. She felt stimulated to go and analyse the morning's test results so returned to her cubbyhole desk and entered them all on to her computer, backing them up immediately to a separate hard drive. Then she entered them into a non-parametric statistical programme, suitable for this kind of small-group data. She was thrilled when, on pressing the key for the result, there was a significant difference between certain groups.

That evening.

She felt giddy looking down, the Gods were unbelievably high, and remarkably uncomfortable. She had put on her newest dress, added the antique earrings inherited from her grandmother and turned up at Covent Garden feeling a million dollars - until she saw some of the other clientele and found herself mounting staircase after staircase to reach their cramped, unbelievably expensive seats. Now she was overawed by the audience in the Gods - not well-dressed, but mostly bespectacled and studious, with musical scores open on their laps. In order to view the whole stage she had to lean out forwards and sideways, this gave her an involuntary idea of opera as a tennis match with the audience facing from side to side according to who was singing and leaning forwards en masse when something happened at the front of the stage, all in time to the music.

"I should never have come," she thought.

Tom had persuaded her that afternoon, pleading that his date could not make it and he didn't want to waste the ticket. He also told her that she must experience opera done properly at least once in her life before she could condemn it as elitist. So here she was, a girl who didn't even like musicals.

There was sudden clapping and leaning forwards, she saw the conductor arrive at his rostrum, raise his arms and instruct the orchestra to begin. Lila relaxed back into her seat and let the music wash over her, releasing her thoughts. She almost missed the opening of the curtains and the revelation of the set which brought forth further clapping from the cognoscenti. When the singing began, she could hardly believe that voices could soar all over the large auditorium without benefit of microphones. Gradually the magic stole over her and she became entwined in the story of Carmen and her lovers.

 By the end "Carmen, my Carmen," sung by Jose over the dead body of his love, brought tears pricking at her eyelids. She was hooked.

"Oh, Tom, that was marvellous, thank you so much."

 He smiled, "De nada, my Carmen; you helped me out."

She forbore to mention that he could probably have sold the spare ticket ten times over outside the theatre.

"Let me buy you a drink," Lila offered.

"Sure, let's move away from here, it'll be too crowded."

So they walked through Covent Garden towards the river and found a pub in a side street off the Strand.

"What can I get you?"

"A brandy please, Lila."

He let her go to the bar and order two brandies, returning with crisps in addition. Neither had eaten much supper. They clinked glasses and sipped the fiery liquid.

"How is your Mum?"

 "Getting worse overall. It's funny, some days she seems much better than others, though it is variable even during the day. She copes badly if she is tired or hungry. I suspect that looking after her is like dealing with a small child: constant vigilance, avoiding confrontation, keeping them happy…."

"Poor you; how did you get away tonight?"

"Mrs Dewhurst, bless her, agreed to come in at short notice. She and Mum really get on well and they watch the same kind of TV programmes. Mrs D. says it is better than being on her own all the time - and I think she does mean it. I will pay her though, just like a baby sitter."

Then, turning her head away to hide the tears which were returning, "Tom, I am so worried about the future. What can I do when Mum needs someone there all the time? I can't bear to think of her in a care home, I'm sure she'd hate it, she loves our house. Yet I can't give up work altogether – it's my career, my future which is on the line, not just a job. I want to do something meaningful in my life and I think that would be through science. It was bad enough that I couldn't do medicine- there just wasn't enough money for me to study all those years - but I did manage a PhD because it was paid a little and we struggled through. Now I'm cooking with gas, getting results, I can feel that avenues will open up for me if I keep going. But if I stop, then it'll be all over, the next wave of bright young things will step on me and I'll be trampled into the dust."

Tom put his hand on her shoulder, he could feel her heaving with suppressed sobs.

"Oh, Lila. I am so sorry, I hadn't realised what a pickle you're in."

He put his other hand on her other shoulder, turned her to him and held her head against his slender,, not so manly chest. She noticed again his particular smell, and allowed herself to lean upon him, sighing gratefully, hoping to be kissed.

 Eventually she looked up.

"Tom, there is one thing you could do for me, if you felt able."

"What is it?"

"Prescribe some colchicine tablets for my Mum. The mice that received it are doing fine, at least as well as the monoclonal- treated ones."

"Lila, I'd love to, but I can't do it."

 "How about if I told you she has gout?"

 "Does she?"

 "Well, she's got painful bunions on both feet."

Tom laughed, got out his handkerchief and wiped her eyes.

"Let me think about it," he said.

CHAPTER 5

That same evening found Susan Armstrong re-doing her make-up in her office, before brushing down the skirt of her suit and spraying on a little expensive perfume. She checked her appearance in the long mirror concealed on the inside of a cupboard door, smiled at herself with a wry conspiratorial grin and left, locking the door carefully.

 Dermot was already seated in the quiet, but expensive restaurant he had chosen for their meeting when she arrived. He stood up, slightly awkwardly as the waiter brought her over.

"Susan, how nice to see you. Thank you so much for coming."

"No problem Dermot, I always enjoy the food here and it is a good opportunity for a frank discussion."

She sat down and chose sparkling water to drink whilst perusing the menu. Dermot persuaded her into a classy Chablis with her seafood and gradually she began to relax. They talked at first of cabbages and kings, then over the main course of IG0047F and its prospects. Susan explained the recent results which Lila had obtained and noted that they augured well; but that was no guarantee of clinical efficacy in man. Dermot nodded and asked,

"Would your hospital be able to undertake a single centre phase 2 clinical study in recent onset dementia?"

"Probably, though you need to talk to Edmund Ferguson about that. He is the lead clinician."

"I'd like you to be involved too."

"Yes, I'd be interested to be involved, but as a scientist and not a clinician I can only be a co-investigator."

"That would be fine."

Susan looked puzzled.

"I thought that Immunogenomics wanted to sell the molecule to Big Pharma?"

"We do, but it seems sensible to have a plan for further investigation, especially considering how long it takes to get ethical approval. Also, your University departments are the crème de la crème – so to have an arrangement would make the molecule more enviable. A bit like selling a house together with planning permission."

"Can you afford to go on with it alone if no bidder turns up?"

"Susan, that is not a question that I should answer; however, strictly between you and me, the answer is no."

She laughed, "I'm glad you are so honest. It is refreshing in someone from the pharmaceutical world."

It was Dermot's turn to laugh.

"I've never been much good at spin, but I can see the wood from the trees when it comes to trying out therapies. We're doing well so far - but we're quite stretched now with several candidate drugs for different inflammatory conditions - so we need financial input. It only requires one of them to do well to make a mint; I wish that we could take all of them into man and reap the benefits of those that succeed, but we simply lack the resources. So, we pass them on to a bigger wealthier company to do the expensive clinical trials. Perhaps one day we'll be able to do this ourselves, but not yet."

"What about using other sources of money - venture capital, crowd funding?"

"That's a possibility, but it's not my area of expertise. I've come up through Big Pharma so I have contacts there in several companies, so I prefer to go down that route."

"When did you leave clinical medicine?" asked Susan.

"I got as far as being a Senior Registrar in Gastroenterology at a time when there were three of us for each job which came up. I didn't want to leave London, or rather my wife didn't want to leave, so when I failed to get the job there that I really wanted I had a rethink. There was an advert for a role in pharma and I applied on the off chance and got it. The work suited me, my wife was happy, at least for a time, so I carried on."

"How is your wife? You married Celia from Newnham, didn't you?"

"God knows, I haven't seen her for 10 years. We'll probably next meet at the wedding of one of our children."

"Oh, I'm sorry, I didn't know," lied Susan.

"Oh, it's all water under the bridge now, though it hurt like hell at the time. She left me for a merchant banker. How about you, are you married?"

"You know I'm not," thought Susan, but she said, "No, I never married."

Inadvertently she glanced down at her fingers, playing with her coffee spoon, not ringless certainly, but with no signifier ring. She looked at Dermot again.

"Tell me about your children."

"I have two, the classic combo, a boy and a girl, both students now – so I see less of them than I'd like. You know what it's like," here he paused, realising that she probably didn't, but ploughed on, "they are away in term time and then in the holidays they spend most days asleep in bed until lunchtime, then go out in the evening and return in the small hours - so we interact very little. When we do though it is lovely, I really enjoy being with each of them."

"Is either of them doing medicine?"

"No, when they were small I was working all hours, coming home late and tired. Celia was the same. She worked as a GP trainee, but it was tough with a family as well. I think that put them both off. James is reading history, Lauren is doing French and Spanish, both at King's. There is only 18 months between them, so they are very close."

"That must be nice."

Susan meant it - she had been an only child, much wanted, much loved and had not felt the need of siblings then, being very self-sufficient and on good terms with her parents. Now, though, they were dead and she had no close relatives; she had begun to feel isolated and wished that she had a sibling with whom to share memories, to face the future. She looked thoughtful.

"Did you keep up with many of our contemporaries?" asked Dermot.

"No, very few. I see Rosemary from time to time when she is in the UK, she lives in the States now. Sometimes I see one or two of the others at meetings or back in College for a dinner, but that's it. I think that you clinicians had much closer ties with each other than we scientists. How about you?"

"Oh, I still keep up with a couple of the other housemen at Middlesex, but none of the girls. They sort of sided with Celia, at least I think they did because none of them sent cards to me at Christmas once we were divorced. I haven't been back to any of the reunions since we split, I don't fancy meeting Celia and her merchant wanker at one."

Susan laughed. "Fortunately, I have no such problems. It is one of the good things about staying single."

"Now, I should really go," she added." Please could you ask them to get me a taxi?"

"Where do you live?" asked Dermot

"Paddington, by the canal in one of those new blocks."

"Oh, I can give you a lift if you like, it's on my way home. My car is parked nearby."

"Thank you, that would be nice."

Dermot paid the bill, which had been enlarged by the two brandies taken with their coffee, and pulled back Susan's chair, offering his hand to help her to her feet. She staggered momentarily, suddenly aware of the two glasses of wine and one of brandy, before regaining her balance and walking to the cloakroom to collect her cashmere coat.

"Do you mind if I go to the loo?"

"No problem"

Dermot waited, fingers playing with the car keys in his pocket, suddenly nervous as a boy on his first date. He hoped that Susan would be impressed by the Porsche. Just as Susan emerged, he felt a sudden cracking and pulling out the keys he saw, to his horror, that he had broken off the ignition key halfway down its inordinate length.

"Oh my God," he said, adding unnecessarily "it's broken."

"Do you have a spare?" asked the ever-practical Susan.

"Yes, but it's at home. "

"Then a taxi it is," decided Susan, turning to the maitre d', "Please would you order us one."

Dermot was so embarrassed by his clumsiness that he spoke little in the taxi, except to apologise profusely. Susan stopped him.

"Dermot, it is no problem at all for me. I can see that it is for you though - where is your car? Is it on a meter?"

"No, thank goodness, it's in a multi storey - it'll be safe, but expensive. At least I won't get a parking fine or be towed away. I can get the train home to Oxford from Marylebone, come back early tomorrow and pick it up."

"In fact, we have probably drunk too much to be driving anyway - I certainly have - so look on it as a good thing."

"Thank you, Susan, it's good that you are always so positive."

The taxi arrived at the base of the smart, glassy block in which she lived and Susan got out, leaned back into the open door and said,

"Dermot, thank you. It was a delicious meal and it was good to catch up on science and on our lives."

"No, thank *you* Susan, I really enjoyed this evening. Goodnight."

The taxi swept away and Susan entered the lobby, greeted the concierge and took the lift up to her spacious, beautifully decorated, soulless penthouse apartment.

****

Lila woke late on Saturday, having been up for an hour or two in the night, persuading her mother back into bed. She checked on Grace who was snoring gently then went downstairs to make her first, much needed, coffee of the day and her usual porridge with nuts, seeds and chopped banana.

As was her custom on non-working days, Lila took the breakfast back to her bedroom and sat in bed, propped up on 2 pillows to eat it whilst reading yesterday's evening newspaper, the free Evening Standard. She loved these rare moments of peace and was deep into the foreign news when she heard Grace getting out of bed. The special mat next to the bed tinkled when trodden on - a very useful alarm mechanism.

"Good morning Mum," she called. "Would you like a cup of tea?"

"Morning sweetheart. Yes please."

Lila got up, leaving her room in time to see Grace disappearing into the bathroom, then went down to put the kettle on. She made tea and toast, spread with coconut oil and strawberry jam, a disgusting combination as far as she was concerned, but acceptable to Grace and possibly helpful in dementia according to an article she had read about certain lipids present in coconut oil.

Grace came downstairs, still in her nightie, slightly damp at the front.

"Here's your breakfast Mum, I'll get your dressing gown."

Lila did this and sat with Grace, now warmly wrapped, while she enjoyed her meal.

"Mum, I have to go out this morning for a little while. Will you be OK if I leave you here with the radio on? Or should I ask Mrs D to come in?"

"I'll be fine darling, don't you worry."

"Let's get you dressed then."

Lila led Grace upstairs again, noticing that her gait had changed and she led with her left foot for every stair, just like a small child learning to climb them. It was the same when she came down again, clean, dry and dressed. She sat gratefully in the comfortable armchair, sighing as though she had run a marathon. Lila put the small table next to her, with the Evening Standard on it, then raced upstairs to dress herself. Unusually, she could not decide what to wear and, having tried on two dresses and rejected them as being too formal, ended up wearing the shirt, jeans and jumper from last weekend since they were still draped over her bedroom chair. She sniffed them carefully before putting them on and decided that they would pass muster, but, just in case, she gave herself a spritz of the Jo Malone perfume which she kept for special occasions. Running down the stairs she called

"Goodbye Mum," but then, needing to check, went into the front room and gave her comfortably seated parent a kiss.

"I'll be back in an hour," she called as she went out.

It was another fresh Spring morning with sunlight filtering through the leaves in the park, lifting her spirits and relieving the anxiety she felt about meeting an almost complete stranger. She slowed down at the park gate, not wishing to be the first to arrive and was rewarded by the sight of Dragan loitering outside the deli, looking worried.

"Hi," he said, "I was afraid that you might not come." He gave her the same slightly shy smile as before that had made her say yes to this meeting.

"Oh, you needn't have worried, I keep my word."

"Good, let's go in. He held open the door for her and let her go in front of him. "What would you like?"

"An Americano please, no milk." Like many people with Eastern genes Lila was lactose-intolerant and could not digest milk easily.

"I'll have the same. Would you like something to eat?"

"No thanks, I've had breakfast."

His face fell, Lila felt sorry for him he was so easy to read.

"Please do eat something if you are hungry, I don't mind."

He gave the disarming smile again and said,

"Thanks, I will. I'm ravenous, haven't had any breakfast, I was too nervous." He smiled again, self- deprecatingly and Lila found herself smiling back.

He ordered their coffees, plus eggs on toast for himself and they went through to the rear room to find a table, navigating, with some difficulty, the large Bugaboos piloted by many customers. There were no free tables, so they ended- up side by side on the stools by the large window ledge which served as a table and which gave a good view of the side street.

"Now," he said, "shall I start by telling you something about myself or would you like to begin?"

"Oh, you go first."

Dragan told her of his birth in Bosnia, how when he was still a baby his family fled to the UK just before the war, having been warned that fighting was likely to break out. They were lucky because his mother was English, so the family had been able to settle in London, living with her parents for a few months, until she and his father Mehmet had been able to find somewhere nearby to rent. Dragan had been followed by another brother, Ferid, and then a sister, Layla. They still lived in a house in Kensal Rise and all the children had been to school locally. Dragan had gone on to study journalism at Middlesex Polytechnic, then done a couple of unpaid internships on the Evening Standard and then the Guardian before finally getting a paid job at the Daily Chronicle.

Lila listened carefully, then asked,

"How did your mum come to meet your dad?"

"She was on one of those rail trips round Europe. It was her first long vacation from Uni, she was reading English at Cambridge. Her parents were very proud of her and trusted her to behave well with her two Uni friends. My Dad was working as a waiter in Dubrovnik in the holidays, earning money for his studies and they met in the restaurant when the three girls had a meal out to celebrate Mum's birthday. He had been learning English and was happy to try to speak to them in their own language. They taught him to sing "Happy Birthday." He told me it that for him it was love at first sight, Mum felt the same. She persuaded her friends to go to the same place for lunch the next day and he asked her to go for a walk with him afterwards. They walked round the walls of the old city two or three times, without noticing, until he had to go back to work. He asked her to stay in the city – so she did. Her friends were worried but could not persuade her to leave with them on the ferry to Split. She said she'd see them back in UK for the next term - but when the day came she wasn't there. There was a postcard telling them she'd decided to stay with Mehmet and that she'd found some work to support her. In fact, she'd found several people who wanted to learn English so earned enough to support herself and lived in Mehmet's little room above the restaurant.

Her parents were furious and anxious and came to see her in Dubrovnik. But they liked Mehmet once they got to know him, and she was adamant about staying. The Uni was persuaded to let her take a year out, with the possibility of returning thereafter - but by that time she had had me and so she never finished her course. It hasn't done her any harm though, she is a writer- Tricia Boone.

"Tricia Boone? I read loads of her books when I was a teenager, she understands feelings so well."

"Yeah, she says that probably staying at Uni would have ruined her as far as that kind of writing was concerned."

"What does your dad do? Is he a writer too?"

"No, he runs a couple of restaurants now."

"We have a lot in common," she said. "My mum also went against her family's wishes when she married my dad. For me it's the other way around. My dad was British, in fact he was a Scotsman, but he went to Trinidad and met my mum there."

Lila explained the instant attraction between them and then brought the story up to date with her birth, her very happy early childhood, then the sadness of her dad's death and her mother's dementia.

"I am so sorry," said Dragan, "it must be awful for you. How do you cope?"

She explained about the wonderful Mrs D. and the pattern of her working life.

"What work do you do?"

Here Lila was cautious, she had been warned not to chat about the details of her experiments, particularly not the animal work.

"Research, into dementia, of all things."

"Gosh, it must mean that you have a good understanding. I was reading about a possible new test in the Guardian yesterday. Is that your work?"

"No, not mine, I read that too - but my mum is beyond the need for that. Though it'll perhaps give us what we need to find early onset patients who are more likely to be treatable. And a cohort of subjects who have one particular kind of dementia, so that it's easier to see whether any treatment works or not. Right now we have to rely on clinical symptoms, assessment of cerebro- spinal fluid from a lumbar puncture and imaging."

"Is there more than one kind of dementia?"

"Oh yes, there are 4 major forms." She ticked them off on her fingers. "Alzheimer's disease, vascular dementia, Lewy body dementia which is associated with Parkinson's disease and fronto-temporal dementia. Also, there are other conditions which can present as dementia."

"What does your mum have?"

"We don't know for sure, probably Alzheimer's because it's the commonest. We'd only find out after a post-mortem, so I'm not in any hurry!"

"You are very matter of fact. I'd not manage that."

"I think it's because I'm a scientist and work with medics. But I do get emotional about her at times, especially when some new feature appears - like not recognising me."

"What? Has she done that?"

"Only once, just recently, but it was really horrible."

"Oh, Lila, you poor thing." He put his hand gently over hers." Can I help you?"

"Do you really mean that?"

"Yes, of course."

She thought for a moment, then took a leap of faith, liking and trusting this young man.

"Would you like to meet her? Why not come back with me now? When you have finished your toast, of course."

"OK," he replied, "give me a couple of minutes." He chewed the last of his crusty bread, they both finished their coffees, then set off back through the park to Lila's home.

CHAPTER 6

It was like Mother Hubbard, thought Lisa, distractedly - when they got there the front door was open and Grace was nowhere to be found. She searched the house, while Dragan went around the garden and checked the shed. They met back in the sitting room.

"She's never done this before. Where can she be?" Lila felt tears pricking at her eyes.

"Can I suggest that you do two things?"

Lila nodded. "What are they?"

"First check with the neighbour whom you mentioned to me, and, if Grace is not there, then ring the police."

"OK. " Lila was about to ring Mrs D when she thought better of it and scooted out of the still open front door and across the low wall to Mrs D's PVC imitation Georgian one. She rang the bell and waited, moving her weight from one foot to the other in anxiety.

The door opened and Mrs D's cheerful face appeared.

"Hello Lila, how are you?"

"Is Mum here?" asked Lila, unable to cope with civilities.

"No, my dear, she isn't. I haven't seen her at all today."

"Thank you, I have to let the police know she's gone missing - please ring me if she comes here."

"Of course I will, I'm going along to the shops now, I'll keep a look out for her."

"Thank you, thank you, " said Lila, already climbing back over the wall.

Dragan had heard this interchange from Lila's doorstep and he immediately handed Lila his phone,

"I've dialled 999", he said.

Lila took it, explained that she needed the police and then explained the problem to a sympathetic, but to Lila, very slow, woman. Finally, all the details were down.

"Is this the best number to contact you on?"

Lila gave the lady her own mobile phone number for first use, with Dragan's as back up. She hung up and returned it to him.

"What do I do now?" She felt incapable of making any rational decision. Dragan saw this and said gently,

"Why don't we go to some of the places that your mum knows and likes?"

 Lila nodded.

"Where do you go for a walk?"

"She likes to go to the swings and watch the children playing."

"Let's go. "

Dragan took her hand and led her off, back into the park, but across to the lower corner where there was a large play area, not visible from their previous trip back from the deli. They walked fast then, as they grew closer, Lila broke into a run.

"Mum, Mum, " she called, hurrying through the gate, which almost slammed into Dragan's face. He watched her run up to a huddled, coatless figure sitting on a bench in the weak sunlight and put her arms around it, tears streaming down her face.

"Oh Mum, I was so worried about you."

Grace just smiled up at her daughter.

"Hello love, " she said.

They helped Grace home between them. She was both cold and tired, so Lila put her onto the bed, under the duvet, still fully dressed, but with shoes off. Dragan found the kettle, filled it and sourced a cup and a teabag. He had almost managed to make the tea when Lila reappeared and took over, adding a spoonful of sugar before pouring on the boiling water. She took it up to her Mum, but did not give it to her immediately, instead she added a little cold water from the bathroom tap. She watched her mum sip it, removing it to a place of safety afterwards. Lila had begun to realize that she could not rely on her mother to be sensible in any respect any more.

"No more, " said Grace when the cup was half empty and turned onto her side, ready to sleep.

Lila kissed her on the side of her forehead and went downstairs. Dragan was sitting in the kitchen, drinking tea, with a cup ready for Lila.

"Thank you, she said, "I'd have freaked out if you hadn't been here to help."

"No problem", he said, "I've let the police know that your mum has been found."

"Oh, I'd have forgotten about that, you are a real help."

Dragan smiled that lovely warm smile, "A pleasure, I'm so glad I was with you too."

They sipped their tea in silence for a while, then Lila said, almost to herself,

"What on earth do I do now about Mum?"

****

That night was long and troubled for Lila, even though Grace slept remarkably well throughout. Lila could not get to sleep, her mind was relentlessly active, going over the same ground again and again. She had to find a carer to stay with Grace all the time that she was at work, but in no way could she afford someone from a care agency. That afternoon she had approached Mrs D but, as expected, she had not wanted to be tied down for so many hours each day, though she had very kindly said she would do this until Lila found someone. Horribly embarrassed, Lila asked about how much payment would be required. Mrs D reassured her that she did not want or need to be paid, but if Lila could buy the food for her and Grace to eat together that would be fine. So, the next week or so were covered - but then what, or rather who? Perhaps a sort of au pair might be possible, Lila could house her - or him - pay pocket money and teach them English in return for her mother's care. But how to find the right person, one who was mature enough to be kind and caring, but with sufficient gravitas for Grace to obey? Maybe there was someone with a grandparent with dementia, so with some idea of the likely problems? Eventually she fell into a troubled sleep and woke late, having somehow switched off the alarm on her phone without remembering doing so.

Grace was up and about, Lila could hear her in the bathroom. TGIS, she thought - Thank God It's Sunday - as she stretched luxuriously, extending her feet into the chilly area at the bottom of her bed and wriggling her toes. She felt like turning over and going back to sleep, but knew she had to see if Grace was OK, so rolled to the bed edge, sat up and swung her legs onto the floor, searching around with her feet for her slipper socks, a welcome Christmas gift from her aunt. Remembering their origin gave Lila an idea - perhaps one of Grace's sisters might be able to help?

She put this idea into operation once she had fed and dressed Grace. The conversations with both Hope and Charity were similar: both were delighted to hear from Lila, but very sorry, neither could spare the time to come and stay to care for Grace, nor did they have any bright ideas about finding a suitable carer. Their children, Lila's cousins, were all either working or in full time education and none had a friend needing work. Lila thanked them – though for what? she wondered. It also crossed her mind that, had circumstances been different, Grace would probably have gone to help them.

She was looking into au pair agencies online when her phone rang. It was Dragan.

"Hi Lila, how are you? Is your mum OK?"

"Hi Dragan, nice of you to ring. Yes, Grace is fine, I'm fine too, but the front and back doors are locked now all the time. It feels like a prison here."

"Oh, you poor thing. I was wondering if you would like to bring your mum round to my house for coffee and a chat. My parents would like to meet her. I told them all about yesterday."

"That is so kind. Of course, I'm sure Grace would enjoy coming to meet your family. What time would you like us?"

"Would 11am suit you?"

"Yes, what's your address?" Dragan told her, and Lila put it into her phone, together with his phone number. "See you soon, bye."

Grace seemed happy to go out and to meet the family of the young man who Lila told her helped to bring her home yesterday, though she was not sure she could remember that event. In her good winter coat with a matching scarf she looked smart, normal, and Lila put her arm through her mother's with an affectionate squeeze. The walk did not take very long, but Grace was tiring by the time they reached the front door. Lila rang the bell which echoed loudly through the house.

A young woman opened it, obviously Dragan's sister. She was beautiful, with large brown eyes and a big smile.

"Hi, you must be Lila and Grace. Dragan has told me about you. Come in please."

Their predominant impression of the house was of bright colour, red walls in the hall, then green walls in the large kitchen-diner at the back of the building, with pictures everywhere - mostly family photographs, some in collages, some large individual ones taken professionally plus some large colourful abstract paintings.

"This is nice," said Grace. She sat down in a bentwood chair by the large table and looked around.

"Very nice."

Dragan appeared in the doorway.

"You made it, well done. Would you like some tea or coffee?"

"Coffee please", said Lila, "what about you Mum?"

"Coffee would be lovely, thank you," said Grace, obviously happy to be there.

Dragan set up the percolator, then sat down beside Grace while it bubbled to fruition.

"Did you manage to get warm again after the park yesterday?"

Grace looked puzzled, Lila came to her rescue.

"Yes, she had a little nap and was fine when she woke up - but I don't think Mum has any memory of it."

Dragan nodded.

"So I see."

He made their coffees and one for himself and explained to Grace about his family, telling her that his Mum and Dad would be home soon. They had gone to the farmer's market to buy some overpriced organic goodies, he explained. Grace was enthusiastic about the market and said she loved the fresh salad stuff from there. Lila laughed and said that her Mum's memory was pretty good where food was concerned.

Then the front door opened and voices called out

"Honeys, we're home."

Tricia had a kind face, that family smile and very blue eyes; Mehmet was tall, dark, handsome and Lila could see how one could fall for him instantly. They were very friendly, warm, welcoming. Lila felt overpowered by acceptance and suspected that Grace might too - but on looking at her Grace showed no sign of discomfort, she was smiling broadly, nodding and replying quite sensibly to most questions. She seemed to be flowering in this environment, Lila thought, perhaps it was like her childhood, lots of people (all three children had come into the kitchen), lots of talking. Evidently Lila was the only person who felt at all uneasy. She sat quietly listening to the conversation about the market, Sundays, food, local events, without saying much. After an hour she thought that they should leave, but when she suggested it there was an outcry - from Grace as well as from their hosts.

"Oh no, please stay to lunch. It is only stuff from the market."

So they stayed and it was mid-afternoon before they were able to make their way home. Grace was unusually bubbly, she had enjoyed the visit tremendously; Lila felt troubled. She liked them all, they were very kind, but somehow she felt her privacy was being invaded. She was not used to large family life, she supposed.

Grace fell asleep in her chair almost as soon as she sat down, so Lila enjoyed the luxury of time to herself. She lay on her bed with the Sunday paper, coffee and a small bar of chocolate on the bedside table. It was amazing how little things made life good, she thought, as she sipped her coffee and read the colour magazine. Her peace was interrupted by her mobile, ringing from an unknown number. She was tempted to ignore it, but curiosity got the better of her and she picked up.

"Hello, "

"Hello Lila, sorry to disturb you but I thought I should ask you something. It's Tricia here, Dragan's Mum."

"Oh, hello. Thank you so much for inviting us round and for the delicious lunch."

"No problem, feeding two more is neither here nor there with a big family. It was our pleasure. The reason I'm ringing is that Dragan told me about your mum wandering off and needing constant supervision while you go to work. He is worried about you both."

"He is such a kind person."

"Yes, he is, and I am very proud of him. What crossed my mind was that we have had several *aux pairs* over the years and one of them is still around locally, having married a British guy. She has children, but now they are at school and when I met her the other day she told me that she'd like a part-time job. She has no experience of dementia as far as I know, but I can vouch for her as a kind and caring human being. If you'd like me to contact her to see if she is interested let me know. You don't have to say anything now, just think about it. "

"Gosh, that sounds possible. Does she live locally?

 "Yes, the school is around 10 minutes' walk from our house - closer in fact to yours - so timing might be good. You need to think about an early end to the day, holidays, illness - but she would certainly be better than your having to give up work or Grace going into a home."

"Yes, I'll think it over and get back to you in a day or two, if that is OK?"

"Absolutely fine, speak soon."

Tricia ended the call. Lila lay back, turning the possibility over in her mind. Her own job was pretty flexible, but there were times that she could not miss - and there was Boston. That could not be covered by a part time helper. If only Grace had not taken a turn for the worse. If only she could go back to where she'd been six months ago, like she had when started on donepezil, the drug that helped some Alzheimer's sufferers. That brought her thoughts back to colchicine and her mice which, on that drug, were doing better than the controls and better than on the Immunogenomics molecule. She resolved to talk to Tom again tomorrow.

CHAPTER 7

Lila was at work reading about dementia from a website for the general public.

"Even if memory is lost, intuition and emotional understanding remain intact for much longer."

 That is so true, she thought, essentially Grace is still Grace, with her personality shining through - a personality which could be difficult at times. As a child, especially in her teens, Lila had had some major bust ups with her mother. When she was small her father was there to intercede; without him there was no-one to pour oil on the troubled waters and they had both said things which they later regretted. I hope those episodes have been forgotten thought Lila. Now they mostly rubbed along together quite well, largely because there was no longer any question about who was in control.

She was waiting for Tom to return from the ward round, having done all her major tasks for the day.

She marshalled her arguments, putting them down on paper, as she liked to do even now, after years of computer use.

1. Grace has dementia, an incurable and, eventually, fatal condition.
2. There is as yet no known curative treatment.
3. There is no suitable clinical trial for Grace to enter. (Lila had checked this again)
4. Colchicine is a drug which has been used in man for decades, its side effect profile is known.
5. There is reason to believe that it might be effective in dementia treatment, based on its properties.
6. Mouse experiments so far support this contention.

7. If Grace waits for a clinical trial of colchicine (and who would fund it?) it will be too late to reverse the changes in her brain
8. Therefore, she should have the benefit of trying colchicine now.

When Tom finally put his head round the door, she smiled brilliantly at him and said,

"Come in Tom, I have something to say to you. Please take a look at this," handing him the list.

Tom felt himself wedged between a rock and a very hard place. He shifted awkwardly from foot to foot, scratched his already tousled blonde hair and rubbed his chin. He was undoubtedly indebted to Lila, without whom his PhD would have floundered, he wanted to help her and her poor mother. On the other side of the weighing scale was the knowledge that there was no licence for colchicine in dementia and he'd be prescribing it on a named- patient basis to someone who was not in fact his patient, in the hope that it would do more good than harm. He longed to ring the BMA and ask for help but did not quite dare to do so. He had anticipated this situation and had read General Prescribing Information online, noting the advice

"When prescribing, there are a number of points to take into account ……

Primum non nocere - First, do no harm. Hippocrates' advice still holds today. Prescribe only where necessary and consider benefits versus risks. Involve the patient in decisions about their care and respect patient autonomy.

Note the patient's age, medical history (especially of any hepatic or renal dysfunction) and any concurrent medication. Think about dosage carefully; manufacturers' recommended doses are based on population studies and assume 'one dose fits all'. However, there are genetic differences. New drugs are often marketed at the highest therapeutic level to demonstrate effectiveness in large numbers of patients but companies are not required to provide data on lowest effective dose.

If this is a new - potentially long-term - prescription, review the patient to assess for effect, side-effects and the need to continue."

"Do you know if Grace's liver and kidneys are functioning normally?"

"Yes, she had blood tests when we saw the neurologist. Everything was fine."

"O.K.", Tom said, "this is what I'll do. I'll write a script for Grace to have colchicine by mouth once a day at the usual dose for gout for two weeks. You will monitor her very closely, testing her brain function if possible. At the end of two weeks we will reconsider. If anything unusual happens stop the drug immediately and let me know. O.K.?"

It was all Lila could do to stop herself hugging him, but she just replied,

"O.K. Thanks a mill Tom."

"It'll have to be a private prescription- that means you pay the cost of the medication, plus whatever the pharmacy adds on."

"No problem."

Tom took a sheet of hospital headed paper

"What is your Mum's full name, date of birth and address? "

Lila told him and Tom wrote these at the top of the page then added the name of the drug, dosage, date and his signature, qualifications and GMC number.

"You can take it to any pharmacy."

Lila folded it, put it safely in her rucksack and left to go home via the local chemist. At the last minute she changed her mind and took the script to one close to Euston Station, preferring the anonymity. The paper was exchanged for colchicine tablets, with the aid of her debit card and she caught the next train home.

When she got there the cupboard was again bare- no Grace, no Mrs Dewhurst either. Then she heard voices from the garden- going out she found them sitting in two garden chairs, rescued from their winter immersion in the shed, enjoying the spring sunshine. Grace was smiling, a newspaper open on her lap, almost falling off. Mrs Dewhurst rose and came across to Lila,

"Hello dear, how was your work today?"

"Fine, Mrs D, thank you. It's all going well. How was Mum?"

Mrs D. took Lila's elbow and shepherded her back into the kitchen, the aid conspiratorially,

"I'm afraid she had a little accident. No problem, I've changed her and put her clothes into the wash."

Lila's face fell. This was the thing she dreaded most - incontinence. She had thought about it and knew that if and when it happened she would find it hard not to treat her mother like a naughty child, even though she knew it was not her fault.

"Oh no," she said. " What do I do now?"

Mrs D. put a comforting arm around Lila's slim shoulders and gave a little squeeze.

"It's not as bad as all that, you know. My husband had incontinence after his prostate op.-the same problem. He was provided with incontinence pants by the health people - they delivered two or three months' worth at a time - it was hard to know where to put all the boxes. Our GP arranged it. There are still some left, I think, in our attic. I'll go and have a look. Grace can use those while you get her own supply organised."

"I'll let the GP know now. Thank you, Mrs D. What would I do without you?"

Mrs D smiled and volunteered to make them all a cup of tea while Lila rang the local GP practice.

The receptionist to whom she spoke was at first unhelpful and tried to put her off with excuses about all GPs being too busy to speak to her, but once Lila began to cry she changed her mind and found one, a young woman who listened carefully.

"When was your mother last seen by us?" she asked.

"Not for a couple of months. Dr Cartwright did a home visit recently."

"Ah, yes, I have just found her letter about that visit."

There was a pause while she was presumably reading the letter.

"OK, first we need to check if your mother has a urinary tract infection. Please could you come down to the surgery and collect a sterile pot with instructions for urine collection and a form to send with it to the hospital?"

Lila agreed to this, but wondered how on earth she was going to manage to collect a sample of Grace's urine for testing.

The doctor was still talking. "I need to authorize the local authority nurses to contact you about supplies of incontinence pants or pads. I'll do that and they should be in touch within a day or two. Now, how are you coping?"

Lila sighed. "Not so well now. I dreaded the onset of incontinence - and now it is here. Also, my mum wakes up in the night now quite often – and I can't get back to sleep easily afterwards. Then I'm tired at work."

"I see. Who is with your mother while you work?"

"Our neighbour, for the time being, she's doing it as a favour - but I'm looking for somebody else. I have one person who might be available, but I haven't met her yet."

"I see. I think that we should see both you and your mother here soon. Please make an appointment with me. I am Dr McKay. I'll put you back to our receptionist to organise one."

"Thank you," said Lila, with mixed feelings. She wanted all the help she could get; but did not fancy explaining to the GP about the colchicine, which was still in her bag.

The appointment was organized for over two weeks' time, there was no suitable slot any earlier. Lila breathed a relieved sigh - she could give Grace the two weeks' worth of colchicine if she started it tonight and then conveniently forget about it at the practice, because it would have finished.

She returned to the ladies in the garden for her cuppa with a lighter heart.

That evening she gave Grace the first colchicine capsule with her evening meal. Grace made no comment even though it was new for her to have medicine at that time and took it without demur. The night was no different to usual - but the wake up was brief and Lila did go back to sleep quickly, despite the excitements of the day.

 Next day when she came home she heard her mother call out,

"Gordon, is that you?"

Lila's heart sank. The first time that Grace did this, asking for her long dead husband, Lila had told her the truth. Grace had been inconsolable, sobbing just as much as she had when he first died. Now Lila knew that she had to find some other way, so she replied.

"No Mum, it's only me."

"Hello darling. I'm worried about Gordon, he's been gone a long time."

"Oh, he's fine Mum, no need to worry. Busy at work."

Mrs Dewhurst appeared from the kitchen, bearing a tray with a teapot and three cups.

"Hello Lila, your Mum has had a good day. We went for a walk in the Park and had a little picnic. I think she is a bit tired now."

"Thank you so much. I am interviewing a possible carer this weekend. I hope that is soon enough?"

"Yes, that's fine. When you have found somebody, I can still help out from time to time, you know. I just don't want to be tied down at my age. "

"Of course, I quite understand."

They had a companionable teatime, Grace seemed to have forgotten about Gordon for the time being, but Lila knew that her worries tended to recycle and was a little on edge. She need not have worried - Grace ate her supper of spaghetti bolognaise with unusual relish and, for the first time in ages, thanked Lila for it. The yellow capsule of colchicine went down with no problem. That night Grace slept through and Lila was woken from deep restful sleep by her alarm in the morning. Like the mother whose new baby sleeps through for the first time, she was terrified that something dreadful had happened in the night and hurried to Grace's bedroom. Her mother was still peacefully asleep and snoring gently.

The week passed quickly, with Grace sleeping well each night. Lila continued giving her the colchicine, beginning to hope that the two things were related. On Friday evening Mrs D told her that she had stopped putting on the incontinence pants because Grace was managing fine with going to the loo - perhaps it had just been a blip, she said. Lila was ecstatic and relieved.

On Saturday morning at 11 am the bell rang. It was the ex-au pair of Dragan's family. She looked about Lila's age and was pretty with long dark hair, but looked even more tired than Lila currently felt. The interview went well, Marjana had had a granny with dementia who lived with her parents when she was growing up, so understood many of the problems. She was also obviously intelligent and seemed caring. Grace was a little reserved at first, sensing that this person was going to replace Lila, but began to warm to Marjana after a while. It was decided that there would be a trial period of a month during which they could each decide if the arrangement was to continue. Marjana would come to the house as soon as she had dropped her children at school, Lila would have to be home in time for Marjana to leave to pick them up. That gave her a short working day, but it would be sufficient for the practical things that she had to do in the lab. Any reading, writing etc could be done at home. School holidays would be a problem - but Mrs D would probably be able to cover those. At that thought Lila decided that Mrs D should meet Marjana and went next door to ask her over. She was pleased to be involved and even asked some pertinent questions. When she had gone Lila approached the delicate question of money. Marjana was hoping for twelve pounds an hour in cash, but Lila would find that hard to provide. They settled on the basic London living wage, with a possible increase if Lila's salary was raised. Marjana left and Lila began to make lunch.

"When will she come back?" asked Grace.

"On Monday Mum, will that be OK?"

"We'll have to see." Lila was surprised by this lack of passivity on Grace's part but didn't question her further.

CHAPTER 8

Monday came, and with it heavy spring rain. Marjana arrived, dripping from head to foot.

"You poor thing. Don't you have an umbrella?" asked Lila.

"I can't manage two children and an umbrella," said Marjana, "not enough hands. I'm sorry to make your floor so wet."

She hung her raincoat on a hook by the door.

"No problem, come and say hello to Grace."

Grace was in the kitchen, sitting at the table finishing her porridge. Lila was about to introduce Marjana, sure that Grace would already have forgotten her, when Grace spoke.

"Hello, you are coming to look after me while Lila goes to work, aren't you? Please remind me of your name?"

"It's Marjana, can I come and sit with you please?"

Grace nodded and Marjana sat down beside her.

"Your hair is wet," Grace nodded towards the far wall. "There is a towel over there."

Lila, pleased by this logical thought on the part of her mother, made her farewells and went out into the rain under her umbrella, having decided against biking.

Marjana dried her hair, washed up, then said,

"Do you like music, Grace?"

There was a nod, so Marjana put on the radio and altered the stations until she found something that made Grace smile. She began to sway and then dance in time to the music, then held out her hands to Grace, helped her up and they danced together to the Beatles' "Hey Jude." Marjana suspected that looking after Grace was not so different from amusing and occupying her children, something at which she was expert.

They were dancing again when Lila returned, in good time for the school pick up. Her mother had drawn a picture using felt tip pens. It was meant to be a still life of the vase of flowers on the table, but it had an odd quality, Picasso-like, with multiple view points and odd sizing - some flowers being bigger than the vase. There were two handles, not one.

"Isn't it interesting the way she sees things, your Mum?" asked Marjana.

"Yes, it certainly is," said Lila, feeling inadequate. Why had she not thought of doing things like this with Grace - her own mother! - instead of just sitting in front of the TV with her? Perhaps the dementia would have progressed more slowly if she had kept Grace's brain more active. Anyway, now I am doing something for her, she thought, with the colchicine every night. It might just be doing some good, as it was in the mice in her laboratory, where the colchicine-treated ones were out performing the Immunogenomics mice as well as the controls.

When Marjana had gone Lila asked Grace a question.

"Did you have a nice day?"

"Yes love, she's a good girl, that one. I'm tired now though."

Lila switched on the TV, made Grace comfortable, then went to make supper. At least she could feed her mother well, she thought.

The days passed in similar fashion, with Marjana persuading Grace to do things: to play cards (snap), to dance, do simple yoga and to read out loud. They went out when the weather was fine, usually to the park, but sometimes further. Grace began to look better, less pale, less puffy, more her old self.

Lila still felt upset that her caring ability was not as good as she had thought - but did spend better quality time with Grace at the weekends and began to enjoy that time more. She was very grateful to Dragan and his family and rang to thank them.

"No problem, you are most welcome. I'm glad that it has worked out well for all of you. Dragan is here, do you want a word with him?"

Lila was about to demur, having not heard anything from Dragan since their lunch at his home she thought that he had regretted making contact, when he came on the line.

"Hi Lila, have you missed me?"

"Ha ha, of course" she said, lightly.

"I've been in Eastern Europe, doing a series of articles for the paper. I meant to ring you, but my phone was stolen on the first day. It was a complete nightmare because I lost all my contact numbers, couldn't ring anyone except home because I knew that one by heart."

"I can imagine."

"Can I come around to see you soon?"

"Yes, when is good for you?

"How about this Saturday, say 10-ish?

"Anyone for ten-ish?" laughed Lila, repeating an old joke. Dragan was good enough to laugh. "That would be fine, see you then."

****

Saturday dawned fair, Lila was still washing up the breakfast dishes when Dragan arrived at the door, bearing a rucksack.

"Hi," he said, smiling his wonderfully complicit smile, which made her smile in return.

"Are you ready"

"Ready for what? I can't leave my Mum"

"Ready for an awayday all together. Your Mum can come too. It's a magical mystery tour."

"But...but...I have things to do, there's the house to clean, the washing..."

His face fell. Then he brightened and said,

"I'm good at cleaning. Tell me what needs doing, give me the equipment and I'll get on with it while you deal with the washing."

So she did. In an hour the vital parts of the house had been cleaned by the two of them and the washing was reaching its final spin. Grace had sat happily looking at the large Saturday newspaper which Dragan had brought.

"Nearly there", said Lila, "should I hang the washing out, do you think, or is it going to rain?"

Dragan consulted his mobile phone.

"The weather app says it will be fine all day, let's chance it."

They hung out the sheets and duvet covers but hedged their bets by putting smaller items inside. Since these included Lila's smalls, she insisted on dealing with this part herself.

Finally, at 11.30 am they set off on their outing, with Lila and Grace unaware of their destination, but wearing walking shoes and comfortable clothes, as advised. An umbrella was put into the rucksack, just in case. Lila felt enormous relief at having the decisions about the day taken from her and was in a good mood; Grace, catching the feeling, was also very cheerful.

The trip involved the Overground, going west. Dragan kept them from catching the train to Clapham Junction, so they waited for the next one to Richmond, admiring the neatness of the Brondesbury Park station garden, with labels indicating where and which seeds had been sown.

"Oh, let's come and pick some mint when it comes up," said Grace. "I like mint tea."

Lila was taken aback - Grace had read the label, understood and formulated a plan based on that comprehension. She must be getting better. She gently squeezed her mother's arm.

"Of course we will", she said. "It's a Community Garden, so anyone can help and use the produce."

The magical mystery place turned out to be Kew Gardens. Dragan had chosen it because of the Orchid show, knowing that Grace was likely to recognise orchids from her tropical childhood. She was enchanted by the displays - huge pillars covered in orchids of one colour or another - but also liked the ponds and the underground tunnel with small aquaria showing what life was like in very ancient times. Again, she understood the concept, once explained to her by Lila, and commented that it would have been good to bring her class here.

The rucksack turned out to contain a picnic - various sandwiches bought from the local supermarket, apples and a bottle of water with 3 paper cups. They sat on a bench in the sunshine to eat it, watching children climbing in the lower curved branches of an enormous cedar.

"This is lovely", Grace exclaimed, "so lovely."

Lila was impressed by Dragan's thoughtfulness and preparedness. She had never known a young man quite like him and felt that he was becoming like a brother to her, a son to Grace.

"Thanks so much", she said. "This is a wonderful day out for us."

"I'm glad" he replied. "I was worried about the weather, but it's perfect."

Indeed it was, the sun shone, but not too hotly and a few fluffy white clouds were being gently blown across the sky.

"Coffee? " asked Lila. "I'll get some if you'd like it."

Grace wanted tea, Dragan coffee, so she joined the queue outside a van parked nearby and waited her turn, covertly watching Grace and Dragan talking quietly. He was obviously telling Grace a funny story because she was smiling, then laughing out loud - something Lila had not heard for ages.

When the warm drinks had been drunk they decided to walk to see the bluebells - the smell of them wafted towards them even before they reached the wooded area where they grew.

"Oh, bluebells, I can smell them," Grace exclaimed. Lila again felt her heart lift - sense of smell was often impaired very early on in neurodegenerative disease. It was good to know that her mother was still capable of sensing a smell and of recognising it. The colchicine must be working!

They were all three tired on the journey home and spoke little, reading the papers instead. Once home Grace retired for a "little nap." Lila offered Dragan tea, made it and took the tray into the garden.

"It has been a smashing day", she said," I am so grateful to you."

 "My pleasure"

They sat in companionable silence for a while, then Lila remembered the washing and fetched it in before the air cooled. She also took a peek inside the fridge.

 "Would you like to stay to supper?"

"I would love to, but I can't - I have to be back at home to help my parents to entertain some rather difficult people. In fact, I should go now, I have promised to make a starter. Another time perhaps?"

"Of course."

He rose and walked into the house, picking up the nearly empty rucksack as he went. By the front door he turned to face Lila.

"Say goodbye to Grace for me please."

He leaned forward and gave Lila a gentle, light kiss on the cheek, spun on his heel and left.

Lila watched his small, jaunty figure going down the path. She was so lucky to have met him. What a pity that she didn't fancy him in the slightest.

CHAPTER 9

Tom returned to the lab late on Monday morning, looking tired and harassed. Lila, who knew he had been on call over the weekend and who wanted desperately to buttonhole him about the colchicine, thought better of it and left him alone for a while. Then, when it was nearly time for her to leave, she approached him,

"Tom, please could I have a quick word?"

"Hi Lila, yes, what is it?"

"I wanted to show you the colchicine data in my mice - I've done a print out for you. Here it is. Also, I think it is definitely helping my mum. She can read more, can understand and link up thoughts; she's stopped being incontinent and hardly wakes up in the night now. Please can I have some more for her?"

Tom sighed. "Could you ask your GP now?"

Lila's face fell. "Not easily, not yet. I want to have incontrovertible evidence of benefit, then I'll ask her. Please, just 2 months' more."

Tom sighed again, then took the easiest option and gave in, writing another private prescription for two months' supply. He handed Lila the paper and said,

"Lila, this has to be the last time, you do understand?"

Lila nodded. She blew him a kiss.

"You are an angel, Tom."

He laughed and went back to his work.

By the time of the GP appointment Grace seemed a little better still: she had begun to take some care of herself again, brushing her own hair, going unaided to the lavatory and singing and humming to herself the way she always had before illness struck. Lila was tempted to cancel the visit but decided to go ahead with it in order to get the GP on her side, if possible, before having later to confess about the colchicine. She and Grace walked down to the surgery, checked in on the electronic board for two sequential visits and sat down to wait. The magazines were at least a year out of date, so Lila spent the time making a few notes about what she wanted to say to the GP. Grace picked up an old copy of Good Housekeeping and was looking through the recipes when they were called in.

Dr Mc Kay was very welcoming, sitting them both down and facing them by turning round her swivel chair.

"How are things going Lila?"

"Surprisingly well, thank you. Mum seems to be a bit better - the incontinence thing was a brief episode – it's not a problem now. Also, Mum is sleeping better."

"Did you find a good helper?"

"Yes, thank you. A friend's mother recommended someone who has turned out to be excellent. She is very stimulating and has lots of ideas for things to do with Mum. They get on really well."

"Perhaps that is why your mother has improved?"

"Yes, maybe", said Lila, thinking that she hadn't considered that before.

The doctor turned towards Grace and asked her a few simple questions – about the date, the day of the week, the Queen. Grace didn't know the first two, but was right about ERII and, surprisingly, the Prime Minister. She consented to be examined and to having a blood test done.

Dr Mc Kay called for a nurse to take Grace down to the phlebotomist, then used the opportunity to talk to Lila on her own.

"Is there anything that you want help with? Last time I spoke to you I felt that you were, quite reasonably, very distressed by your mother's illness and all its ramifications."

"Not really, right now, thank you. The circumstances have improved a lot. However, please can I come back to you if I need to?"

"Yes, of course, just make an appointment. Now, I'd like to give you a quick check up, if that is all right?"

Lila assented and had her heart and chest listened to and her blood pressure checked.

"All fine. What I suggest is that we try giving your mother an additional medication. I know she is on donepezil, but we could add in a statin. They reduce cholesterol which is slightly high in your Mother's previous blood sample. There is evidence that they help to prevent heart disease, but also that they may reduce dementia. Perhaps a statin might help to slow down the progression of your mother's disease."

"Fine", Lila nodded.

She thanked the doctor, took the prescription, which she noted, unlike the one from Tom, was written on the computer and printed out, and went downstairs to find Grace. They went together to the pharmacy near the station and picked up the new tablets, then walked home across the park.

That evening Lila handed Grace her usual colchicine tablet and was about to give her the statin too when it occurred to her to read the package insert first. This unsettled her, so she went to the internet for more advice and found several worrying paragraphs:

"Very rarely, statins can cause life-threatening muscle damage called rhabdomyolysis (rab-doe-my-OL-ih-sis). Rhabdomyolysis can cause severe muscle pain, liver damage, kidney failure and death. The risk of very serious side effects is extremely low and calculated as a few cases per million patients taking statins. Rhabdomyolysis can occur when you take statins in combination with certain drugs or if you take a high dose of statins, and also if:

You are taking multiple medications to lower your cholesterol

Are female

Have a smaller body frame

Are age 65 or older

Have kidney or liver disease

Drink beyond recommended limits of alcohol

Drugs and food that interact with statins:

Grapefruit juice contains a chemical that can interfere with the enzymes that break down (metabolize) the statins in your digestive system. While you won't need to eliminate grapefruit entirely from your diet, ask your doctor about how much grapefruit you can have.

Some drugs that may interact with statins and increase your risk of side effects include:

Amiodarone a medication for irregular heart rhythms

Gemfibrozil another variety of cholesterol lowering drug

Protease inhibitors, such as saquinavir and ritonavir

Some antibiotic and antifungal medications, such as clarithromycin and itraconazole

Some immunosuppressant medications, such as cyclosporine.

There are many drugs that may interact with statins, so be sure your doctor is aware of all the medicines you take when being prescribed with statins."

She then went to the websites on colchicine which she'd found previously.

"The effects of some drugs can change if you take other drugs or herbal products at the same time. This can increase your risk for serious side effects or may cause your medications not to work correctly. These drug interactions are possible, but do not always occur. Your doctor or pharmacist can often prevent or manage interactions by changing how you use your medications or by close monitoring.

To help your doctor and pharmacist give you the best care, be sure to tell your doctor and pharmacist about all the products you use (including prescription drugs, non-prescription drugs, and herbal products) before starting treatment with this product. While using this product, do not start, stop, or change the dosage of any other medicines you are using without your doctor's approval.

Other medications can affect the removal of colchicine from your body, which may affect how colchicine works or increase the risk of serious side effects. Examples include certain azole antifungals (such as itraconazole, ketoconazole), cyclosporine, HIV medications (such as ritonavir), macrolide antibiotics (such as clarithromycin, erythromycin), telithromycin, verapamil, among others.

Colchicine may rarely cause a certain serious (even fatal) muscle damage (rhabdomyolysis). This muscle damage releases substances that can lead to serious kidney problems. The risk may be increased if other drugs that may also cause rhabdomyolysis are taken along with colchicine. Some such drugs include: atorvastatin, digoxin, gemfibrozil, pravastatin, simvastatin, among others."

She looked down at the new tablets, noted that they were called simvastatin and filed them carefully at the back of the medicine cabinet in the bathroom. Fortunately, Grace did not ask about the new tablets, but went to bed after the evening's TV without complaint.

CHAPTER 10.

Susan Armstrong's mood matched the thundery weather - she had an imminent migraine, her new Louboutins were pinching her incipient bunions and she had heard nothing from Dermot Banks since their tête-à-tête over dinner. She was sitting at her computer, shoes now off, devising her talk for the neurology conference and having problems with the slide design. Deciding to seek help she marched down the long corridor of the laboratory section, hoping to find Tom who was good at PowerPoint. Instead she found Lila, hunched over the computer in her tiny room.

"Good morning", said Susan.

Lila, who had been intently working on her data, was startled by this intrusion.

"Oh, good morning Prof", she said.

"Are you good with doing PowerPoint slides?"

"Not great, but I can do most things, given time."

"Excellent", said Susan. "Please could I borrow you for a few minutes?"

"Of course", Lila replied, saving her work and rising awkwardly from her chair.

"It's the backgrounds", explained Susan, "I have amalgamated slides from several different previous talks and I cannot get them to look uniform without losing things from some of them."

"No problem", Lila sat at the professorial desk, feeling very grand, and checked the slide set. She made a few keystrokes, altered one or two individual slides and asked,

"Does that format suit you?"

Susan examined the presentation, clicking through it to check each slide.

"Yes, that is just what I wanted. Thank you so much. What exactly did you do?"

Lila explained slowly and carefully. Susan made notes in her diary.

"Thanks, I'll manage it myself next time. Funny how one always has to go one generation down to get IT stuff done."

Then, cheered by this success, she asked,

"How is your mother?"

Lila thought that perhaps this was her moment.

"She's a little better, thank you. "

Susan did not ask why a person with a neurodegenerative disease had improved, she merely said,

"Good. Thank you, Lila."

This was a dismissal. Lila returned to her room and her calculations. These showed that the control , placebo- treated mice had worsened considerably in their performance over the weeks, that the ones treated with IG0047F were doing better, but those given colchicine were undoubtedly the best performers in the swimming test. They had not worsened since the initial test, indeed there was significant improvement in their timings.

The planned treatment and assessment phase would shortly end, the mice would then have to be sacrificed for detailed examination of their brains. Lila hated ending the life of a creature herself. She told herself that it was for a good purpose - to enable better understanding and treatment of human disease, but it was only when she brought the personality of her Mum into the equation that she was absolutely convinced. She needed help for this part of the work, there were lots of mice and all of the sacrificing, brain extraction and preservation had to be done in one day. Terry kindly agreed to be available on the following Tuesday for the purpose. Lila was relieved, he was an old hand - the mice would be dispatched expertly with a quick and painless death and their brains saved properly for immunohistopathological analysis.

With her plans made, Lila was able to return home. She asked Marjana whether there was any possibility that she could stay late next Tuesday. Marjana thought that might be possible if she could organize for her children to be collected by a friend to go and play with their schoolmates, she would let Lila know. As back up, Lila also trotted over to Mrs Dewhurst, who was similarly obliging, saying that she'd be happy to spend a little time with Grace whom she hadn't had a cuppa with for several weeks now.

Reminded by her experience with Susan, Lila began to make her own talk for the Boston meeting on her laptop whilst sitting with Grace in front of the TV. The subject was her previous experiments, but she was tempted to include the most recent data - she would have to ask Susan. Still uncertain about whether to confess to having a colchicine group, Lila carefully made a separate file which excluded them from her current results, justifying this to herself as a stop- gap measure until she saw what their brains looked like.

In the event Tuesday went smoothly. Lila returned home about 7pm to find that, as requested, Mrs D had taken over from Marjana at 6pm. Grace was pleased to see her and said,

"That was a long day, love. Are you all right?"

Lila wanted to weep - it had been a while since her Mum had noticed much of Lila's life - but she just went over to Grace, hugged her and said,

"I'm fine Mum, thanks. It was a tough day, but it went well and I'm hopeful about the results."

"Will you get them tomorrow?"

"Oh no – not for some weeks. There's a lot to do still."

"Should we have supper? I'm hungry."

"Yes Mum, give me 5 minutes and I'll have your supper on the table."

Lila had bought fish and chips near the station. The wonderful vinegary smell was permeating the room.

"Is it F&C?"

Lila laughed at this abbreviation which had long been used by them both. Grace's sense of smell was obviously working.

"Yes Mum, you've got it in one."

CHAPTER 11

At last October arrived. Lila had still not confessed about her mother's use of colchicine to the GP, nor about the colchicine-treated mice to Prof. Armstrong. She had focused on the Boston meeting and persuaded herself that it needed to be over before she came out with both confessions.

For months Lila had been anticipating the trip to Boston with Tom. The cheap flights had been organized and she had succeeded in seating them together. She was a little worried that they'd not find enough to talk about for 7 hours, but then there were films to watch and discuss, food to be eaten etc. In the event her disappointment was severe. Not only had Tom let her down by being too late to accompany her on the cheaper Underground trip to Heathrow, but once seated on the plane, in narrow uncomfortable seats with little leg room, Tom turned to her, smiled and said,

"Do you mind if I'm a bit anti-social? I want to go over my talk, eat and then sleep, if that's all right with you. I am bushwhacked, the ward has been very busy and I've not had a proper night's sleep for weeks."

"No problem, " said Lila, hiding her disappointment. She picked up the book she had bought at a charity shop and began to read it, ignoring Tom completely. Once they were safely airborne she too checked her talk on her laptop, spoke it through a few times in her head, then put the laptop away and busied herself with the in-flight entertainment, choosing a film she had wanted to see but had missed. She found the small screen and poor quality sound prevented her from concentrating on the action so switched to music instead, choosing the classical channel. Whilst listening her mind drifted away to reflections on the previous busy weeks. She had managed to deal with all the mice, removing their brains and preserving them for histo- and immunopathological analysis. Then a trained colleague had made serial sections of each brain, carefully labelling them, and staining them for different forms of analysis. Lila had started on this - because of the coding she was blind as to the nature of the treatment each mouse had received. There were literally hundreds of hours using the microscope ahead of her. It was when she thought of the sheer drudgery involved in some aspects of scientific research that Lila wished that she had followed her dream and done medical training. Tom's life was hard, but he seemed always to enjoy it, other than the laboratory aspect. There was no possibility now of Lila returning to do clinical training - she could not afford it. Wistfully she remembered Joanna, a friend who had done the same B.Med Sci degree as her - though medicine was what she really wanted she had not been admitted to the course. However, Joanna had gone into the City for a few years, worked really hard, made lots of money, got extremely dissatisfied and was now funding a 4-year medical training place for herself.

 Lila's thoughts turned to Grace who was still continuing on colchicine, courtesy of Tom, whose arm she had twisted yet again by telling him of the definite improvements. Grace very rarely woke in the night now, she was continent and had recovered some of her mental acuity. There was still no way she could help Lila with the crossword anymore, but she could read and make sense of a broadsheet newspaper now - the hated Daily Chronicle had been abandoned. Last week Marjana and Grace had been cooking – Lila enjoyed the apple pie and spaghetti bolognaise, made, she was informed, nearly all by Grace with a little help. In truth Lila was enormously grateful to Marjana, but also a little jealous, that she and Grace had such a good relationship. Lila felt her own relationship with her mother was gradually going back to where it had been, with good and bad times, ups and downs, but regular, like a healthy ECG - and infinitely preferable to the low grade flatlining one they had reached prior to colchicine, with Grace taking little actual notice of her presence and even failing to recognise her. Dragan was another friend with whom Grace could talk and laugh. He teased her often and Grace, and indeed Lila too, was always pleased to see him. He tended to drop in on his way home from the station, staying for a cup of coffee and a chat. He and Lila could usually finish the Guardian quick crossword between them. He had also made the effort to take the two of them out at the weekend again; but had not asked Lila out on her own. She was to some extent relieved, she liked Dragan, but did not fancy him, unlike Tom. She turned to watch Tom's sleeping face - he looked cherubic with his blonde curly hair and a peaceful smile on his sleeping face. He had such charm, all the nurses on the ward liked him. One of them had told Lila how lucky she was to be going to Boston with him. She replied coolly, but was in fact over the moon about it and hoped that it would be the start of great things between them. Lila longed to bend over and kiss him.

By this time pre-lunch drinks were being served so she allowed herself a rare gin and tonic, followed by a glass of white wine with her lunch. Post lunch and with the film over she found herself wanting to tell someone about the flight, so digging out her computer she began an email to Dragan.

"Hi Dragan,

I'm writing to you from the plane! Old-ish one – a jumbo jet, Boeing 747, I think, is its proper name.

I couldn't believe how many people were able to get on board, nor how long it took before we were all in our seats. Probably a good thing since it took me ages to get as far as the plane. We are near the back. I am in the middle of a row of three people, next to Tom who is by the window. The man on my other side has barely spoken to us, seems either shy or grumpy. Hope he can't read this!

Thus far (c. 2/3 way) we have been served with boiled sweets (for take-off), cold towels, free booze, peanuts, lunch with wine, tea or coffee, with choc. mints called Ovation - slightly unfortunate name, makes them sound like a contraceptive.

The pilot's cabin is sadly out of bounds, but I peeped in as we boarded. There were 2 people in it: pilot and a co-pilot, the latter is female (hurrah!). The pilot has grey hair and is of coronary age – not confidence-inspiring. Nor is the fact that my ceiling light doesn't work & the safety sheet is missing from all 3 of the seats in our row. However, the air hostesses are v. chirpy and helpful.

Tried my 50p book which was a feminist black comedy (& not v. funny) by Fay Weldon. Tried to watch a film but the sound is poor and the screen is small, so I'll wait and see it properly another time. Read the Grauniad can't do all the Xword without you."

Unsurprisingly she now felt post–prandial sleep beckoning and tried to get a little more comfortable by tilting her seat back as far as it would go. This was not very far, but was obviously annoying to the person behind her who complained loudly.

"You could tip your own seat back too," Lila retorted, unusual unhelpfulness being provoked by her alcohol intake. Tom was no help as by this time he was asleep, head resting against the window.

A compromise was reached whereby Lila's seat was less tilted and she wriggled around trying to find somewhere to put her head. Tom's shoulder was the only answer as the man on the other side of her was a stranger and seemed determined to remain so. Gingerly she nestled into Tom, lightly at first, and then, as sleep overcame her the weight of her head descended upon him. It was thus that they found themselves when the pilot announced that they were 40 minutes from landing. Lila feeling groggy and realising she needed the loo, asked to be let out and the man beside her rose to make way for her. She joined the queue for the loos. Tom followed, patted her on the shoulder and said,

"Did you get some sleep?"

"I must have, I think. Sorry about using you as a pillow."

"Absolutely no problem. I slept for most of the flight and I feel better for it."

"Good", Lila replied." Then you can lead the way into Boston to our Airbnb."

Landing was not simple or smooth as there were gusting crosswinds. Lila felt more and more sick as the plane lurched from side to side during the descent.

Tom noticed and advised her to use the acupuncture points near her wrist.

"What? " Lila was amazed.

He showed her how to measure three fingers down from the middle of her wrist crease and then to stimulate that area by moving her thumb, pressing on it gently, sometimes rotating the thumb.

She tried and the nausea withdrew considerably, but she was very glad when they landed with a bump and another lurch and began to roll rapidly along the runway, folding down the wing flaps to slow their progress. The engines roared in reverse, it was rather frightening - but soon their speed reduced and the huge machine turned towards its landing bay. Lila heaved a sigh of relief and said

"I don't want to do this too often."

 "Nor me", this from the man on her left. "I have been terrified the whole flight."

 Lila was sympathetic.

"Oh, you poor thing. You could have told me, I'd have tried to help."

 "There was nothing you could have done. In any case I am so loaded up with Valium that I can hardly think, let alone speak. It is wearing off now though. "

He stood up as the seatbelt signs had gone off and opened the flap of the luggage compartment.

"Do you want your suitcase?"

"Yes please, it's the red one."

He handed it down and put it on his seat. Lila gathered together the things she had put beneath the seat in front - making sure to find her handbag, phone and laptop and put them into the large blue imitation leather bag she had bought specially from Primark. Tom was getting his belongings together too. There was then a long pause while the stairs were fixed to the plane doors and people began filing out. They were way back in the queue to get through passport control and it took ages for them to gradually edge forward towards the desks. Lila took the opportunity to go back to the crossword, Tom looked over her shoulder and together they managed to solve several more clues. Frightened Man, as Lila had christened him, turned round and asked to help. He managed to get the last few and they cheered as the puzzle was finally completed. This aroused the ire of the uniformed guards in charge of the queue who told them to quieten down in impolite terms. Lila became less sure that she wanted to enter the United States. Finally, her turn came and a taciturn man asked why she wanted entry, got her electronically fingerprinted and stamped her passport, saying

"Have a good visit."

"Thank you, said Lila, very relieved. Tom was also just emerging from another desk so they went together through baggage collection without stopping and on to the exit, both travelling with hand luggage only. The instructions from their Airbnb host told them to take the subway, so they made their way to the entrance and bought tickets to ride.

The flat when they found it was small, but clean and looked comfortable. Tom had done all the online interaction with their Airbnb host and had explained en route that it had only one bedroom - which would be Lila's - but that there was a sofa bed in the living room for him. Lila began to hope that he would not occupy it after the first night but said nothing. She was very tired - that morning in the UK she had been up at six to finish packing and check through the arrangements for Grace, ensuring that there was plenty of food for the 6 days of her absence. Marjana was coming each weekday morning as usual, Mrs D was looking in each afternoon, giving Grace supper and staying overnight.

Lila had left a note for Mrs D. about Grace's medication in the evening, the precious colchicine; Marjana was already familiar with the morning tablets. She had then left at 6.30 am for Heathrow, using the Overground first, then a walk of nearly a mile to get the Piccadilly line from Acton Town, as the Heathrow express was too expensive. The journey took ages; luckily she had her paperback with her and was able to sit down on both trains. She had arrived just after 8am to find a long queue to check in, as she had no hold luggage she tried to do this on a computer terminal- but was stymied by the need to have her documents checked by a living being. She joined the queue, reading standing up, and was checked in just in time to hurry through security, then take a shuttle to the far away gate just as boarding was starting. She had felt exhausted before the flight took off, now, after 7 hours 45 minutes airborne and all the business of getting into the USA, she was beyond everything except sleep. Oddly it was still only mid-afternoon in Boston. The joys of travel are greatly overrated, she thought.

Tom, who had used the faster but expensive Heathrow Express because he woke late, realised how shattered she was and was solicitous, taking her suitcase, and walking them, fairly slowly for him, to the apartment. He guided her to the lift and up to the 7th floor, worked the self -check-in lockbox using the code which he had been sent and opened the door, shepherding Lila inside. She was suitably impressed by the views of what turned out to be Boston Common from the window and relieved to find a comfortable queen-sized bed in the bedroom.

"I need to sleep," she said, "even though I dozed on the plane."

"Of course you do", Tom replied. "Your body clock is on UK time. Would you like to try melatonin?"

"No need just now."

"Yes, but you'll wake very early and might be glad of it then."

"OK, please give me one then. Thanks"

Tom handed over a small white capsule with instruction to put it into her mouth and let it dissolve if she woke before 2am Boston time. Lila adjusted her watch, said goodnight and retired into the bathroom.

"See you in the morning about 7.30?" Tom shouted through the door.

"OK."

She emerged to see Tom putting a sheet onto the opened sofa bed.

"Goodnight"

"Goodnight."

 She shut the bedroom door, undressed fast, leaving her clothes on the chair by the desk and gratefully lay down in the bed which had already been made up. She was asleep in minutes, having resolved to contact home in the morning.

CHAPTER 12

The next morning she woke and for a second or two had no idea where she was, then the knowledge returned and she checked the time on her phone. 8am, she was late. She remembered waking in the night, about 1.30pm, sending a text to Mrs. D (how lucky that lovely lady had a grandchild who gave her an old Nokia and showed her how to use it), having a pee, then taking a melatonin tablet as directed by Tom. After a while she had gone back to sleep, obviously deeply and refreshingly as she now felt fine.

Having no dressing gown, she wrapped herself in her parka and ventured into the kitchen from whence came a tantalising aroma of fresh coffee. Tom was standing by the hob, stirring something.

"Good morning madam. Breakfast is almost served." He gave a mock bow.

"Good morning Tom. You have been busy. Did you get much sleep?"

 Staying in character Tom replied, "Yes, my lady, as much as my heart – or rather my brain - could desire. How about you?"

"Wonderful night", Lila replied. Your melatonin worked like a charm in the middle of it."

 "Good, now sit down at that little table and I'll give you your scrambled eggs on toast and a cup of coffee."

Lila did as she was told. The eggs were just right, creamy and delicious. The toast was wholemeal, her favourite. The coffee was also to her liking.

She was very happy sitting there with Tom beside her in a scene of cosy domesticity.

"Airbnb is amazing if all this was provided" she commented.

"No such luck. There was instant coffee, bread and milk only - so when you went to bed last night your humble servant, being less rat-arsed, went out on an "expotition" to the locality and did a little light shopping."

"Wow Tom, thanks. How much do I owe you?"

"Nothing", he replied," but we can set up a kitty from now on for meals in the future if you like."

She did like, and the kitty was established in the plastic bag which had held Tom's liquids for the flight.

"The Conference starts at noon," Tom pointed out. "I think we can walk there in about half an hour from here, so we'd have time to do some sightseeing first if you like.

Again, Lila agreed. "Should we walk the Freedom Trail? Trip Advisor says it's the best way to see the sights especially for first timers. It starts at Boston Common, we can pick up a map or just follow the red bricks in the pavement. It's two and a half miles, covers 16 sights."

"Sure, sounds perfect. Let's take the stuff we need for the Conference with us and we can just go straight on from the end of the trail or if we run out of time we can finish it another day."

"I'll wash up quickly, then I'll need 5 minutes to get ready."

"Fine, I'll check my emails."

The morning passed happily - the October sun warmed them and the trail was of interest to them both. They had roughly equivalent paucity of knowledge of American history and both of them always enjoyed being educated, so the time flew by. They were nearing the final item, the steps up to Bunker Hill, when Lila checked her phone and noticed that it was already 11.30am.

"Tom, it's 11.30, we'd better head to the Centre or we'll be late for the Opening Ceremony."

"OK Lila, it's no big deal, but I guess we'd better show up so Susan knows we aren't just having fun here. I think it's too far to walk in time, let's take a cab." Tom's vocabulary had definitely veered towards the American, Lila thought.

It was easy to find a licensed cab. The driver was from Afghanistan, a fact which surprised them both, but he knew the way and they were at the Convention Centre with 10 minutes to spare, and 10 dollars lighter in the kitty. The Centre was huge and magnificent, like something out of Star Wars. What they hadn't bargained for though, were the registration queues to check into the Neurodegeneration Conference. They were in the adjacent queues, E-H surnames for Lila being a Fraser and I-L for Tom as a Jayne, so could chat as they slowly progressed towards the Reception desks.

"Gosh, I hadn't realised how many people would be attending. We should have got here earlier."

"Never mind," Tom reassured her, "we'll just be missing the introductory remarks from all the big cheeses involved."

Lila occupied her time checking out the centre on her smartphone.

"The BCEC was designed by world-renowned architect Raphael Vinoly and HNTB Architecture. The beauty and symbolism of the building's modern, glass-lined interior is reflected throughout the 2.1 million square feet of space. The 41,000 square-foot ballroom overlooks the Boston Seaport District, offering breathtaking views. And with 516,000 square-feet of column-free, contiguous exhibit space, and 82 meeting rooms, the BCEC has the functionality to accommodate your event, your way."

At last it was Lila's turn, Tom's followed swiftly. They put on their Conference badges, picked up their Conference bags from a separate desk and followed the signs and many other people to the main hall. This was massive and full of people, many sitting, but some standing, greeting friends, looking for friends, looking lost. She led Tom as far forward as possible, but even so the stage was a long way off. She was reminded of the time she saw Bob Dylan at the Excel centre - a small Stetson wearing figure seen as though the wrong end of a telescope. Then it dawned on her that it didn't matter because there were huge screens showing the stage suspended at intervals along the sides of the room. She spotted 2 seats in the centre of a row and, apologising regularly to those whose feet she nearly trod on, Lila made her way to them, followed by Tom. They sat down and Lila sighed with relief at having found somewhere good to sit.

"Phew, it's a bunfight, isn't it?"

"Yes, Lila you are very skilled at getting where you want to."

"Thank you." Though she was not sure how much of a compliment it was.

Soon the anaemic background music which had been playing quietly changed to loud, beaty stuff, followed by an announcement.

"Welcome to the 5th World Conference on Neurodegeneration. Please take your seats for the Opening Ceremony which will begin in 5 minutes."

The screens flickered into life, together with a central one revealed at the back of the stage when the curtain was lifted. They showed a photomontage of Boston, then of the previous meeting in Toronto, accompanied by more muzak.

The voice came back, giving a two-minute warning, then one minute, then the film stopped and onto the stage walked a dapper young man. He announced himself as their compere for the ceremony, then proceeded to introduce the movers and shakers who had put the Congress together. Each entered to applause and gave a brief speech of welcome.

"This is very tedious", Lila whispered to Tom, who smiled, but put his finger to his lips to quieten her.

She felt rebuked and tried to concentrate. There was now a scientific part in which there were going to be 3 speakers - all top notch, each giving a named lecture. The pattern was similar for each: the Someone Middle initial Somebody lecture on xxxxxxxx. At the outset the speaker explained who Someone Middle initial Somebody was or had been, showing slides of their face, their major papers before embarking on the talk proper. She fantasised about giving the Charles H. Schulze lecture on Peanuts. It was hard to take much in; she was feeling tired again and very hungry. It would be supper time in the UK now and her stomach was reminding her.

Finally there was some entertainment - a local jazz band who were very good. Lila longed to get up and dance and was tapping her feet and jiggling in her seat. The band finished and the compere advised them that tea, coffee and snacks were now available outside the auditorium, but that they should return in half an hour for the first pharma symposium, given by Tempus.

It took an age to file out, Lila realised the unwisdom of being in the centre of a row and resolved to sit near the end of one for the next session. She would have liked to go back to the Airbnb flat, eat and then sleep - but Susan was a main speaker in the next session, so she had to stay and listen.

While queuing again for tea her mobile vibrated. She found a text from Mrs D,

"Shd I give G the evg tabs in b'rm? "

Lila recalled that Mrs D's granddaughter, aged 14, had taught her how to text. She had left the colchicine in Grace's bedroom as they were taken at night, so she replied,

"Yes please. Hope all well?"

"We r doing fine"

"Good, thank u v much."

The tea was made by putting a bag into a paper cup and pouring hot water from a large cylinder onto it using a tap mechanism. It tasted foul but Lila needed something to keep her awake so drank it, having thickened it first by dunking a biscuit in it. She looked around for Tom and saw him chatting animatedly to a dark, handsome young man. She made her way over to them and stood waiting to be introduced, then realised that they were conversing in French. Tom spoke French! Of course he did, he was the product of a public school education and had probably been to France many times, Lila theorized. She was about to melt back into the crowd, feeling inadequate to the task of French conversation, when Tom spotted her and beckoned her closer.

"Lila meet Jean Jacques, an old friend of mine. Jean Jacques this is my esteemed colleague Lila – who has picked up the pieces of my research project many times."

Lila and Jean Jacques smiled politely at each other and said hello.

"We should go back", Lila said, "Susan is speaking first."

"I'll join you", Jean Jacques stated, "If that is OK?"

"Of course, let's go." Tom wove his way through the crowd back into the auditorium closely followed by his two friends.

Susan Armstrong was very impressive - she looked elegant In a dark sult and high heels and spoke clearly and with conviction to a set of slides which Tom had largely provided. She explained current knowledge on Alzheimer's disease and briefly enumerated the failures in previous trials of therapy, thus setting a background for the next two speakers. The first of these was Japanese, a very nervous gent who spoke with such a marked accent that he was hard to understand. Fortunately his slides were largely self-explanatory and the basic message that epigenetic changes ('environment-induced changes in gene expression due to changes in DNA accessibility, rather than changes in the code itself) were important came through. The final talk was largely theoretical, backed-up with data from worm *C. elegans,* used for so much genetic and epigenetic research.

Afterwards there were drinks available on the way out of the auditorium. Lila gratefully took a cold glass of white wine and sipped it, while waiting for Tom and Jean Jacques, who turned out to be known as JJ, to make their way out. They took a long time, so Lila wandered round, smiling vaguely at strangers, hoping to find someone to chat with. A girl of roughly her own age returned the shy smile and asked,

"Hi, do you work for Tempus?"

 "Oh no, Lila replied, I'm a scientist from the UK."

"Welcome to America! I'm Dolores, from Scientific World."

 This was a magazine devoted to Science, explaining it in ways that could be understood by a general audience.

"What did you think of the session?"

 "Well, I'm biased because Susan Armstrong is my boss - but I did think she gave a very clear overview of the current situation."

 "Sure, I agree. She is one smart lady. What about the other two?"

"The middle speaker lost me most of the time because I could not understand what he was saying, but the worm data was elegant. Sorry, unintentional pun."

Dolores looked blank.

"*C. elegans*," explained Lila.

"Oh, yes, I see. Are you working on Alzheimer's too?"

"Yes, I am now. It was MS before."

"OK, both incurable diseases. Are you getting anywhere?"

 Lila was tired, empty and had just consumed most of a glass of wine too quickly. Her habitual reserve deserted her.

"Possibly, it's too early to say much - but I am getting interesting results in mice. I'll be speaking about some of them on Monday. There is more though..." she broke off, having seen Tom and JJ emerge from the hall accompanying Susan as part of her entourage.

"Excuse me, I have to go. Nice to meet you."

She hurried to join her group, aware that she had nearly spilled the beans about colchicine, and to a reporter at that. She would have to be more careful.

Susan received her congratulations with a smile.

"Thanks Lila, good to know it was comprehensible. Are you enjoying things so far?"

Lila affirmed that she was and that she had seen something of Boston that morning.

"Good, always make sure that you see something interesting wherever you go, otherwise the round of meetings gets very tiresome."

At that point Dermot Banks from Immunogenomics appeared, took Susan's elbow and steered her away for what looked like a confidential chat. Lila, Tom and JJ were left together with various would- be questioners for Susan. It was a fact that, although questions were encouraged during the meeting after each talk, many listeners preferred to ask theirs privately of the speakers at the end of the session. One could tell whose talk had reached the most people by the size of the huddle round each speaker. Realising that their chance had been lost, those who had gathered round Susan gradually dispersed, one or two asking questions of Tom, who had obviously been involved with Susan's talk as his name and picture was on the thank you slide. Mostly they wanted copies of the slides. He dealt with these quickly by telling each one his e-mail address and asking them to write and ask him, since that way he would not forget.

Finally the three of them were left together, Susan and Dermot having disappeared.

"Let's go home," said Tom." I can make us spag. bol. for supper, I got all the ingredients yesterday."

"Fantastic," Lila was delighted to have someone to cook for her for a change, but her delight was reduced when Tom went on,

"JJ, why don't you join us, if you have nothing better to do?"

JJ was delighted to be invited and volunteered to provide a bottle of vin rouge for the feast. They walked back to the flat together through the streets, which had darkened quickly as they went. The streetlights came on, the air cooled and they were glad to reach their block and go inside. JJ went off to find wine, promising to return soon. Lila and Tom smiled at each other.

"Good to be home, eh?" said Lila.

"Indeed ma'am", Tom was treating her with the butlerish courtesy he had employed earlier. She was aware that it was his way of gently distancing himself from her but was unsure why.

He began to prepare their meal. Lila freshened up, then set the table - it was really a 2 person table but would just about seat three at a pinch. The bell rang - it was JJ bearing not one, but two bottles of wine, one white, one red.

"I noticed you drinking white earlier," he explained to Lila, "I thought that perhaps you did not like red wine?"

Lila was pleased at his thoughtfulness.

"That is so kind of you. I do prefer white wine."

"It is Californian, a Chardonnay, I hope that is OK?"

Lila preferred Sauvignon Blanc but kept that fact hidden and said it was perfect, as indeed it was once opened and tasted. She was both hungry and thirsty, but instead of getting herself some water and waiting for the food she drank the wine. The mellowing effect was excellent and she was on good form through the meal, but the second glass (her third that evening) made her sleepy and she yawned surreptitiously.

"Lila, if you're exhausted please feel free to go to bed. JJ and I will wash up."

She accepted gratefully, bid them goodnight and retired to her peaceful room. There was a knock on the door.

"What is it?" she asked.

"Only me", Tom replied, with tonight's melatonin. "Do take it if you wake in the early hours, you'll feel better in the morning if you do. "

She opened the door, half wishing that her nightie was a more glamorous affair than the shirt type she was wearing, took the tablet and wished them a repeat goodnight. She was asleep in minutes, but wide awake again at 2am, 8am London time. Remembering the melatonin, she reached for it on the bedside table, then thought that she should pee first and have a drink of water. She climbed out of the warm bed, shivering in the autumn night, and opened her door to creep to the bathroom. The end of the sofa bed was just visible from the corridor. On it were two sets of feet, intimately entwined.

Refusing to take this in at first, Lila entered the bathroom and sat on the loo. Her thoughts were racing. She put her head into her hands and sat still for a while, wanting to cry. Then she took in a deep breath, told herself it didn't matter, that it explained why Tom had never made any advances to her and why he would not in the future. She had been a blind fool to hope. Returning very quietly to her room she took the melatonin and lay down again, but further sleep remained elusive while she went over all her past interactions with Tom in her head.

CHAPTER 13

In a smart hotel adjacent to the Conference centre things were going rather better for her boss.

Dermot had swept her away from the meeting, ostensibly to discuss business, but had then confessed that what he really wanted to do was to take her out to dinner. He explained that he had been too embarrassed by the previous occasion to make contact, then his time had been taken up by travelling, but that he wanted a further chance to show her that he was not always a complete idiot, just a partial one. Spoken in his warm Irish tones it made her laugh. She was also happy and relaxed now that her talk was over and had gone well, so Susan agreed to accompany him to his chosen venue, an Italian restaurant called Mamma Maria. Dermot had chosen well, the setting was a beautifully decorated town house, warm and intimate; the food was to die for and Susan loved good Italian cooking.

This time their conversation flowed more easily. Dermot talked about his recent activities with his children, he had been seeing more of them with benefit to them all, including his ex-wife who was becoming more approachable as they were taken off her hands so often. Susan explained about her involvement with an Arts charity and the fact that she was a passionate devotee of art and music as tools to improve the lives of those who were mentally ill. They began to become real people to each other, instead of the ciphers which they had been.

Both felt suddenly tired as the wine kicked in and the exhilaration of the successful talk dissipated. Susan stifled a yawn, but Dermot noticed and said,

"Should we leave now, or would you like pudding?"

His use of the upper class old fashioned word, rather than dessert, pleased Susan.

"I'd like to go back to my hotel please," she said. "I'm all in."

Dermot paid the bill, organized a cab and helped her into it. It was nice to be taken care of, for once, she thought. It turned out they were in the same hotel.

Dermot climbed into the cab beside her, asked for The Intercontinental and they were whisked to it with very little time for further conversation - or had she dozed off, Susan wondered? Dermot saw her to her room, gave her a gentle peck on the cheek and waited while she opened the door and slipped inside before going to his own.

"Dermot is a gent," was Susan's last coherent thought as she drifted off to sleep.

Hi Mrs D, how are you? How's Mum doing? Lila texted the next morning, at what must have been lunchtime in London.

The reply came within a couple of minutes. *Hi Lila. Grace is a bit withdrawn today, seems tired, maybe she just needs a rest?*

Lila was concerned.

Does she have a temp? Is she more confused?

No, neither, just seems worn out.

OK, thanks. Please let me know how she gets on. I'll be in touch at dinner time. Is she taking her tablets?

Yes. Hope u r having a nice time!

Perhaps the colchicine isn't going to work, thought Lila. Then she checked herself, it was just one small setback, overall Grace was so much better since taking it – don't be prematurely negative she told herself.

Lila returned to her laptop and reviewed the slide set for her talk, still deliberating whether to cut out some slides. She had realised that going slowly was good because English was a second language to many attendees. She had not yet dared leave her room, wishing to wait for the two boys to get up first. At last she heard noises and was able to emerge from her room and greet them with the cheery "Bonjour!" that she had been rehearsing.

Tom looked somewhat abashed, but JJ greeted her smilingly, oblivious to her heart problem.

They breakfasted together then walked to the Conference Centre just in time for the morning plenary session. Again, Lila found it hard to concentrate - her mind kept wandering to her Mum and to Tom. She forced herself to take notes as a way of keeping focused and was glad that she did so, because several new areas of interest were revealed to her.

After the coffee break there were multiple sessions, so Tom suggested that the three of them should split up to cover as much as possible. Lila heard a set of talks on animal models of dementia but did not learn much more than she already knew.

During the conference lunch break, having found a small grocery shop a little way from the conference centre where she bought a sandwich and an apple, Lila sent another message to Mrs Dewhurst.

Hi Mrs D, how is Mum?

Hi Lila. Grace hasn't eaten much, has back pain. 0 to see, she's not fallen. Can I give her paracetamol?

Thanks, think it wd be OK, but pl. check package insert on her other tablets first.

OK– it'll take me a while, pl. be patient!

Of course! Thanks. What would I do without you?!

Lila went back to eating her sandwich. Her thoughts drifted to Tom and JJ. Good for them, she told herself, don't be bitter; but it was easier said than done, the human heart was pretty much ungovernable. She chastised herself – why am I thinking about this? I should have my mind on what I'm here to do, give my talk and learn something, not worrying about heart-pangs for someone who will never have any interest in me, particularly with Mum not at her best. Just then a text arrived.

Simvastatin paper lists loads to avoid, not paracetamol tho. Should I give her some? 1 tablet?

Simvastatin?

Yes, the one you left in b'room cupboard.U said I should give to Grace.

Oh no! Sorry -my fault. Please don't give her simvastatin, just the colchicine; in fact, please stop both of them for now.

OK. Will do.

Lila was on her way back into the centre when another text arrived with a ping.

Grace passed red urine,?blood! What should I do?

Oh shit! Thought Lila, then she quickly typed a reply.

Grace needs to see a doctor. It's too late for the GP and I can't ask you to take her to A&E. Hold on. I'll ask if a friend will take her.

Lila typed a message to Dragan, knowing she was asking an awful lot, but hoping he would help.

Hi Dragan, hope you are well. May I ask a huge favour of you? Mum is peeing blood and I can't ask Mrs D to take her to A&E. Is there any chance you could take her? I know it's outrageous of me to ask…

Within a minute a reply came: *Of course. If you let Mrs D know I will be there in 10 minutes or so that would be great x*

Lila waited anxiously. She was due to speak in just 30 minutes. She headed back to the conference centre and followed the signs to the Speaker Preview Room where she had her lanyard barcode scanned and handed her USB to one of the computer technicians. After opening the file, she did a final check of the talk and let the technician transfer it into the presentation sequence for the session of research abstracts she was in. She left the room and headed for the toilets – the anxiety of speaking, particularly presenting her own data to a potentially critical audience, provided an urgent need to open her bowels. Sitting on the toilet seat, noting a mild degree of nausea, she sent a text to Dragan:

Hi. Any news? Thanks again for your help, I'm so grateful.

The reply came swiftly: *Hi Lila, it's Tricia here, Dragan's driving us to St Mary's. We'll update you when Grace has been seen. I'm sure she'll be fine, don't worry.*

Thank you both! Texted Lila in response. What wonderful people, she thought, then wondered what she could do to thank them when she was back. She finished in the toilet, washed her hands a touch excessively, then headed to room B3 of the conference centre.

Lila took a seat in the second row from the front. She was third of 5 speakers, each with a strict 10-minute talk slot plus 3 minutes of questions. She became more and more nervous as her time to speak approached, by the time she reached the lectern she was shaking. Tom and JJ were in the audience, both gave her friendly encouraging smiles. As the chair read out the title of Lila's talk Susan entered the room at the back, accompanied by Dermot Banks. Lila took a deep breath and began with slide 1 containing a brief introduction to the immunopathology of Alzheimer's disease. Once she started to explain the slide Lila felt she was on home ground, her nervousness vanished and she dealt with each of the subsequent slides simply and clearly, noting the changes found in control mice and the lesser ones found in those treated with the Immunogenomics monoclonal antibody. She said nothing at all about the colchicine-treated group.

There were one or two questions, nothing she could not cope with, then Lila could sit down to listen to the remaining talks. She longed to leave the room and ring Dragan, but thought it would be rude and probably unhelpful, so stayed put, fretting inside while the next two speakers had their moment on stage.

When the session finished Lila turned round and saw that Tom and JJ had vanished. Susan was bearing down on her, Dermot in tow.

"Well done, Lila," said Susan. "Good data, beautifully presented."

"Thank you," said Lila, blushing.

 "May I add my congratulations," said Dermot Banks. "I thought you were very clear and concise."

"Are you free this evening", asked Susan, "and if so would you like to come and eat with us?"

"That is very kind, but I have already promised to help cook a meal for Tom and JJ. We've bought the food already."

Lila was relieved to be able to decline with a real excuse. The thought of a whole evening with Susan was excruciating, especially when she was scared stiff about Grace.

"I should really go now," she said. They made polite goodbyes and Lila fled home to the little flat, which was beginning to feel like home. She made cottage pie as well as she knew how, trying to remember not to salt it twice, because she was too upset to concentrate.

CHAPTER 14

It wasn't until a good three hours after the session finished that Lila heard back from Dragan in an e mail.

Hi Lila. Your mum is in good hands. She has a problem with her kidney and some blood in the urine, they are checking for infection. We showed the doctors the tablets she has been taking, they said they might be the cause, but they weren't sure. They are giving her antibiotics and intravenous fluids. She is going to be admitted because she is a bit more confused, but they hope not for very long. Have you done your talk yet?

Lila replied:

Thanks so very much. Talk over.

Should I bring forward my journey home - I'm booked for tomorrow overnight?

I think she'd like to see you as soon as possible, if you can make it earlier please do.

Just then Tom and JJ arrived back to the flat. Lila told them the news, including the fact that Grace had been given both colchicine and the simvastatin and that rhabdomyolysis was a possibility.

Tom's face became ashen.

"OMG Lila, poor Grace. I can't remember much about rhabdomyolysis, but I know it is very bad. This could be my fault for giving her colchicine, I should never have let you persuade me. This could be the end of my career."

"Tom I am so sorry, I will leave you out of it. I'll say I got the colchicine from an experimental supply in the lab."

Sorry as she was for him, Lila did not fail to notice that his thoughts were for himself as much as for Grace.

She offered them the meal, which was pronounced delicious by JJ, but which tasted of ashes to both Lila and Tom. Whilst eating, Lila, without apology, went onto the website of the Canadian airline to see if she could fly home earlier. It transpired that her cheap ticket was neither changeable, nor refundable and that there was no earlier flight with that airline. Looking at alternatives she found that the prices were astronomical, far more than she could ever afford. There was nothing for it, she would have to wait 24 hours in Boston, then fly back as originally arranged.

Lila told this to Tom and JJ.

"What about your travel insurance?", asked JJ. "Would it pay up for this?"

It was a thread of hope. Lila found the policy which she had downloaded onto her computer and read through it hurriedly, then more slowly, trying to take it in.

"No, I don't think so", she said, sadly.

JJ leaned over her shoulder and scrolled through the policy details.

"No, I am afraid you are right."

Lila burst into tears. It was all too much - her poor mother in hospital, probably because of what she had done, Tom angry with her, now a delay before she could reach Grace who might die, alone, without the daughter she loved there to comfort her.

She was sobbing too loudly to hear what Tom was saying on his mobile, but when he told her to go and pack immediately she understood. The cab he had ordered was downstairs, the ticket he had bought her was at the BA desk at the airport and the plane was due to leave just before midnight. It took her little time to fling her possessions back into her suitcase.

"Passport?" Asked Tom.

Lila nodded.

"Thank you so much. I don't know how I can repay you."

He went downstairs with her, saw her into the taxi and said,

"Shove over Lila, I am coming with you to make sure the ticket pick-up goes OK. They want to see my credit card."

She shifted sideways and Tom climbed in beside her then waved to JJ who had come to see them off.

"You can do the washing up, JJ" Tom laughed. JJ nodded and waved.

Tom turned to Lila,

"I am sure your Mum will be fine. I am so sorry to have sprung JJ on you like this - I honestly didn't know he was coming. I feel you need some explanation."

He gazed at her interrogatively and Lila nodded, unable to say anything.

"We met a few months ago when I went to a small meeting in Paris."

Lila nodded again, she could remember his going there and her sadness at not being asked to go too.

"Well it was, it really was, love at first sight. I think we were both stunned by it, the immediacy of the attraction, the need to keep seeing each other. Neither of us had fallen in love before. I had only been out with girls, trying to persuade myself that was where my interests lay, without a lot of success. JJ had had boyfriends, but nothing serious. We just had to keep in touch, and we did, meeting at weekends whenever possible, courtesy of Eurostar. Then I felt that he was cooling towards me: he called off our meeting in London last time - that's when I took you to the opera."

Lila nodded again, beginning to feel like a puppet.

"JJ was not supposed to be coming to Boston at all, but one of their team couldn't make it because of illness, so JJ was substituted to give his talk. It was wonderful to see him again and to find out that his reasons for not coming to London were connected with that illness - he genuinely could not leave Paris. We realised that nothing had changed, we still felt the same way, so I just invited him to supper. You know the rest, I think."

Again Lila nodded, finding it a safe means of communication without crying.

"I should have asked you first, warned you. It was very unfair of me and very good of you to put up such a brave show. I am very, very fond of you and, had JJ not happened, I'd have gone on taking you out, trying to make myself fall in love with you. My family would find a girlfriend so much more acceptable than a boyfriend.

"You haven't told them?"

"No, not yet. My grandfather was a builder, my father turned that business into a big success and wanted me to carry it on. It certainly does not interest me at all - so I am already something of a disappointment to him. When I said I wanted to do medicine he became very keen that I should do surgery, something like orthopaedics. Neurology, "nervous diseases", means little to him. This might be the final straw. "

"What about your mother?"

"She'll be upset at first, but she'll come round. We are very close. I only hope she can make the old man see sense and not do something drastic, like disinheriting me."

Lila realised that the Jaynes family was seriously rich and felt much better about accepting the airline ticket home. She relaxed back into her seat, took Tom's hand and gave it a little squeeze.

"It will all work out in the end Tom. I'm sure that what your parents want is for you to be happy."

"Oh, I hope so. Thanks Lila, you are a brick."

She hoped that was complimentary.

Tom was fiddling with his mobile.

"Rhabdomyolysis, " he said, "it says here….. *is the breakdown of damaged skeletal muscle. Muscle breakdown causes the release of myoglobin into the bloodstream. Myoglobin is the protein that stores oxygen in your muscles. If you have too much myoglobin in your blood, it can cause kidney damage. The overall prognosis of **rhabdomyolysis** is favourable as long as it is recognized and treated promptly. Most causes of **rhabdomyolysis are reversible**. Severe cases of* *rhabdomyolysis* may be associated with kidney damage and electrolyte imbalance and hospitalization and even dialysis can be required....

The cab was slowing, Tom told the driver which airline and they stopped outside the correct entrance. Lila emerged, clutching her computer, and opened the trunk to get her suitcase.

Tom paid the driver from the kitty, now seriously diminished, then guided her into the airport and to the BA ticket desk. It did not take long for Tom's card to be accepted and the ticket produced.

"Now for check – in," he said, again guiding her gently, his hand on her elbow. Lila felt very safe and cared for, wishing that Tom had never met JJ, despite what she had just said to him.

At the check in area Tom steered her into a queue with a handsome young man at the desk. When it was Lila's turn Tom smiled at him and told him why Lila was flying home in a hurry. The young man, whose

badge read John, was sympathetic.

"I don't suppose there is any chance of an upgrade? "asked Tom." Lila will

need to get some sleep in order to cope with tomorrow."

John looked at Lila who was still wearing the smart trouser suit in which

she had given her presentation.

"Let me check," he said and went back to his computer. There was a long

pause while he clicked various keys. Then he looked up at Lila and smiled.

" You are in luck ma'am- there is one spare seat at the back of Club class-

I'll put you into it. Tell no- one please."

Lila nodded (she felt she was getting good at this) and thanked him

profusely as she took her boarding pass. She and Tom moved off towards

departures. He turned to her and advised

"One more thing, here is some melatonin and one tablet of zopiclone.

Take only half of the zopiclone and one melatonin soon after you sit

down. The flight back is usually shorter as the winds from the west blow

the plane home."

She took the proffered tablets and put them into her handbag, then stopped and turned sideways to face him.

 "Tom you have been marvellous, I cannot thank you enough. I'll leave you out of it as far as the colchicine is concerned, don't worry about that. A far as JJ is concerned, I wish you all the luck and love in the world. I am very happy for you. Good luck with your talk tomorrow- and thank you again so much for getting me home. I'll repay you when I can."

She reached up and kissed him gently on both cheeks, then fled up the escalator towards departures before he could see her tears. During the journey to the plane via security and passport control she was on autopilot and only surfaced when the time came to board and find her wonderfully comfortable, spacious seat in the upstairs section. In other circumstances she would have enjoyed exploring all the options open to her: music , films, TV, champagne etc- but she remembered Tom's warning and dutifully took a glass of water proffered by the attentive attendant and swallowed the tablets as instructed, using half a zopiclone and a whole melatonin, allowed to dissolve in her mouth. Just before switching off her phone she texted Dragan to let him know about her flight and likely arrival time.

As soon as they were airborne, with the seat belt signs off, she pressed the button to recline her seat to the horizontal, put on the eye mask, wrapped herself in the blanket and attempted to go to sleep. Her thoughts were whirling- would Grace survive long enough to see her? How could she explain the colchicine to the hospital and to Susan? Then they switched to Tom- he was a good person, she must protect him at all costs, how sad that he loved JJ and not her. Finally she became introspective: both Tom and Dragan were her friends, but was there something wrong with her, did men find her great as a friend, but not someone to fall in love with? With this unsettling idea her reticular inhibitory system finally got the upper hand and she was asleep.

It seemed only a short while later that she was woken by an announcement that they were 1 hour away from Heathrow. Her watch informed Lila that she had slept for 6 hours, but she felt unrefreshed, dopey and disorientated. Coffee from the attentive air hostess helped, together with a brief power breakfast concoction. Once more semi-upright she availed herself of the TV possibilities, watching the news, with half her attention. The remainder was thinking about Grace and how to reach her as quickly as possible. There was a delay in landing, caused by overcrowding of incoming flights so the plane had to make an uncomfortable low figure of eight holding pattern over the South East. Lila hated this part most- it felt as though a thoroughbred was being held in check on a slow hack- and there were other planes doing the same thing and looking horribly likely to crash into them. At last they were permitted to land, following the route of the Thames- from her window seat Lila had good views of Epping Forest, the M11, then later the Wembley Arch. She had a wonderful feeling of belonging to the part of the world just below Wembley – then realised that she could make out Hyde Park with the Serpentine, from that she found the Edgware Road, followed it with her eye northwards and , to her complete amazement she could just spot Queen's Park itself, where she absolutely did belong.

"Stop the plane, I want to get off," she thought, as she did on trains running into Euston without stopping at Queen's Park. The absurd thought of parachuting out to land in the park made her smile, despite all her worries.

Finally they dropped/descended lower and lower, almost grazing the tops of lorries on the A4, she felt, and landed gracefully on the main runway, with the sudden reverse engine thrust she'd noticed at Boston.

The plane rolled to a near stop, then turned suddenly sideways to its bay. There came an announcement which included gratitude from the captain and the entire crew. Lila again had a funny thought- a castrated crew would be unlikely- but might have reduced the worldwide spread of the HIV virus.

"What's wrong with me today? "she wondered. "Why am I so flippant and cheerful?"

When she switched on her mobile she received part of the answer: a message from Dragan

"Hi – I'll be waiting for you in the Arrivals Hall, wearing a red carnation in case you've forgotten what I look like. Your mum is much better this morning."

Lila smiled, Dragan was in a flippant mood too- must be something in the air. She thought how he often made her smile and how wonderfully kind he was to her and Grace. She was really looking forward to seeing him.

It took a while for this to happen.

CHAPTER 15

As soon as he received the text from Lila telling him about her flight, Dragan had set his alarm for 5.30 am, reckoning that if he left within 10 minutes he could be at Heathrow in time to pick her up.

He knew she would be in a state, having flown all night, worried stiff about Grace, and thought that she should not have to cope with public transport, particularly during the morning rush hour. His mother had agreed to lend him her little car and he'd worked out where to park it for a short-stay pick up. Just before leaving he rang the ward to find that Grace had improved considerably overnight- with a sigh of relief he added this to his text to Lila, which he hoped she'd be able to pick up before she caught the Underground or the Heathrow Express.

He put his travel-cup filled with coffee into the car's drink-holder, inserted the key into the ignition and set off. He had rarely been to Heathrow by road, since he usually went on the Express, but he knew that the way there was along the M4. Only problem was how to reach that. He'd forgotten to put the journey into his mobile and didn't want to stop to do that now.
Realising that time was running short he decided to go the way he did know out to the M40 - from trips to Oxford- then, although it was somewhat roundabout- round the M25 , onto the M4 to approach Heathrow from the west. Unfortunately, the fates were against him and he became stuck in traffic about a mile from home, in Tubbs Lane- a one way street with no possibility of turning back. He gritted his teeth and shuffled forward each time the car in front moved, turning on the radio to relieve his mixture of tension and boredom. Once out of Tubbs Lane traffic flow improved, but it was still a journey of stops and starts all the

way to the A40. Finally he reached the 50mph speed limit sign there, just after the Hoover Building, with its ugly new roof, and was able to press down harder on the accelerator. The garage on his left sailed by, making him think about petrol. Startlingly the gauge was reading very close to zero. He'd not thought to check before embarking on his mission to retrieve Lila.

"Bloody hell," he thought," what else can go wrong?"

He knew that there was not another garage before the M25, then nothing before the M4. He had to go back. He shifted into the left hand lane, annoying the person close behind in the middle lane and peeled off to the left. With one or two false starts he managed to find his way back onto the A40, now going homewards, back to the large roundabout and then right round until he was heading west again,-before the garage. The process took a good ten minutes. He was lucky in finding a spare pump and quickly put £20 worth of fuel into the tank. Locking the car door he strode quickly towards the cash desk, feeling in his pocket for his wallet as he did so. Nothing was there- he felt in the other side, still empty. With mounting horror he remembered that this morning he'd donned his better pair of trousers because he was meeting Lila, but had not swapped the wallet into them.

"What the hell do I do now?" he thought, almost speaking out loud.

There was nothing else for it- he had to get Lila – so he wheeled round, got back into the little car and drove off the forecourt, back to the A 40.

"I'll ring and explain when I get to the airport", he decided.

The rest of the journey went fairly smoothly- the M25 for once not living up to its reputation as the largest car park in Europe. Dragan managed to find the short-term parking, locked the car and strode rapidly into the terminal.

Lila had made the mistake of not using the loo before landing- so had to do so soon after disembarking. Of course, there was the inevitable queue for the ladies, so she was slow to reach passport control and the queue there was also long. She was unsure about the e- gates so opted to join the line slowly creeping forward to pass by a real person. This turned out to be a man who frowned, looked her up and down and asked where she had just flown in from. Lila's mind went suddenly blank- then she remembered,

"Boston, "she said.

The man nodded, smiled and let her back into the UK.

Having nothing other than cabin baggage Lila went rapidly through to the Customs Hall, feeling smug when she saw the other passengers waiting by the carousel. No- one stopped her as she passed through Customs and past the not- very- tempting duty free offerings displayed in the corridor after that. Then she was hailed by a uniformed man selling Heathrow Express tickets.

"No thanks", she said, glad that Dragan would be waiting for her.

She passed through a set of 'no return' doors and was in the Terminal 5 Arrivals Hall.

There were meeters and greeters lined up along the rail separating the hall from the walkway. Lila glanced along the row and did not see the expected face of Dragan. She walked slowly along, checking each board for her name, in case someone else had been sent - nothing. Suddenly she felt very tired and sad, a bit nauseous too, the breakfast coffee rising back into her throat. Pulling herself together she decided to stroll about the large area, looking for Dragan, in case he had been diverted by someone or something. Whilst doing this she pulled out her mobile and switched it back on. No messages. She called Dragan's number- it went to Voicemail. She sighed, what should she do now?

Feeling weary she sat down and closed her eyes.

That was how Dragan found her 20 minutes later. Fortunately, for she had begun to reconsider the Express, Lila had dozed off almost immediately she sat on the bench. Blue bag on her lap, head forward onto the bag and she was fast asleep. Dragan had failed to notice her and had waited for a while watching the new arrivals, some wheeling suitcases with Boston labels, until he remembered that she had boasted about hand luggage only so she should already be out. He turned to survey the space and recognised, with a little thrill in his chest, the small curved form of a dozing Lila. For a brief time he watched her, able to do so without her careful gaze on him, then, very gently, touched her head and spoke her name.

Lila was jolted out of a dream in which she was searching, for what she was unsure. She opened her eyes and looked up, smiling sleepily as she recognised her friend.

"Dragan, I thought you hadn't come for me."

"So sorry Lila, I was delayed. I'll tell you all about it on the way home. Up you come."

He took her hand and the bag and helped her to her feet. Lila grabbed her small wheelie suitcase and they made their way hand in hand to the exit.

Lila felt wonderfully relieved to be taken care of, Dragan was ecstatic at seeing her again, but careful not to let this show. His mother, whom he trusted in these matters, had warned him that Lila was a reserved and private person who would react badly to any attempt to sweep her off her feet, so he must gently gain her trust and befriend her before trying to woo her. He had arrived at the airport, worried about being late and with such thoughts running through his mind he had failed to make a note of where he had parked the car. After they had tried a couple of floors he had the bright idea of using the key fob – and fortunately found that they were quite close to the vehicle. He fingered the parking slip, realised that he had no way of paying and asked Lila if she had any UK money.

"Yes, some, here you are. This is what I have"

She handed him a ten-pound note - more than he needed. Gratefully he paid in the machine and handed the change back to Lila. He remembered then about his need to go back and pay for petrol- but did not like to ask Lila if she had a credit card with her- so resolved to try to do it by phone once he reached home and his wallet.

Lila and bag stowed in the car, Dragan drove carefully round the twisting ramps and out past the barrier, once he had managed to insert the paid ticket. Lila asked him exactly what the ward had said that morning about her mum, then reassured by his reply, leaned back and closed her eyes. Dragan was able to concentrate on finding the way out of the massive airport complex. He had decided to return the way he came, to avoid any chance of invoking the congestion charge if he got lost on the way in from the M4. He had successfully negotiated the way onto the westbound M4 and was signalling to turn onto the M25 when he became aware of a police motorbike in the middle lane, alongside him. The driver was alone, but was talking, probably to a phone contact via a headset in his helmet.

"Typical," thought Dragan, " he is doing what we are not supposed to. "

Feeling virtuous he made the exit onto the slipway and round to the M25. The policeman came too, close behind him.

Suddenly, as Dragan was about to insinuate himself into the traffic flow the bike's siren began wailing, its lights flashing. In the mirror Dragan saw the policeman signalling to him to pull over to the left.

"OMG," he thought, obeying the instruction and parking on the hard shoulder.

The policeman had alighted from his bike and was striding towards Dragan's car. Remembering what he'd been told to do Dragan wound down the window and smiled politely.

"Good morning officer, is anything the matter?"

Lila stirred.

The man's face was stern, impassive.

"Is this your vehicle sir?"

"No, it belongs to my mother. She lent it to me to pick up my friend from the airport."

"Can I see your driving licence please sir?" There was nothing servile about the sir, this man was in charge.

"I am sorry but I forgot to bring my wallet when I left in a hurry this morning, so I don't have it on me."

"Have you filled up the tank today?"

"Yes, on my way to the airport- the garage on the A 40."

"How did you pay?", No sir this time.

"I didn't – but I will once I get home and back to my wallet. When I put the petrol in I thought that my wallet was in my pocket- it was only when I was going to the till that I realized I'd changed my trousers and forgotten it. Then I was in such a hurry as I was late for meeting Lila that I decided to leave and pay later. I promise you that I will pay."

Lila was by now awake and had cottoned on to the problem.

"Officer my mother is very sick in hospital, she might die. I have just flown back from America and we are on our way there. Please could I pay now over the phone with my credit card?"

The policeman turned his gaze to her.

"Which hospital?"

St Mary's. I think she has acute kidney failure from rhabdomyolysis ."

He nodded, turned away and spoke into his headphone for a couple of minutes, then dialled a number, spoke to the recipient, then handed the phone to Lila.

"OK, give them your credit card details. "

The transaction was swiftly accomplished.

"I'll pay you back, said Dragan.

"No need, Lila replied. "It was for me."

When she handed the headphone back the policeman checked that all was well, then nodded to them.

"That's done. Now to get you there quickly. Just follow me please and keep up."

He switched on the engine, the siren and the lights and pulled out into the traffic which had slowed to allow this. Dragan just managed to squeeze out behind him, then to follow the racing bike, doing at least 70 mph. It was exhilarating and also fairly terrifying as they switched lanes to avoid queues, squeezed past lorries and reached the turn off to the M40 in no time at all. Again the policeman led them all the way into Paddington, leaving them in Praed Street with a farewell wave.

Lila responded with a wave and blew a kiss, which Dragan though highly inappropriate.

"Thank you so much, Dragan", she said." Please drop me off here and I'll go to mum. There's no need to wait. I'll ring you later."

She leaned over and gave him a kiss on the cheek.

"You are a sweetheart," she said.

Dragan watched her run into the main doors and followed her with his eyes until she was hidden by other people. He found he had tears in his eyes.

Lila raced to the lifts and up to the ward, Dragan having told her which one. She paused at the nurses' station to check which bed her mother was in and that she was allowed to see her. She was panting and her heart was racing as though she'd climbed the 4 flights of stairs up to the ward.

"Let her be still alive. Please let her be still alive." She was repeating these words over and over in her head.

"Grace, Grace..." the nurse checked the computer screen. "Oh yes, bed 10, you can visit her now. "

Lila thanked her and hurried towards bed 10, fingers crossed. She reached the 4 bed bay and could hardly believe what she saw. Her mother was sitting up, reading a newspaper, with a cup of tea on her bedside locker, looking for all the world as if she was resident in a smart hotel, not someone supposedly at death's door.

"Mum, oh Mum," Lila leaned forward and kissed Grace's forehead. "I was so worried about you."

Grace gave a smile. "My darling girl, it is so lovely to see you. They tell me I am fine now. I might go home today"

She pulled Lila towards her and they hugged for several heartbeats.

Then Grace gently disentangled Lila and asked,

"Did you come back specially for me?"

Lila nodded, now unable to speak. Her throat seemed choked by conflicting emotions - relief that her mother was alive and sensible, plus regret that Tom had spent so much money on her needless journey. She hugged Grace again and finally blurted out.

"I thought that you might die and it was all my fault."

"Oh child, hush, I just had a waterwork infection. It did make me ill though. I was on a drip all night with antibiotics in it, worked like a charm."

"Thank God," Lila slumped into a chair beside the bed.

"Oh Mum, I love you so much. I couldn't bear to lose you."

Grace smiled," I know sweetheart. I feel the same way about you."

They held hands and were quiet together, both thinking of their lives together.

"Have some shuteye", Grace suggested," you look worn out. "

"I am."

Still holding her mother's hand Lila shifted in the chair until she could rest her head comfortably and closed her eyes. She slipped into sleep quickly, still under the influence of zopiclone.

A passing nurse saw her, smiled at Grace and said jokingly

"Perhaps you should change places."

It was over an hour later that the ward round reached Grace's bed. She had seen the procession of tired-looking young people, led by a middle-aged suited man as it passed from bed to bed. When they arrived at hers, she gently tapped Lila on the arm which was still draped over her own. Lila woke up, groggy and disorientated. The junior doctor was telling her consultant about Grace.

Lila listened, unable to take much in at first, but as her wits returned she attended carefully to what was being said. The urinary tract infection was the cause of the hospital admission. Grace had a prolapse, whatever that was, which might have contributed. The gynae team had seen her and inserted a ring pessary. Lola winced. Grace's dementia was mentioned, but the young doctor was also saying that Grace had done pretty well on some simple mental tests, so the dementia diagnosis was questionable. She was going to organize a review outpatient appointment with the neuro team to reassess Grace. Lila's spirits soared- perhaps the colchicine really was working?

There was no mention of it, nor of the statin, nothing about rhabdomyolysis. Lila's relief was liberating - she wanted to jump up and down and cheer. Of course, she did nothing of the sort, just smiled weakly at the consultant who introduced himself to Grace and then said.

"Is this young lady your daughter?"

"Oh yes sir, she is. She has just come back from America to be with me."

"Well done. Does your mother live alone?"

Lila explained the situation and he nodded.

"Good that you have each other. Your mother is much better and she can go home with you today."

"Thank you very much. Thank you all for looking after her, " Lila said, looking particularly at the young doctor who had done most of the talking. At the back of her mind was the thought, *that could have been me.*

She pushed it away.

CHAPTER 16

It took a while to get things organized so that Lila could take Grace home. The young doctor had to write out a brief discharge summary for Lila to hand to Grace's GP plus her "TTAs", which turned out to be medicines to take away. Being paramedical made everyone think one spoke the lingo, Lila realized. Then Lila had to take the prescription to the pharmacy and wait for it to be dispensed. Grace was persuaded to dress, and her minimal belongings put into a grey plastic bag. Finally they were ready to go. Lila felt she had to order an Uber- it did not feel right to get on the bus or tube with Grace just out of bed - and she could not ask Dragan for yet more help. The car arrived quickly and whisked them home in 20 minutes. Lila still felt quite disorientated: in Boston it was not yet lunch time, here she was expected to make supper soon and get Grace back into bed. She struggled to find the house keys in her bag, eventually locating them and opening the front door to a chilly house. Lila sighed, Grace wandered over to her usual chair and sat down.

Once the heating was turned on and some lamps lit the place looked better and both their moods improved. After rootling in the freezer Lila found a pizza, added some fresh tomatoes, grated cheese and a little olive oil to the top and waited for the oven to get hot.

"Are you hungry Mum?"

"No, darling, just tired."

 Lila felt like saying

"Oh! you are always tired," but managed to stop herself and said instead,

"Well we have pizza for supper, and I think there's some salad to go with it. After that we can both go to bed. I am tired too after all the travelling."

She waited to see if Grace would ask her where she had been or if she had remembered anything about the Conference, but Grace just nodded, leaned back and shut her eyes.

They ate supper in front of the TV, grateful for the mindless relaxation. Lila gave Grace her antibiotic, but no colchicine and no statin. Then she put Grace to bed. Lila gave her a hug and a kiss and settled her among the several pillows on which Grace liked to sleep, slightly propped up. Once settled, Grace slipped quickly into sleep. Lila checked on her once she had put on her own pyjamas and cleaned her teeth - Grace was snoring gently.

Lila climbed into bed, still feeling odd, somewhat out of space and time, and weary. She remembered to send a text to Dragan to thank him and to let him know they were home, then she copied the same words to Tom, hoping he'd read it before flying back. Tomorrow she'd speak to Mrs D and Marjana. She knew that there were decisions to be made – but for now all she could do was sleep and think about the future tomorrow.

She was woken when it was still dark by noises from the bathroom. It took her a few seconds to recall where she was, then, realising that Grace might be in difficulty, Lila sat up, slid her legs over to the edge of the mattress and put her feet onto the chilly floor. Without bothering to locate her slippers she hurried to the bathroom – to find the door locked.

"Mum, Mum, are you OK?"

A fresh thump occurred from inside the room.

"Mum, please open the door. Can you let me in?"

Some more noises, possibly of someone moving.

"Mum, it's me, Lila, please can I come in?"

Silence.

All sorts of scenarios were going through Lila's mind. What was she to do? If she tried to break open the door her Mum might be just behind it and get hurt. She knocked gently.

"Mum, Grace, speak to me. Are you all right?"

"Yes, I am all right. I just dropped something. Go away."

"OK Mum, I'm going."

Lila made noisy footsteps away from the bathroom but then tip-toed back and waited quietly in the corridor. More thumps and a clunk of something landing in the sink. Lila waited, getting colder. She was just going to get her dressing gown and slippers when the bolt rattled for a while and was eventually drawn back. The door opened. Lila withdrew into her bedroom and watched her mother pass by to her own room. Once Grace had closed her bedroom door Lila went to inspect the bathroom - there were loo rolls scattered all over the place, the soap was on the floor and the soap dish lay, cracked, in the sink. The loo needed flushing. Also, the bathroom cabinet was gaping with the pack of simvastatin half out. Three tablets had been removed. Lila wondered if Grace had felt she was being deprived of a medication and had self-treated. She resolved to put a lock on the cabinet, tidied up the bathroom, then crept to Grace's door and opened it quietly. Grace was already asleep. Lila pulled the covers up to keep her warm and returned to her own bed and fortunately back to sleep.

Next morning started grey and overcast. Lila's mood matched the weather, but she was careful to seem cheerful to Grace who seemed no worse for her nocturnal activity. She rang Marjana to let her know that Grace was home and that she was needed again tomorrow, if that was OK. It was.

Lila popped round next door to Mrs D and told her as much as she knew. It had not been rhabo- whatever, just a urinary tract infection which had been nasty and had got as far as Grace's kidneys. Now the antibiotics had kicked in Grace was fine to be at home and finish the course there.

"What about the other tablets?" asked Mrs D, "the ones you thought caused the problems?"

Lila sighed. "They didn't, but I don't know if Grace should go on having them. I need to talk to someone about it. Just for now she's only on the antibiotic three times a day."

Mrs D nodded.

"How was your trip?"

Lila gave her the edited version: it had been great fun, the talk had gone well, Boston was a lovely city.

Mrs D nodded again.

"What about the young man who was going with you? Tom, I think you said."

Lila cursed herself for having given so much information. It had happened because she was so happy about travelling with Tom and needed to mention his name to someone.

"Oh, he's fine. I didn't get to hear his talk- but I'm sure it would have been good. He'll be on his way back today."

Then, to change the subject,

"I've got a day off tomorrow because I wasn't expected back yet. Do you think Mum would like to go somewhere? If so would you like to come with us?"

"Where were you thinking of going?"

Lila remembered their day out at Kew with Dragan. It had been a big success, so she suggested the same. Mrs D was delighted. She loved gardens and gardening and wanted to see the autumn colours, so the plan was made to set off in an hour when the washing up was done and a picnic made.

That evening, lying in bed waiting for sleep, Lila reflected on the Kew trip. It had certainly been a success for her mother and even more so for Mrs D. who turned out to be very knowledgeable about plants. There was an initial hiccup when Lila realised just how expensive it was to enter the gardens (Dragan had had a pass which had allowed the two of them in free, so she had not noticed before). Mrs D had been incensed, saying that it used to cost one penny, something Lila found hard to believe. The solution came when Lila asked about getting a pass – and found that this could be used to pay for two people for repeated visits. This seemed a good option and she was about to buy one in her name when suddenly she had a brainwave and put Grace's name on it. That meant that Grace and Mrs D or Marjana could go at any time they fancied, even if Lila was working. The pass covered two of them for that day- so there was only one extra visitor to pay for. Lila's debit card funded all this. Although she was bothered about just how low her bank balance now was, she managed not to show it and they entered in a jolly mood.

The autumn colours were lovely once the sun had come out. She blessed Dragan for having brought her here and reminding her what a lovely place it was. She had wished he was with them to enjoy it too. His gentle teasing of Grace often brought out her laughter and made Lila happy too.

There had even been some colchicums, pointed out to her by Mrs D. Pale lilac crocuses, larger than the Spring ones; they formed delicate drifts in the grass. There were similar flowers in Queen's Park. Lila wondered whether she could herself extract colchicine from them for Grace- but abandoned the idea as it would be difficult to obtain a reliable, stable preparation- and what would she do when the supply ran out? Grace had become tired after a while so she and Mrs D had sat down for coffee and a sandwich while Lila had taken hers and wandered freely around, enjoying the space, the trees, the low autumn sunlight as the day wore on. It occurred to her that she had very little time like this now- she was either working or looking after Grace- and it was marvellous to be free for a moment. The "voice in her head" that spoke thoughts normally suppressed told her that if Grace had died, she would be free. Lila hated that thought but reflected that her love for Grace was mingled with resentment and that the latter was gaining ground again now that Grace was back in her care. Then the voice reminded her that for years Grace had cared for her, as a hard- working single parent, with little or no time out and Lila felt ashamed. She inwardly acknowledged that her struggle to save Grace by using colchicine was also about saving herself.

Tomorrow she was going to have to work hard and efficiently. As far as she could see the only way to get more colchicine for Grace from now on was in a clinical trial, as she was certain Tom would refuse to prescribe any more, even though it had not been responsible for Grace's illness. She could no longer twist Tom's arm-after the panic in Boston and his purchase of her ticket home. The only way to get a trial going in man was to provide data that suggested the drug was effective in animals- and she still had several sections from her mice to analyse and count. She hoped fervently that the data would be good and said a little prayer to that effect, though to whom or what she was praying she had no idea.

CHAPTER 17.

The next few weeks were busy, but boringly routine for Lila. Each day she spent looking down a microscope, counting plaques and cells, noting results. Every slide was numbered, but she was not privy to the coding, so she had no idea of which treatment had been given to the mouse whose brain she was analysing. When she had been through all the slides once she took out a random sample and re-analysed them, comparing the results with her previous effort to make sure that she was consistent. Tom offered to help- but his initial efforts were slow, laborious and not repeatably accurate- so Lila simply thanked him and said she could manage.

Grace was being looked after mostly by Marjana and that was going well but it seemed to Lila that Grace was not as astute as she had been whilst on the colchicine. She said nothing of this to Marjana but did ask her one day how she thought Grace was getting on. Marjana had not noticed any changes - or, if she had, was too polite to mention anything. Lila wondered if she had imagined the improvement - a kind of what her father had called "thinkful wishing."

At last it was all done. Lila entered the results into a spreadsheet, locked them so they could not be altered and sent them to the statistician who held the code. He promised to start work on them soon and to get back to her by the end of the week.

Lila returned to her mouse swimming data and plotted graphs of how long it took the Alzheimer's Disease-like mice in each group to find their way out. It was obvious that both groups of treated mice: those who had IG0047F and those who had colchicine, were faster than the controls, many of whom had not found the exit and had been removed from the bowl by Lila after the statutory time.

 She resolved to show all her colchicine data to Susan Armstrong when she returned from a working trip to Japan and through Ann she arranged an appointment for Wednesday in the next week, allowing a couple of days for any jet lag to resolve so Susan would be in a good mood. Now Lila wished that she had at least asked Susan if she could do something besides the IG0047F work, not just embarked on her own project without permission. What had made her do that? Partly, she thought, it was her independent nature, partly because she had thought the answer would be negative and there would have been no need to take things any further. Anyway, it was too late now – she would soon have all the results and, if the histology of the brains backed up the swimming data, then she just had to come clean.

The weekend, usually enjoyed by Lila and Grace now that they had frequent contact with Dragan and his family, passed very slowly for Lila.

The statistician had apologized and said he had been too busy to look at her results but would do so on Monday. At times Lila was sure it would all be fine, the results would tally with the swimming and Susan would be initially cross but then delighted. At other times, that the results would tally, but Susan would be furious and sack her. Sometimes she half hoped that the histology would reveal nothing and she could quietly let it all drop without having to see Susan - but then Grace would stand no chance of getting more colchicine. In the end that was what mattered, because Lila was more certain than ever that her mother was slowly going downhill again, now she had stopped taking it. The incontinence had returned, much to Lila's distress. Grace seemed very little disturbed by it.

On Monday morning Lila was anxious and distracted. Dragan met her by chance on the platform at Queen's Park where she was waiting for a train, her bike being out of action again. He greeted her, asked after Grace and got onto the train with her. Talking was difficult with the press of people all around but he managed to apologise for not seeing them both at the weekend - they had on the spur of the moment gone north as a family to visit Ferid who was in his first term at Manchester University. Ferid had gone there by train at the start of term but now needed lots of his "stuff" so they had driven up with it, stayed overnight in a hotel, had a look round the city and met old friends. Dragan had intended to come round on Sunday evening but they had returned too late.

Lila smiled and said it didn't matter, she hoped they'd had a good time. But it had mattered, Saturday had been OK with things like cleaning and washing to do, but Sunday had dragged on and she and Grace had bickered over silly things.

They stopped talking as the crowded train had stopped and people were pushing their way off before yet more pushed their way on. Dragan held her arm and drew her towards him to stop her being knocked by a rucksack swinging round as its owner turned. She smiled her thanks, surprised by the jolt of pleasure the action had given her.

Just before they parted, Dragan said,

"Should I call in tonight after work?"

"Yes, Lila replied. "Come to supper."

"Thanks." Dragan disappeared into the crowds leaving the platform, Lila followed more slowly, wondering what she should cook that evening.

Once installed in her cubby hole she went through her e-mails, replying to each immediately, knowing that if she left any they would slip down the list and might be forgotten altogether. Nothing from the statistician yet. In the coffee room she made her Nesmess and sat for a while listening to the lab gossip, some science-related, most not. Ann came in and told her Susan was back and that the Japan trip had gone very well. Susan had managed to see some famous gardens as well as attending the conference and giving a talk, so she was very content. Lila hoped that the mood would last until mid–week. At last, unable to wait any longer, she ventured over to the statistician's office and knocked quietly on the door.

"Come in."

He turned away from his computer, saw who she was and said,

"Just the person! I have been analysing your results, here they are. They look interesting."

He pointed out, as Lila knew, that the mice were in 3 groups. Group 1 showed a lot of brain changes associated with dementia, both the other two had significantly less. When the coding was broken the badly affected ones were those treated with placebo, the others had been given either IG 0047F (group 2) or colchicine (group 3) respectively.

Lila heaved a sigh of relief, then asked,

"Is there any difference between Groups 2 and 3?"

"No," the statistician replied, "group 3 has a lower mean but has more variation. Possibly with bigger numbers it might have been less affected than group 2. You can see- if you look at the individual values for each mouse in group 3 when all its brain slices are combined- that some mice have practically no neurodegeneration, others have quite a bit. The changes in group 2 are more uniform."

Lila nodded." Please could you e – mail all this to me?"

"Of course."

"Thank you very much."

Lila practically skipped back to her cubby hole. She found the e- mail, extracted and saved the data and settled down to plotting figures to show to Susan.

CHAPTER 18

Wednesday came at last and Lila was armed and ready for the fray. She had written up an abstract of her results, together with explanatory figures and graphs. She had also begun writing the paper which she wanted to submit to a reputable scientific journal with a good impact factor.

Dragan had proved invaluable on Monday evening. Lila had been much too excited to cook so they'd all had fission chips (another of Lila's Dad's puns) and when Grace had gone to bed Lila had explained the whole colchicine story. She started with her idea about its possible activity in the brain- which she had tested out in brain slices and found positive results. Then, she explained, came the mistake which occurred when Grace phoned her and she inadvertently injected 6 mice with colchicine instead of the monoclonal antibody, IG0047F. She had managed to obtain more mice from the technician who was sworn to secrecy. Dragan raised his eyebrows but seemed to accept this. The outcomes were just as positive for colchicine, both with the mice when alive and in their brains *post mortem*, as for the monoclonal. Then came the part which she stumbled over, the fact that she had given colchicine to Grace, although there was no clinical trial to support its use, and it was known to have possible severe side effects. He looked at her very sternly as she confessed to this but his face softened when she told him of the, to her mind, obvious, probably consequential improvements in Grace's mentation, continence, ability to read and interpret, and reversion to a proper newspaper. At this point Lila remembered, with horror, that Dragan worked for the Daily Chronicle- but he only laughed at her revulsion for it.

"All newspapers try to influence their readers; some are subtler than others."

Lila explained her fear that Grace had developed rhabdomyolysis, a possibly fatal condition, when the colchicine and a statin were given, and her relief when this turned out not to be the case. Now, she told him, it was no longer possible to give colchicine to Grace outside a clinical trial.

"Why not?" he asked.

This led to an explanation of Tom's role as prescriber and the fact that she could not ask him to jeopardize his career any further.

Dragan nodded. He looked a little sad and said,

"Lila, I did not realize that you were so manipulative. I see why you have had to be though. Just how much of this will you tell your Professor?"

"I'll simply tell her about the animal work, not about Mum. That might get Tom into trouble. But I'll ask if Mum could be enrolled in any forthcoming clinical trial."

"Well, best of luck Lila. I hope you get what you want."

"I hope I don't get the sack."

"If you do, I'm sure the Daily Chronicle would find you a job as a science writer."

"Piss off!" she said with a smile.

Now Lila waited at the door of Susan's office for a response to her knock. Her heart was thumping , she was sweating and wishing herself somewhere, anywhere else.

"Come in."

Susan greeted her from behind her big desk, motioning Lila to a chair beside hers.

"Is this to go over your data?"

Lila nodded.

"Then come and sit by me and we can see the screen together. Do you have it on a stick or have you sent it to me?"

Lila produced the USB stick, gave it to Susan who plugged it in and opened it up.

"OK, fire away."

Lila took a deep breath and began to confess.

Susan's body language was eloquent, she became more rigid, sat up straighter, a little away from Lila as the tale unfolded. She said nothing until the spiel was finished.

"Lila you know that what you did was wrong. Not the fact that you decided to experiment with an old drug-I don't mind you using your brain to innovate- but the fact that you failed to inform me of this at any point up until now. I suspect that if the drug- colchicine- had not produced good results then I would never have heard about it. Am I right?"

Lila nodded.

"Does that mean that you have been experimenting with several old drugs and this is the only one to show any benefit? "

"Oh no- I have only tried colchicine."

"Thank goodness for that."

There was a pause while Susan considered what to say next.

"Lila, I am cross that you did not trust me to listen to your hunch and support you. I would have done so. However, the work you have done is good- and the main thing is that IG 0047F appears effective in a mouse model. We can let Immunogenomics know about that. I am unsure of what to do regarding the colchicine and will take advice from my clinical colleagues since I have no real knowledge of this drug."

"Thank you." Lila was disheartened, she had hoped that Susan would show rampant enthusiasm for a clinical trial involving both drugs.

"Do you think there will be a clinical trial of the monoclonal?" she asked.

"Probably, though it depends on funding, as I understand it."

"Perhaps colchicine could be tested in parallel?"

"Unlikely, I think, given that the trial will be pharma-sponsored."

Lila nodded again, she had not really thought of the implications for Immunogenomics- but why should they want to test a rival, cheaper drug?

"Have you written this up yet?"

"I've made a start. "

"Good, please finish the paper and e-mail it to me when you have. Thank you."

 Lila was dismissed.

In the outer office Ann wanted to know how it had gone.

"OK, I suppose. At least I still seem to have a job."

Inside her room Susan was sitting, twirling a pen in her fingers. She had to decide what to tell Dermot. He would be happy with the full results of his pharma molecule. Should she leave it at that- or reveal the, for him, awful truth that a cheap old drug worked just as well in mice?

Dermot Banks was meanwhile engaged in telephone negotiations with Big Pharma. Another of Immunogenomics monoclonal antibodies had given excellent results in animal experiments, not this time for dementia, but for multiple sclerosis. This, a relatively common and often debilitating disease, starting in young adulthood, currently lacked any therapy for the secondary progressive form. Dermot's firm's molecule looked promising in that area, consequently several Big Pharma firms were keen to take it on further into human trials. Dermot was in his element, juggling the offers like an auctioneer, aiming to get the best deal possible. He was therefore slightly taken aback when his secretary asked if Susan

Armstrong could speak to him. Dermot asked his secretary to ask if he could return the call somewhat later.

Susan was not accustomed to being put on hold, still less to having to wait for a call back. She had, quite accurately, realised that Dermot still held a candle for her and had expected to be warmly greeted when she rang. Her opinion of Dermot diminished, meanwhile her slight desire for him increased a little. She returned to the paper on which she had been working, a review of Tom's, which needed corrections.

They finally spoke via mobiles that evening, Susan by then being at home. Dermot apologised, revealed the reasons for the delay and his delight at what he had achieved for the firm. Susan congratulated him then told him briefly that she had called to let him know about Lila's further work on IG0047F.Dermot, feeling expansive, suggested that this would be best done over a good meal- so tomorrow evening was agreed upon and a venue selected. Susan, having decided that she had to tell all, felt a mixture of relief that the confession could be postponed and frustration that she could not free herself of the anxiety about it immediately.

CHAPTER 19

As expected, Dermot took Susan to a good place, Rules Restaurant in Maiden Lane. She was impressed by the décor and enjoyed looking at the numerous Spy cartoons as they were led, very formally to their table, with a banquette by the wall. Susan was glad that she was wearing her designer coat with an elegant dress beneath. Ann had raised her eyebrows when Susan appeared that morning,

"Going somewhere smart, are we?"

Susan had merely smiled and nodded, not wanting to allow Ann to tell the whole department about what she thought of, despite herself, as her date.

Now Dermot said,

"I thought we'd sit side by side – so you can show me the data while we have a drink. Is that OK with you?"

"Perfect."

They settled themselves in comfortably, ordered gin and tonics. Susan brought out her small laptop, oblivious to the frown on the face of the maitre d'.

Dermot was smart. It did not take long to show him the IG0047F data. Susan had brought the slides which showed only placebo and IG0047F. She had decided to test the water before revealing that colchicine had performed equally well.

"That's excellent. Almost too good - are you sure it is real?"

"Oh yes, Lila is a good scientist, very accurate and careful. If you want me to check one or two of the data points, then I am happy to do so."

"I'd be grateful Susan. One cannot be too careful when the outcome is so important."

"I am sorry I should have already done that."

"No problem. Now what would you like to eat? My favourite here is the kate and sidney pie."

Susan looked temporarily bewildered, then light dawned and she said,

"Oh, I haven't had that for years. I'd love to try it. "

Being on the back foot because she had not checked Lila's findings, Susan did not feel able to come out with the whole truth, about the colchicine-treated mice. She mentally promised herself that she would do so when she next talked to Dermot, having checked some of Lila's results, and proceeded to enjoy her supper and the very fine burgundy provided with it.

Over the meal Dermot revealed the details about another of his monoclonals which had also performed well in animal studies and was being bought by a much larger company to take into man. He was unable to name any names, but Susan had a good idea which molecule he meant, having seen some work presented in Boston. She congratulated him warmly and wished him further success. They drank to that. By the end of the meal both were slightly inebriated. Dermot revealed that he had booked himself into a nearby hotel because he had another meeting next morning in London.

"Not because you are afraid of breaking your car key?" Susan asked archly.

"No, not because of that. The manufacturers were astonished. They thought it could not have happened- but I persuaded them that I am the Uri Geller of car keys- and now I have two more spares, just in case."

"I bet one is tucked on top of your nearside rear wheel, just under the wheel arch."

Dermot was surprised and worried.

"How did you know?"

"Because that is what happens in spy stories."

"OMG, I had better find a different place quickly."

"Inside the rear light is another one, but you need a screwdriver."

"You obviously read a lot of thrillers."

She laughed but did not deny it. Dermot asked if she would like a night cap at his hotel. Susan felt too awkward to accept because she was keeping a secret from him. She thanked him for a lovely evening and he accompanied her to the door, where she was reunited with her coat. They stepped outside and Dermot hailed a taxi, succeeding remarkably quickly. He took her hand, pulled her slightly towards him and kissed her on the cheek, then helped her into the cab. It was a speedy goodbye and Susan felt obscurely disappointed. She wondered to herself what Dermot would do next - would he simply go to the hotel and sleep, or did he intend more excitement? How little I know him, she thought.

Dermot also felt let down. Somewhere in his mind had been the idea that Susan would come to his room and that maybe they could start a late-blooming physical relationship. He still fancied her, always had, and he'd begun to think that perhaps she had begun to find him attractive, but obviously that was not the case. He sighed, wondered idly about going on somewhere to – to what? Drink? Gamble? None of seemed very attractive and he needed a clear head for tomorrow when contracts would be agreed and signed so he walked slowly to his hotel and went alone to bed.

Next morning Susan was in early and asked to be notified when Lila arrived. Unfortunately, it was the morning when one of Marjana's children was taking part in the class assembly – so she had arrived later than usual, meaning Lila didn't appear at work until after 10am.

Summoned to Susan's office, Lila knocked tremulously on the door and entered when told to come in.

"Good morning" said Susan meaningfully.

"I am sorry to be late", Lila apologised. "My mother's carer was late and I cannot leave Mum alone."

"Oh, I thought that you said she had improved?"

"She had, but now she is going downhill again."

"Oh dear, I am sorry. I guess it was an acetylcholinesterase inhibitor that helped for a while? "

Lila was suddenly fed up with concealment and blurted out.

"No, it was colchicine."

"What? You mean that you gave your mother colchicine?"

Lila found herself lying again - she had wanted to tell the whole truth, but Susan's face was so aghast that she'd got to do something.

"Yes and no. It was not the lab stuff. She had a proper prescription from her doctor. I think it was for her gout, but it helped with her dementia a lot."

"I see."

Susan, as a scientist, knew very little about colchicine, other than its laboratory use. She resolved to find out more.

"The reason that I wanted to see you was to ask if I could do a recount on a random sample of your mouse brain histology slides. Dermot Banks suggested this and I think it is a good idea."

"Of course. How many do you want to see?"

Susan told her and Lila went to retrieve the tissue sections from the relevant boxes. She was trembling inside, but outwardly managed to seem calm. The slides should not be a problem. Lila was satisfied that she had done a very careful, accurate job with them. She wondered what would happen with regards to her mother and the colchicine and hoped that Susan would not ask the name of the doctor who had prescribed it.

Susan meanwhile had rung Edmund Ferguson, her clinical neurologist colleague. He was a dry old stick, but clever and well- informed. He was on a ward round but promised to drop in to see her when it had ended. She sat down at a microscope in the main laboratory and busied herself reading Lila's mouse brain slides, carefully counting abnormalities in each one. By the time Edmund arrived she was thoroughly fed up with this activity despite having only completed two slides. It gave her pause to remember how much routine dog work went into some forms of research. She greeted him,

"Edmund, thank you for coming over. Coffee?"

Once they were settled in Susan's room with a mug of coffee each, she began to quiz him on the subject of colchicine. He admitted that, as he'd not used it for donkey's years, he was not very familiar with its properties, though could easily look them up online. He did so on his mobile and showed Susan.

"There you are, mainly used for gout in the past. Has some serious side effects - so it has been supplanted by newer anti-inflammatories."

"Is there any reason to suppose it might help in Alzheimer's disease?" Susan asked.

"None whatsoever. Mind you, having said that, sometimes drugs do turn out to have unsuspected properties. For example, Viagra was originally developed as an anti- hypertensive. There has just been a judicial review of Avastin which has a marketing authorisation for the treatment of certain types of cancer, but not for wet macular degeneration of the retina. Roche holds the intellectual property rights in Avastin and have never applied for a marketing authorisation for Avastin to treat wet AMD. Avastin is, however, used throughout the world, including in the EU, as a first-choice treatment for wet AMD and NICE has recognised the drug as clinically effective and safe. The use of Avastin to treat wet AMD is much cheaper than the two other drugs which do have a marketing authorization. Using Avastin will release tens of millions of pounds per year to be spent supporting other NHS patients. Bayer and Novartis, who make the other drugs, challenged the policy as unlawful, but lost."

"So, if colchicine did work it would represent a cost-saving to the NHS?"

"It would represent a miracle. We have, as you well know, nothing that really treats Alzheimer's."

Susan told him of Lila's unauthorized work using colchicine in mice in parallel with that which she was supposed to do using the monoclonal from Immunogenomics.

Edmund Ferguson smiled.

"I know of that young lady. Tom has mentioned her. I think she helps to keep him going with his research. Good for her trying out something new, shows initiative."

"That is not all."

Edmund cocked his head and raised one eyebrow, a trick that endeared him to his juniors, none of whom could do the same, but they knew that it meant they were to go on.

"Her mother has dementia. Lila told me this morning that when she was given colchicine the dementia improved."

Edmund looked thoughtful.

"Presumably she had gout. Perhaps the pain was making her worse - colchicine relieves it fast - and then her dementia might well improve."

"Oh, I see. So, it would not be worth thinking about a clinical trial?"

"Could I have a chat to Lila, do you think?"

"Of course. Do you want to see her now?"

"No time like the present. Could I borrow your room?"

Susan realized that she was not to be part of the conversation.

"Yes, that is no problem. I have to go and finish some work in the lab. I'll send Lila in to you."

Edmund Ferguson stroked his chin thoughtfully. He thought it unlikely that Lila's mother had been given colchicine for gout. Certainly, a young scientist who organized her very own experiments might well be willing to try out the same drug on a sufferer. How to find out?

Lila entered the room, he stood up and shook her hand, introducing himself, like the good clinician he was.

"Please, sit down", he said, indicating a chair.

"Susan has been telling me about what you have been doing" he began deliberately vaguely.

"I find it most interesting. Please could you tell me in your own words?"

Lila began hesitantly to tell him about the IG0047F project. He nodded, raised the one eyebrow and she continued, explaining why she'd had an idea that colchicine might be effective. He nodded again, said nothing and waited.

It was said by the junior staff that no-one could extract a history from a patient as well as EF (as they called him). He did not interrupt, rarely prompted, but just had that quality of listening with interest that allowed the patient to bring forth everything, even the little nuggets that they had unwittingly failed to reveal earlier to the junior doctors, which held the clue to the diagnosis. Lila succumbed to this approach, revealing not only the mistake that led her to inject mice with colchicine, but in the end also coming clean about what had happened with her mother. She did not implicate Tom, but EF understood.

When Lila had finally finished, she fell silent. A great sense of relief washed over her. She looked up into the long, rather equine face of her confessor.

"Well Lila,that is quite a story. Did anyone else notice your mother's improvement?"

"Yes, my neighbour remarked on it. She helps me with Mum sometimes. Mum said she felt better too."

"Please could you allow me to see the mouse data, if Susan is willing?"

"Of course."

"Thank you, Lila. I will look into this and see if we can make any further progress with it."

"Thank you," said Lila fervently. She left the room with a much lighter heart.

CHAPTER 20

It took 2 days work for Susan to re-assess Lila's slides - but the results were remarkably similar to Lila's - so the exercise was worthwhile in showing the veracity of the results.

Susan e-mailed Dermot to inform him and used the opportunity to let him know that she had also found out that Lila had done parallel experiments with another drug, one that had given equivalent results. He was on the phone within minutes, very angry, demanding to know how this had been allowed to happen and the identity of the other drug. Susan attempted to calm him down, without success. She declined to name the colchicine, thinking that it was better to have it in the scientific domain in a publication first. Dermot ended the call abruptly.

An hour later he rang again. This time he was calm and controlled. He wanted to know whether the second drug was also going into clinical trials. Susan was able to tell him honestly that she did not know. Dermot then said that he would only fund them to do a clinical trial with IG0047F if they agreed not to do another trial, or another arm of the same trial, with a competitor molecule. He explained that to do so would increase the numbers of subjects needed and reduce the chances of including good patients in the IG0047F study. He felt that under such circumstances he would prefer to have his molecule tested at a different centre.

Susan replied that she understood perfectly. As a non- clinician she was not responsible for the clinical trials in the unit, but she would put Dermot's point of view to those who were. She put down the phone and sighed.

What a mess Lila had got them into, she thought. Dermot's trial funding would be useful and the IG molecule stood a chance of working. If so, the resulting paper would be accepted by a top journal and would be widely quoted - good for all the authors. The costs of the IG treatment would doubtless be extremely high - so it would have to be rationed, certainly until Immunogenomics and its shareholders had their pound of flesh.

 Balanced against this was the wildcat colchicine, with no interested pharma firm to pay for a good trial, but with the possibility that if it worked the cost of treating Alzheimer's would be negligible and widely accessible.

She rang Edmund Ferguson.

Lila meanwhile was writing up her latest papers. It always took about ten times longer than anticipated, because one had to go back and check every detail, then the whole thing was far too long and had to be shortened. After that the boss usually wanted changes, or chose to send it to a different journal, with different requirements – that meant re-jigging the sections and sometimes the references too. All in all, it was not a pleasant process. She was quite glad therefore to be interrupted by Ann asking her to come and speak to someone on the phone. She hadn't caught the name, but she had heard Immunogenomics.

"Hello, Lila here.

Hello, Lila, this is Dermot Banks from Immunogenomics. You probably don't remember but we met in Boston after your talk."

"Yes, I do remember. Hello Mr Banks."

"Lila, I have something that I'd like to discuss with you. Would it be possible for you to come and visit me here in Oxford, say tomorrow?"

"Yes, I think so. I'd have to ask permission to take time off."

"Please do, but if possible don't say where you are going. I'd like to keep our meeting a secret for a little while. Should we meet at 11.30 am in my office? Do you have the address?"

Lila said she did.

"Good. You will need to come to Reception and they will ring me. See you tomorrow."

Lila slept very little that night. Her mind was hyperactive, trying to work out why Dermot Banks wanted to see her. Without knowing how much he knew about the mouse trials this was impossible- but that did not stop her brain from running through different scenarios. What she did resolve was not to give away any information, especially none about Grace. The morning arrived, with Lila, having finally fallen into deep sleep in the small hours, groggy when the alarm went off. Coffee helped a little and she took Grace her usual tea in bed, plus some toast, partly as a treat, but also to keep Grace there while Lila washed and dressed. If she got up, Grace tended to wander around after Lila, anxiously, repeating the same question,

"Where are you going?"

"Work, "Lila would reply, and Grace's face would fall.

It seemed kinder to avoid this if at all possible, and breakfast in bed sometimes did the trick.

This time it worked and Lila emerged from her bedroom in her interview garb of black suit and white blouse to find that Grace has sunk back into sleep, propped up on pillows decorated with a few crumbs. This morning sleepiness had become more common since Boston. It was a mixed blessing - it meant that Lila could leave Grace for Marjana to wash and dress, but made Lila feel guilty that she was not pulling her weight in Grace-care. Today however she took full advantage of it, greeting Marjana with the news when she arrived that Grace was asleep. Marjana did not seem to mind, she merely said that was fine, she'd help Grace to dress when she woke up and would make lunch in the meantime. Lila thanked her, reflecting on how lucky she was to have such good people around to help, and left for the trip to Oxford. Timing was crucial, in order to reach Immunogenomics by 11.15 she had to catch a train from Paddington in the next half hour. She ran to the tube, finding that by doing so her anxiety transmuted into exhilaration as she flew past the yellowing trees in the park. The Underground train was just pulling in as she hurried downstairs to the platform so she felt as though the Gods were with her as it carried her to Brunel's beautiful mainline station with the Moorish arched window she had loved since a small child. Once she had asked if she could have one like that in her bedroom, but Grace had just laughed and said no. Lila felt then, as she had done quite often, that things would have been different if her father was still alive. She had probably said just that. Realising just how often she had hurt her mother by such remarks brought a blush of shame to Lila's face.

She hardly noticed the journey to Oxford, being intent on going over what she might be asked and how she would respond. The train was delayed, but by running again, she made it to "Fortress Immunogenomics", as she thought of the building with its highly controlled entrance system, in time. She was asked to wait in the lobby and sat on a slippery leather sofa, pretending to look at the Times, until a red-haired temptress in stilettos came to collect her. The RHT turned out to be Dermot's PA, Lila wondered if she was as efficient as she was glamorous as they made their way via the lifts to the top floor. The RHT knocked on a large door, then entered, holding it open for Lila to pass through. The views through the windows on two sides were extensive, including the famous Oxford spires, but also, closer to home, several other utilitarian buildings on the commercial estate. A metaphor for Big Pharma, Lila thought.

Dermot Banks, as expected, sat behind a big desk. He stood up, smiled, shook her hand and indicated that Lila should sit in a comfortable chair facing the desk and asked if she would like coffee or tea. She chose the former and the RHT went off to obtain some.

"Well Lila, it is nice to meet you properly. I very much enjoyed your talk in Boston and the way you dealt with questions. You obviously know the field very well."

"Thank you."

"Susan has shown me the results of your mouse studies with our molecule and I understand that she herself has verified the data, which is impressive."

"Yes." Lila was determined not to be expansive in her answers.

"Immunogenomics will need to follow this up with clinical trials. Until now we have transferred the ownership (Lila noticed that he avoided the word sold) of such putative therapies to larger organizations since we have been too small for clinical trials. However, I think that the time has come for expansion in that direction and I am wondering whether IG0047F is the first molecule we should try. That could be in collaboration with your institution, with Susan Armstrong and some of the clinicians in the attached hospital. We might need to make it a multi-centre study, depending on statistical advice"

Lila nodded.

The coffee arrived and gave her pause for thought. Why was he telling her this?

As if he had read her mind Dermot continued.

"The reason I asked you to come here was that I thought you might like to be involved in this process. We would be collecting samples for analysis during the study - these would include blood, cerebro-spinal fluid, possibly others such as saliva, and would ask for post mortem samples of the brains of all subjects included when they died. You could be responsible for organizing the work done on these and would have technicians working under you to do most of the actual dogsbody stuff. It would provide a rich source of information on dementia and you could be the first author on some of the papers."

He paused and looked at Lila expectantly.

"It sounds very interesting, "she said, somewhat lamely." Would I be an employee of Immunogenomics?"

"Certainly, "Dermot replied, "we can tempt you with a very good package, a salary far in excess of what you receive now and with extra benefits such as a company car, pension scheme, membership of the onsite gym here."

Lila was about to tell him about her personal circumstances and the difficulty in moving to Oxford when he went on.

"Why don't I show you around our set up here?"

Lila assented and he rose, shepherding her out into the corridor. They explored the recently built facilities, Lila commenting favourably on the laboratories themselves and also on the break out areas where staff could chat and exchange ideas. These were light, airy and painted in bright colours; Lila was reminded of Dragan's house. Dermot introduced her to everyone they met, she was impressed that he knew all their names, until she realized he had good long sight and was reading their badges. Some were working on MS and Lila began to interact with them on the science involved. Dermot was pleased and indicated that if she came to them, she could also continue her previous investigations into MS too.

Lila was beginning to think it might be a good idea to accept, even if it meant a long commute each day.

As they rose back in the lift Dermot remarked,

"Of course, drug discovery is a very expensive process, as you are no doubt aware, and not always successful. It has happened that after long and costly studies, molecules which seemed very promising in animals have not succeeded in man."

Lila replied,

"Of course, I am well aware of that."

"Immunogenomics would not be able to fund such studies if there were a cheaper competitor molecule in the wings."

Lila looked at him. He was smiling down at her, holding the lift doors open, giving no indication that he had just threatened her, or rather, had tried to buy her off. She decided to say nothing, as if she began to speak her Scottish blood would boil and she would later regret an outburst. Instead she smiled back and returned to the big office to collect her coat.

"Thank you so much. It has been most enlightening."

Lila held out her hand.

Dermot was unsure of her intentions, just as she wished. He shook her hand and said,

"It was a pleasure Lila. Should I pop an offer in the post?"

"Thank you," Lila replied, deliberately oblique. She turned and left him looking after her, still uncertain.

CHAPTER 21

The conversation with Edmund Ferguson had left Susan in no doubt as to their future plans. He was horrified that anyone should attempt to block the development of any drug that might help patients with dementia. Once she told him of Dermot's caveat that the Immunogenomics trial would only proceed in their hospital if any further research on colchicine were shelved, Edmund determined to explore the effects of colchicine. Like Dermot, he was impressed with what he had seen of Lila and her work. He recognised her determination and dedication in the face of adversity, having heard details of Grace's problem from Tom.

"Leave it with me please, Susan."

She was very happy to do so, not wanting to be the person to turn down Dermot's offer. Once the clinicians had refused there was no way she, as a scientist, could run a clinical trial, so she was off the hook. However, she felt that her budding relationship with Dermot was about to be secateured.

Lila was still furious when she arrived back in the lab. She could not speak to Susan as the trip to Immunogenomics had been kept as a secret between her and Dermot Banks, but she needed to talk to someone. Tom ended up as the recipient of her story as he came to the lab in the late afternoon. Lila poured out what had happened and how very angry she was that Immunogenomics would only use their facilities for a clinical study if competing molecules, i.e. colchicine, were abandoned and that Dermot had tried to buy her off with the offer of a lucrative and interesting job.

"I'd rather die," she said dramatically.

Tom calmed her down.

"Look at it from Dermot's point of view for a minute. It makes sense for him to do all that," he said.

"His job is to make money for the company, not to cure dementia. In fact, what he and other pharma companies would love is a long term treatment rather than a cure."

"That's why we have to find a cure, or at least a long term treatment that is affordable for everyone"

"Of course, that's why we are here."

"Oh Tom, what should I do? I really think colchicine helped Mum- how can I get her some more?"

"That is also why I am here," Tom replied. "Edmund Ferguson asked me to find you. He wants to speak to you again."

"When?"

"Now, if possible. On the ward."

"I'm on my way." Lila grabbed her coat and rucksack and hurried into the hospital.

EF was finishing the ward round with a cup of tea in Sister's Office. When Lila appeared in the doorway he beckoned her in and asked Sister if they could speak in private briefly. Sister rather reluctantly agreed and left, closing the door behind her.

"Now Lila, come and sit down. I have been thinking about what you told me and what I suggest is this - first of all, I see your mother as a patient if possible. Do you think your GP would refer her?"

Lila nodded.

"Yes, I think so."

"Good. I would assess her carefully, including a session with a clinical psychologist, check her bloods and if all was well, prescribe some colchicine for her for a few weeks. Is that how long it took to work?"

"Yes, it made a difference quite quickly - in days, I thought." Lila's heart was leaping in her chest.

"Fine, let's say one month. Then I would reassess her using the same tests to see if there was a discernible difference. If so, we should think about instigating a clinical trial."

"Would Mum be included, to ensure that she stays on colchicine?"

"No need. As a doctor I am allowed to prescribe medications which I believe will benefit the patient even if they are not licensed for that indication. I can continue to prescribe for your mother or persuade your GP to do so."

Lila's spirits were soaring.

"Oh thank, thank you"

It was hard to stop herself from hugging this tall gent lounging in his hospital chair, feet outstretched.

"Don't thank me yet. Let's see what happens. Ask your GP about a referral and let me know quickly. I shall need it in writing but an e – mail will suffice. This is my address."

He handed her a card with an impressive number of degrees after his name.

"Off you go." He waved her towards the door. "Sister is wanting her empire back."

Lila left, pausing in the entrance hall to find the number of her local GP practice on her mobile, then calling it. The ringing continued as she hurried towards the station, interrupted by various admonitions about flu jabs and using the internet for contact, but was finally answered. She asked for Dr McKay.

"Dr McKay is back in the surgery in half an hour, please ring then."

The receptionist had put down the phone before Lila could reply. She resolved to catch the train back to Queen's Park and go into the surgery in that half hour – with luck she could catch the doctor as she came in. Fortunately on the train she had second thoughts about the wisdom of this approach. Being seated she managed to get out a notepad and pen and wrote a brief, but polite, letter, giving Grace's details and explaining that Edmund Ferguson, a neurologist at her university hospital, had asked if Grace could be referred to him in order to investigate a possible treatment. Lila put her mobile number at the end in case there were questions. She dropped into the surgery, borrowed an envelope from the receptionist, enclosed the letter and addressed it to Dr McKay.

"Please would you see she gets it tonight?"

"Sure", said the receptionist. "She'll be here any minute. I'll hand it to her when she arrives."

Lila wondered if the interview suit she was wearing had helped with this easy interchange. She hurried home to Grace, who, by this time, as arranged, was with Mary Dewhurst, Marjana having left earlier to pick up her kids. They were sitting companionably on the sofa with the 6 o'clock news on the TV, neither really watching it. Lila went in and kissed Grace on both cheeks.

"Hello Mum, I missed you today."

"Hello darling." Grace beamed at her.

Mary was full of questions about the trip to Oxford, having been informed about it by Marjana.

Lila replied as best she could, explaining the smart set-up there, but not mentioning the job offer. She did not want Mary to think they would leave the neighbourhood. In order to stop that line of questioning she mentioned Edmund Ferguson's offer to see Grace. Mary Dewhurst was impressed.

"You know he looks after some of the Royal Family."

This was news to Lila.

"How do you know that?"

"Oh, from the TV, I think. I remember his name."

Grace suddenly spoke.

"I'd like to see a Royal doctor."

They all laughed.

CHAPTER 22.

There was no problem about the referral. Dr McKay rang Lila next day to say that she had sent an e – mail to EF and that she hoped it would be a useful visit. The outpatient letter took several days to arrive and when it did the appointment was for the next week.

Lila asked for the day off work and she and Grace travelled in together on the Tube, thankfully after the early morning crush. They checked in at the desk in outpatients and sat waiting in a room full of people, some obviously incapacitated: in wheelschairs or with walking sticks some with trembling limbs, others not. Lila wondered if some of them had MS, the disease she had worked on for her PhD. Most of the crowd were in couples, with an obviously devoted husband or wife caring for a sick spouse. How much better it would be for Grace if Duncan were still alive, thought Lila.

After what seemed a very long time Grace was called into the consulting room. EF greeted them both warmly, then talked to Grace, allowing her to explain her problems to him. Lila was surprised at some of what her mother said - there was a complete denial of most difficulties, but Grace did admit to problems remembering things. This was followed by an examination. Grace was behind a curtain so Lila could hear, but not see, what went on. Finally, EF asked if Grace would mind going for some tests. She agreed readily and they went on a round of various departments: haematology for blood tests, radiology for a pre-booked PET scan and then, after lunch, a long session, with Lila excluded, with a clinical psychologist. By the end they were both feeling exhausted and had a cup of tea in the café nearby before embarking on the journey home. EF had also ordered a lumbar puncture, but this had to be on another day. Lila realized that being a patient was quite a tough job, as was being a carer.

It was two weeks later that EF called her into his office. The results were in keeping with Alzheimer's disease and he was prepared to prescribe some colchicine for Grace for a trial period of one month. Lila accepted the prescription gratefully and obtained it from the hospital pharmacy, glad to do so without feeling underhand. She gave the first dose to Grace that evening.

In the days that followed Lila watched Grace like a hawk, trying to notice any smidgen of improvement. Nothing seemed to change. Lila was despondent, so much so that after a week she even cried when updating Dragan, who dropped in most evenings on his way home from work. He tried to cheer her up, saying that perhaps it would take longer to work this time. As usual Grace responded with laughter to his gentle teasing. Then, unexpectedly she teased him back, calling him a dragon. He and Lila looked at each other - surely this was a sign of better mental function? They whooped and high fived, Grace was startled by the success of her wit. After that she gradually came back to her usual self, taking an interest in newspapers, commenting on what was on the TV, moving more and more easily. Her incontinence persisted until the 4th week, when Lila noticed that Grace had begun to have clean pads and stopped putting them on her. In fact, she stopped helping Grace to dress - merely putting out her clothes for the next day was now sufficient. Grace even brushed her own hair now; Lila felt slightly sad as doing this gently and lovingly had been therapeutic for them both.

The next appointment with EF was scheduled for December 15th. This time, knowing how tiring a day it would be, Lila took them in an Uber. They were both nervous, Grace more so than last time because she understood much more, Lila because she hoped that there would be objective changes in some of the many measurements made, so that EF would organize a proper trial. They sat in the depressing waiting room again. Lila wondered how anyone could face a career as a Neurologist, it must become suicidally depressing after some years. EF however showed only pleasure at seeing them. His chat to Grace was longer than before: since Grace was no longer monosyllabic, she insisted on telling him the minutiae of her current life. Lila was horribly embarrassed; EF simply listened carefully and encouraged Grace when necessary. The rituals of examination, blood tests, PET scan and clinical psychological assessment were gone through and they were free to go home. Grace however was less exhausted than on the last occasion and asked if they could go home on a bus so as to see some of the Christmas lights along Oxford Street. The number 6 took them home in style, on the top deck at the front. It was a surprisingly magical experience - the illuminated angels passing above them, the dressed shop windows, especially that of Selfridges, and the crowds of cheerful people out buying presents all contributed to their happiness.

Walking back from the bus took them near to Dragan's home so it was no surprise to meet him in the street, coming from the opposite direction, having used the Underground. He was eager to find out how the visit had gone, so turned round and walked back with them to their house, chatting to Grace about the bus ride on the way. Lila realized that her mother had been out and about so little in recent times that almost any experience was special. She suddenly had an idea for a good Christmas gift for Grace, and perhaps for Dragan too: a trip to Kew at night when the light shows were on.

Once home, Lila offered Dragan some supper - she had made some bolognaise the night before, knowing that they would be hungry on their return. He accepted, having rung his Mum to let her know. Dragan went out and bought a bottle of red wine to celebrate while Lila heated up the bolognaise and cooked spaghetti. The three of them found themselves laughing a lot, enjoying the food (Lila was a competent, if not inspired cook), the wine and each other's company.

Grace later declared she was tired, so Lila accompanied her up the stairs to bed and made sure that she got undressed, did a pee, brushed her teeth and took her colchicine before getting into bed.

"You are such a good girl, my darling."

"And you are such a good Mum." Lila bent to kiss Grace.

This was an interchange they had had many times over the years, but tonight it had a special resonance for them both.

"And the dragon is a very good young man." Grace looked meaningfully at her. Lila nodded, but did not comment.

"There are not many like him."

This time Lila replied, thoughtfully,

"Yes Mum, you are right, as usual."

She blew another kiss and slipped out of the room and quietly down the stairs. The dragon was washing up.

"Please could I watch something on your tele?" he asked. "If I go home now I'll miss the start."

"Sure, which channel?"

It turned out that Dragan wanted to see the news, since a subject on which he had been reporting was likely to be mentioned. They sat companionably on the sofa, Lila was reminded of her Mum and Mrs D, watching the news in just the same way. Only Dragan was genuinely engaged, commenting quietly under his breath. The subject was fracking and the protests against it which had led to imprisonment for a few stalwart objectors for a minor offence. Dragan was incensed at the heavy handed way in which they had been dealt with, muttering that the UK was becoming a police state.

Lila was relieved, she had been wary of engaging with him on political subjects, particularly since he worked for such a right wing paper as the Daily Chronicle, but she now felt that his ideas were similar to her own. So she did not object when he slipped his arm behind her along the back of the sofa.

Once the news was over, Dragan rose to leave, saying he had a busy day tomorrow, and was sure that she had too. Lila concurred, though in fact her job involved correcting proofs of an accepted article and re – revising another, nothing very arduous. They stood up, awkward for a moment in the narrow space, then Dragan picked up her hand, lifted it to his lips and kissed it.

"Goodnight sweet princess, " he said, with a theatrical bow.

He turned and left the front room, picked up his coat from the rack in the hall and tried to open the front door to vanish quickly into the night. Unfortunately, he did not know about the deadlock which Lila had got a locksmith to put on, at the same time as obtaining locks for the bathroom cabinet and the cupboard under the sink, all to keep Grace safe. Dragan's attempts to open the door provoked hilarity in Lila, partly the result of wine, but also the bathos of his descent from Prince Charming to Mr Bean. She stood laughing helplessly as he fiddled with the levers. In the end he turned to her and said, laughing too,

"Madam, I am your prisoner. Do with me what you will."

Something dissolved inside her brain and let another part of it guide her actions.

Lila stepped forward, took his face in her hands and planted a gentle kiss on his lips.

Then she opened the door.

"Goodnight sweet prince", she said, giving him a little push towards the outside world.

CHAPTER 23

That night Lila could not get to sleep, going over her feelings for Dragan and for Tom in her mind, as well as those for her previous boyfriends. Finally she managed to produce a kind of scientific hypothesis which satisfied her. Thinking this important she jotted down one or two phrases in the notebook she kept by her bed, then lay down again; soon sleep overtook her analytical mind. Next morning she had all but forgotten her ideas - but seeing the note reminded her and the thoughts came flooding back, amplified now by work done on them by her brain while she slept. She had previously noticed this unconscious brain-activity-during-sleep phenomenon in relation to crosswords, which she loved to puzzle over. Sometimes trying to elucidate the answer to a clue late at night she had given up, gone to sleep, only to find that the answer was there in her mind in the morning. That had led her to the notebook by the bedside scenario – so she could record the gems that her unconscious mind had provided. The new ideas made her cheerful and she hummed as she rose and made breakfast for her and Grace - the latter's still taken in bed, as this was what Grace had come to like and expect.

 Finally ready for work Lila hurried to the station; she had abandoned her bike in the dark and cold winter months. As hoped, she met Dragan on the platform. Somewhat suspiciously he was standing there alone as a train pulled out, Lila thought he might have been waiting to see if she came.

"Hi!"

"Hi, how are you this morning?" Dragan asked.

"Fine", said Lila," and you?"

"I'm good. "

"I know you are good, but how are you?"

This was a game her mother had played when Lila began to use the Americanism.

Dragan laughed. "OK, Miss Pedant. I am well too."

During this short interchange the platform had refilled and they had to concentrate on getting onto the next train which was now pulling in. As usual there were few seats so they stood together in the centre of the carriage between the doors, hanging on to a pole and swaying as the train ran fast from station to station. It was hard to talk, let alone say anything meaningful. They managed an exchange about Grace's health and Lila's hopes, plus some comments about what was in the Metro that day. The anti-frackers had been released on bail and Dragan was delighted, so too was Lila. All too soon it was time to get off and they parted amicably.

"Perhaps see you tonight?" asked Dragan as she went.

She nodded.

"Yes, drop in if you like."

He nodded and called after her,

"I'll bring supper."

She gave him a thumbs up.

The working day passed slowly. Lila was still writing and correcting scientific papers, checking references, answering referees' queries and complaints. It was annoying (when the referee had misunderstood), boring, yet worrying (in case the outcome was rejection by that journal) and occasionally illuminating (when the referee had pointed out some new facet that she and her co- authors had not seen). Eventually she felt she had done all she could, so sent the revised version to all the co-authors for their comments, before she could return it to the journal.

It was already 2 pm and she had not eaten anything since breakfast. She hadn't made sandwiches, so she headed to the canteen, intending to have some soup. Tom was there, next to EF, both eating their way through mountains of food - the hospital Christmas dinner for staff. Lila had completely forgotten about it and had failed to buy a ticket. She was turning to leave, but Tom saw and stopped her, offering a ticket which he had in reserve.

"The F1 couldn't make it, so you can have it instead."

"Thank you."

Lila's plate was heaped with turkey, stuffing, brussels, potatoes boiled and roast, carrots, cranberry sauce and gravy. She felt obliged to sit next to Tom, though they had not interacted much since the trip to Boston, both of them somewhat embarrassed: Lila by her financial obligations, Tom by her knowledge of his sexuality. EF smiled benignly at her.

"Wow, this is some feast," said Lila.

"Yes, it is the best meal here all year", replied EF." I think it is meant to keep the staff onside. In the old days the junior doctors were well fed for free, especially in the chest hospitals, like the Brompton, so that they did not catch TB. The medical staff had their own dining room which made interaction and discussion of cases easy. Now we share one room with everyone, including patients and relatives – so no- one can talk freely about their patients and get advice from colleagues."

"Would you like to go back to the old days?"

"Yes and no. As always there were good things, like junior doctors being a part of a firm - a pyramid structure with the consultant at the top. That gave a sense of stability and belonging - you knew who to report to, to ask questions of. You admitted patients, clerked them, saw what happened to them. Now foundation year applications are done online, and juniors end up wherever they are sent for a few months at a time, on rotas; they don't belong to anyone, they look after patients briefly, especially in A&E, and may never find out what happened, whether they made the right diagnosis, unless they have time to chase things up, which they mostly don't. In addition, they become shift workers, just doing their time and leaving, with no sense of being part of the team. That way they don't get enough experience and we do not get to know them very well."

Lila nodded, her mouth full of food.

EF continued,

"I think the changes to core medical training which will come into effect next year will be beneficial, certainly to those beyond F1 and 2. However I must not bore you with all that. How is your dear mother today?"

"She is fine, thank you. The visit tired her less than last time and we saw the Christmas lights on our way home. They made her very happy."

EF replied, smiling,

"I think of dementia as a return to childhood, with the adult patient initially becoming difficult like an adolescent, then exhibiting a childlike delight in simple things, finally, sadly returning to infancy."

He was about to expand on this theme, but, seeing Lila's face, thought better of it and said instead,

"She certainly seemed improved to me. I have to look at the PET scans this afternoon. Would you both care to accompany me? It should be a learning experience for all of us."

Both Lila and Tom agreed willingly and got on with their stolid eating.

The PET scan involved something called positron emission tomography, they were informed by the erudite Consultant Radiologist.

"PET differs from CT and MRI in that it examines active, living cells and evaluates how they function, whereas CT and MRI are used to detect damage caused by a disease," he told them

"The advent of tau-targeted tracers such as flortaucipir have made it possible to investigate the sequence of development of tau and amyloid-β in the development of cognitive impairment due to Alzheimer's disease", he informed them.

"For Aβ+ subjects, flortaucipir neocortical uptake appears significantly higher with more advanced clinical stage. Moreover, the pattern of its distribution in the inferior and lateral temporal lobes reflects the post-mortem distribution of tau. Further, the results of tests such as the mini mental state are consistent with the hypothesis that cortical tau is associated with cognitive impairment."

Lila, Tom and EF all nodded.

"Currently PET scanning in Alzheimer's is a research tool. I was able to undertake it in your mother's case under a small grant programme of Professor Ferguson's. Here you can see the scan which she had a month ago-note the uptake in the outer parts of the temporal lobes."

He pointed at the screen and they all nodded again.

"Now yesterday's scan"- the screen switched to another similar picture.

"Here there is still some uptake outside the mesial temporal lobe - but it is less. This is very important - development of tau beyond the mesial temporal lobe may be dependent on amyloid accumulation. The regression could mean that amyloid is also unravelling and reducing - that the basic changes of the brain in Alzheimer's could be reversible."

Lila's eyes widened. It looked as though the colchicine was turning back the clock and restoring Grace's brain to some extent - that fitted with her improvement in understanding things, in the restoration of continence too. It was exciting, marvellous. She was afraid to say anything in case she had not understood properly.

Tom spoke.

"Has your Mum changed at all clinically during the time between these scans?"

Lila dared to speak.

"Oh yes, she has improved - lots of little things: she is more with it, her speech has improved, she even made a joke yesterday. The big thing is that she is continent again - that makes our lives so much easier."

EF nodded sagely again.

"I support that. Her mini mental state score has risen. The full report of the clinical psychologist will take some time, but I think there is no doubt that Grace has better mental function than she had a month ago. You know as well as I do that few patients with Alzheimer's improve, other than the usually transient benefit when they are first given acetylcholinesterase inhibitors. I doubt they would alter the PET scan. In any case Grace has been on donepezil continually throughout the past year - the only factor which has changed recently is that she has received colchicine - so we now need to see whether colchicine can benefit other sufferers, and, if so, how much and for how long."

"What sort of trial are you proposing? A randomized DBPCT?" asked Tom.

"A double- blind, placebo- controlled study would be ideal- but long, involved and costly. Currently we do not have much in the way of funding, but we do have a drug which is readily available and can be given to patients and I think we should start soon. There are so many Alzheimer's patients out there, needing to try something. I wonder whether the next step is more n of 1 studies, just to see if the results in 100% of one patient can be generalized."

Lila decided to reveal her ignorance.

"What is an n of 1 study?" she asked.

"It is similar to what I did with your mother", EF explained. "An individual patient is studied for a length of time, with careful observations, then given the new treatment and the study continues with measurements over a similar time period, sometimes then the treatment is stopped and the measurements continue. Occasionally a placebo is used instead of treatment to see if existing treatment is working."

"Does it need ethical approval?" asked Tom.

EF pondered,

"I am not sure. Perhaps Tom you could check that for me. If so I'd like you and Lila to work on that together. Lila knows what tests her mother had- we would repeat those in the new subjects, including the PET scans if I can find funding for them."

"Are they expensive?" asked Lila.

"Yes, around £1000 a time, so, with one before and one after treatment, it would cost 2k for each patient we include. I'd like to study 20 subjects, so we need 40k. That is 40k we do not have at present."

"Do you have any ideas for suitable grants for this project?" Tom enquired.

"Some, but I have a nasty feeling that we have just missed the boat for one of the most likely ones. I will look into it, but do let me know if you have any bright ideas. Please excuse me, I have to go now."

EF rose, bowed his head courteously to Lila, and loped out of the room on his long legs.

"He's a funny old stick, isn't he?" observed Lila.

Tom was affronted,

"He is one of the best and most respected neurologists anywhere, Lila. Your mother is extremely lucky to have been taken on by him."

"Sorry, I didn't mean to be disrespectful and I am very grateful to him. All I meant was that he seems to belong to an earlier age."

"One when people were polite and kind to each other."

"Yes."

Lila was aware of having upset Tom and, not wanting to worsen things, fell silent. She continued to savour her mega-meal, but was becoming increasingly full.

"Would you like some pudding or mince pies?" asked Tom.

"No, thank you. I couldn't."

Then, thinking of that evening,

"Do you suppose I could smuggle a couple of mince pies out for my Mum?"

Tom laughed,

"I'll get some. Do you have anything to hide them in?"

Lila indicated her bag, big enough to put in A4 papers and with space for extra contents.

Tome returned with 4 mince pies and insisted on keeping only one for himself to eat there and then. Lila wrapped the remainder in a paper napkin and hid them in her bag. She told Tom that Grace loved mince pies and until then she had forgotten to get any.

"Don't you make them? " Tom was surprised. "My mother always does. We used to help her when we were little, it was very messy and great fun." He looked wistful.

"We?"

"I have a brother and two sisters. My brother is older than me, my sisters are younger."

"Is any of them medical?"

"No- I'm the only fool in the family", he laughed." My brother is what you might call an entrepreneur- he sees business opportunities and takes them, my sisters haven't really decided yet, but both are on the Arts side. Lily, the youngest, is still at Uni."

"Lily- that's like my name!"

"Yes, I thought about mentioning it, but somehow never got round to it. She is nothing like you, though. She's a dreamy, artistic blonde- or was when I last saw her. Sometimes she has flaming red hair."

Whereas I am a hard, dark scientist thought Lila, but did not say so.

"I must go", she said. "Nice to talk to you, Tom. When should we meet to discuss the plan for the possible study?"

"Tom checked the calendar on his mobile phone.

"How would tomorrow at noon suit you?"

"Fine- where should we meet?"

"I'll come to your little office if that's OK. I am likely to be bothered if we stay on the ward or nearby."

"See you then."

Lila moved off, weaving her way through tables of satiated people, few of whom she had ever seen before. Behind her she could hear greetings called out to Tom who was progressing more slowly, exchanging a few words with someone here and there. She thought again about her career choice- and how lonely a path it often was, compared to that of a doctor.

CHAPTER 24

The meeting next day in the cubby hole started well. Lila searched for "NHS ethical approval" on her computer and found the NHS Health Research Authority site easily.

A photo of a pretty girl with pink top and matching lipstick, wearing mascara plus a pair of oversized spectacles adorned the site. She was obviously cold in her sleeveless top: the hairs on her arms were erect, and she appeared to be using a pen which was strange, given that the site was electronic.

"Why do they feel the need to put in these staged photos? No- one I know looks like that at work. I bet that cost them a pretty penny from some agency- taxpayer's money that could have been better spent," Tom grumbled.

Once the site was entered there were questions to answer to determine whether the n of 1 study proposed would need to go through the rigours of an Ethics Committee. The link took her to an MRC site and then she clicked on

Is my study research?

Question 1 was

Are the participants in your study randomised to different groups?

The answer was obviously NO.

To Question 2

Does your study protocol **demand changing treatment/care/services from accepted standards for any of the patients/service users involved?**

They had to answer YES.

The site informed them that:

Your study would be considered Research.

You should now determine whether your study requires NHS REC approval.

Follow this link to launch the '*Do I need NHS REC approval*?' tool.

Lila did so and found another question

Firstly, is your study research?

She answered affirmatively and received another question:

Is your study a clinical trial of an investigational medicinal product (CTIMP)**?**

Since underneath it stated that this can include studies involving drugs with Marketing Authorisations, which colchicine had, the answer was YES again. The computer told her

You have answered *'YES'* to the following questions which would indicate that you need NHS approval and you may require other approvals:

Applications must be made using the Integrated Research Application System (IRAS).

Lila entered this site and found that the Integrated Research Application System (IRAS):

Is a single system for applying for the permissions and approvals for health and social care / community care research in the UK

Enables you to enter the information about your project once instead of duplicating information in separate application forms

Uses filters to ensure that the data collected and collated is appropriate to the type of study, and consequently the permissions and approvals required

Helps you to meet regulatory and governance requirements

"That sounds good," she said.

"Just you wait, I have done this before" said Tom. "It is not as easy as it seems. It'll take us a week, at least"

"Perhaps I should stick to mice," laughed Lila.

"Too right, they at least do what you ask of them."

Lila had been looking through the IRAS document - it was clear that they had pages and pages to fill. Only one person could work on it at a time.

"Why don't I take it home and do what I can then pass it to you?"

"Good idea kid, call me if you have any questions. You've got my mobile no haven't you?"

Lila nodded.

"OK, see you tomorrow."

She picked up her laptop, stuffed it into her rucksack and left for home.

In the event the IRAS form took over 2 weeks. There had to be discussions with EF and Susan about the protocol and approval of the Patient Information Sheet and Consent forms, plus a new form for public data and more besides. When they had finally finished it, plus all the other documents needed by the hospital and the Research Office, had received insurance and had chosen an available Research Ethics Committee, Lila pressed SEND with a huge feeling of release. She and Tom high fived.

"We deserve a drink," he stated firmly. "And I know just where to get one," he paused and Lila's spirits rose-"at our departmental party." Her face fell.

"Oh, you cheapskate! Oh God, I should not have said that- you paid for my flight home and I can never thank you enough for that. I will repay you someday, I promise."

"Come on Lila, forget that. The Xmas do is always a good party. The consultants stump up for booze and food and everyone is invited, so it's great opportunity to meet people and their nearest and dearest."

Lila had received an invitation but hadn't thought much about it. She thought that hospital parties were usually sad affairs with lonely people, a few mince pies and rough wine. She had not dressed up, nor had she arranged cover at home. When all the female staff had come in that morning wearing dresses she had wondered why. Now she knew.

"I need to ring and see if Mrs D can come in to sit with Mum."

"OK, I have to pick up my sister. It starts in an hour. See you there."

Lila made two phone calls. Mrs D was able to oblige. Lila asked her to heat up the left- overs in the fridge and share them with Grace for supper, together with some fresh rice. It turned out that Mrs D liked a good dhal curry, so was happy to comply.

Lila looked at herself in the mirror. She was in a jumper, T- shirt, jeans and trainers, hardly party wear. In a rush she slipped out to the Tube, found her way to Oxford Circus and entered the crowds there doing Christmas shopping. The atmosphere was one of excitement mixed with exhaustion and the aroma of roasting chestnuts. It was chilly and she drew her parka around her. The shop windows were as she had seen them with Grace on their bus trip, when Lila had noticed a green dress in a window, but did not remember the name of the shop. It must have been between Oxford Circus and Marble Arch, she thought and set off westwards. Progress was slow, as everyone seemed to be walking in the opposite direction. After a hundred yards she began to think that she was being stupid and should return to the hospital, but then there was the window with the dress, dark green, simple, elegant. She entered the shop, which turned out to be Monsoon, found a suitably- sized dress on the rail and held it up against her. It looked to be the right size. There was no time to find out so she joined the queue to pay.

"If it doesn't fit can I bring it back?"

"Yes", said the assistant," keep the receipt." Lila tucked it into a side pocket of her purse, feeling guilty at having spent so much money on herself when things were tight. Her normal shopping these days was at pound shops and the cheaper supermarkets.

She hurried back to the hospital via a horribly crowded Oxford Circus station – which she had to queue to enter. Once back she changed quickly into the new dress in a cubicle in the Ladies loo. She emerged and looked at herself in the mirror. The dress suited her well, just as she hoped. While she was twirling round, admiring her reflection Ann came in.

"Wow, you look great."

"Thanks."

"You are going to lose the trainers, aren't you?" asked Ann.

"Oh no, I forgot about them. I don't have anything else."

"What size are you?"

"Six, 40 European, I think."

"Lila, it is your lucky day "

Ann kept a spare pair of smart black stilettos in her locker- for the occasions when she went out from work. She brought them to Lila who tried them on, Like Cinderella. They fitted. Once these were on her feet she felt party – ready, but Ann stopped her and said,

"Make –up?"

"Did we fall out?"

"No, Lila, do you want some make –up? Hold on, let me just make your eyes look even bigger"

Ann approached her with a palette of eyeshadows, then a mascara wand. Lila submitted to her eye ministrations, but cavilled at the idea of lipstick.

"No thanks, it'll just end up on the wineglass."

"You look just wonderful," Ann told her.

Lila, feeling beautiful and light- hearted for the first time in ages, went off to join the fray in the Reception Room where all hospital events took place.

She could hear the buzz of conversation from several feet outside the room; once in the open doorway it looked a lot like Oxford Circus tube station with wall to wall people, most of whom she did not know. She had paused, uncertain what to do, when she felt a hand placed gently on her forearm and a familiar voice said,

"It's quite a scrum, isn't it?"

She turned to see who had spoken and found Dermot Banks at her side. Since she had turned down his offer of a job she had not given him a second thought. He spoke again

"I have never been to this party before, have you?

"No," Lila replied, wondering how he came to be there and thinking that she was very likely not going to go to it now if she could escape.

"Allow me to get you a drink," Dermot steered her towards the bar area, found a glass of white wine that she requested, then steered her away into a quieter corner.

"I was very sorry that you did not accept my offer."

Lila told him the truth.

"I am sorry too, but the colchicine study is too important to me. My mother, who has dementia, has undoubtedly improved whilst on it, so I feel that it should be formally tested. Your offer would have meant shelving any colchicine research, so I could not accept."

Dermot nodded.

"You are a very principled. I admire that. However you need to understand my point of view- I have to do my utmost to come up with a successful treatment and in order to do that I cannot allow minor studies on unlikely substances to distract from the main trial. That is now going to take place in Oxford at the John Radcliffe – which is very convenient for Immunogenomics."

"I wish you luck."

"Thank you Lila, as I do to you. Oh there is Susan, I am her guest so should go and speak to her. Happy Christmas Lila."

He walked over to the door where Susan Armstrong had just entered and was surveying the throng. She was wearing a glistening silver sheath dress and looked at least a million dollars.

Lila wondered why Susan had invited Dermot. She must by now know that he had vetoed the colchicine study and taken his expensive clinical trial elsewhere, but, once she saw the delighted expression on Susan's face as she saw Dermot, she knew why. While she was observing them a hand landed on her shoulder.

"Lila, "

She spun round. It was Tom.

"Wow Lila, you look gorgeous! What a transformation."

Lila felt this was a rather backhanded compliment, implying that she normally looked otherwise. She merely smiled her thanks as her attention was drawn to Tom's companion.

"Meet my sister, Lily"

"Lily, this is Lila who has got me out of many scrapes during my PhD."

Lila was so taken with Lily's appearance that she almost failed to offer her hand. Lily was a prettier younger female version of Tom- blonde haired , blue- eyed, with that same charming, effortless smile.

 They exchanged small talk; it transpired that Lily was studying in London, but hated living in a small dark room in a shared flat with no garden. When asked where this was situated she replied,

"Kilburn."

"Oh that's near to where I live – in Queen's Park, "said Lila. "You must come round."

Lily said she would be delighted to do so, then Tom whisked her away to meet EF and Mrs EF, who was a petite grey-haired lady wearing beautiful shoes. Lila looked around for someone to talk to and saw Dragan hovering near the door. She waved and hurried to him.

"Thank you so much for coming at such short notice." She kissed him on his cheek.

"No problem. I am happy to escort you anywhere, dear Princess."

"I hadn't intended to bother with this party but today everyone told me it was good, so I made a last minute effort."

"You are looking stunning. I love the dress. Is it new?"

Lila liked this about Dragan. He noticed things, made her feel good, without implying that she normally looked rubbish.

"Yes, I bought it about an hour ago."

"Good move. "

By this time they had made their way to the bar where Dragan chose a beer and Lila recharged her wine glass. She was trying to indicate to him various people whom she had previously mentioned to him in their evening chats, realising as she did so that Dragan knew more about her life than anyone else.

"Can we speak to the glamorous Susan?" he asked.

"We can try" replied Lila, leading him towards her boss who had an entourage surrounding her, including Dermot Banks. They ended up standing next to Dermot, so Lila introduced Dragan. Soon the two of them were chatting away like old friends, the subject being football. Lila felt excluded and so moved on, chatting to some of the other laboratory staff who were nearby. She took the opportunity to watch Lily in action, still in a group with EF. There was something about her which compelled attention but Lila could not easily put it into words: her face was mobile and expressive, she smiled often, shrugged her shoulders, laughed. Suddenly Lily looked round, caught Lila's gaze and gave a dazzling smile. Lila felt her heart warm to this girl, little more than a child. From the way those around her were reacting Lila was not alone in this view. Shannon likewise was surrounded by others, mostly young men, probably admiring the red dress she was nearly wearing. Lila checked on Dragan - he seemed happy with Dermot, so Lila went over and joined the group around Lily and EF. The talk was of research and the current difficulties in funding, staffing and so on. Worries about Brexit had caused some of the very good European scientists to rethink their careers and move back to continental Europe. Mrs EF turned out to be Spanish and she spoke with sadness of the rifts within Spain about Catalonian independence.

"We are all tribal," Lila found herself saying, courtesy of 2 glasses of wine. "Even if it is only as a supporter of a particular football team."

This provoked laughter.

"Which tribe do you belong to Lila?" asked Lily.

"I don't know. I am not sure that I have found my tribe yet. Maybe the eco- warriors."

They were joined by Dragan whom Lila introduced to EF and his wife, to Lily and to Tom, who had now joined the group.

EF explained to his wife and Lily that Lila and Tom were in the process of setting up a research project on dementia. There was great interest. Tom supplied the bare details of what was intended, leaving out the roles of Lila and Grace in initiation of the project. Dragan, obviously thinking this was unfair, asked

"This is all because of what happened to Lila's mum, isn't it?"

EF stepped in, sounding rather pompous.

"It was fortuitous that Lila's mother was given colchicine for her arthritis and that Lila was perceptive about the consequent improvement in her mental state. When this therapy was repeated the benefit was again seen and so is highly likely to relate to the drug. We need now to see if this is idiosyncratic or if it is a general phenomenon in other Alzheimer's patients."

"Do you think it will work?" Dragan asked.

"I don't know," EF replied," but I do think it is well worth finding out."

"How will it be funded? "

"That is a problem. The timing is just wrong for the most likely sources such as the NIHR- that is the National Institute for Health Research- I hoped that perhaps a patient charity might be interested – but so far no luck. Their funding for research has all been awarded for next year."

"How much is it likely to cost to perform?"

Lila wondered why Dragan was so interested.

"Around 50-60 k in total, I think. Actually prescribing colchicine to a number of dementia subjects is not in itself expensive, the costs come from the testing needed to confirm benefit beyond doubt, especially the PET scans."

"Will you include a placebo- treated group?"

"Not at this stage. I think if we do what is called an n of 1 study in a number of patients and get positive results then it might be necessary to go on to a double- blind, placebo- controlled study proper to convince the sceptics."

Dragan nodded.

"Would you consider crowdfunding for this trial?"

EF looked surprised.

"What is crowdfunding?" he asked.

"It is the practice of funding a project by raising small amounts of money from a large number of people. It is often done via the Internet. However I was wondering whether I could help you via a newspaper."

EF blanched slightly. He had not realised that he had been speaking to a journalist.

"Which one?" he asked.

"I was thinking of the Evening Standard. I used to work there." Dragan was defensive. "Lila teases me about it, but in fact it can be a force for good sometimes. The owner likes to find projects that help people- you must have seen the campaigns against food waste, for the lonely elderly and for helping kids into work."

EF had not -reading the free papers was obviously not his cup of tea - but his wife had and was enthusiastic.

"Oh yes Edmund," I have read about these things." The paper does good work. You should take a look." She continued to expound about what she had read in some detail. Dragan looked relieved.

Lily asked if such funding would be ethical.

EF replied that they would have to check with the Ethics Committee to which the project had been submitted. Lila sighed inwardly - more form filling - and glanced at Tom, who obviously felt the same.

Worried Lily may be bored with all the medical talk, Dragan asked her what she was studying – English, it turned out - and the conversation segued into books and writers via the topic of the usefulness or otherwise of an English degree.

Lila enjoyed seeing Dragan and Tom together, interacting with Lily. She realized that one tribe to which she did belong was the Watchers. Perhaps that was why she was a scientist? Lila also noticed that her feet were aching in the unaccustomed high heels and longed to get back into her trainers.

An hour later and the party was dissolving, people were saying their goodbyes, giving Christmas greetings or Seasonal ones, and departing. EF, as a host, remained standing close to the door, thanking the attendees for coming and wishing them well. Tom suggested that the four of them should go somewhere together to eat. Lila said sadly that she did not think she could do that as Mrs D did not want to be late to bed; but they could all come back with her and have a takeaway. That proved readily acceptable, so they made their way to Euston, once Lila had changed her shoes.

From the train she phoned Mrs D and asked

"Hi Mrs D, is all well? How is Mum?"

"All fine here Lila, we are watching a film together. The curry was great - we had it with rice, and your Mum asked for peas too, so that's what I did."

"That's part of her Caribbean heritage coming out," laughed Lila. She told Mrs D what was happening and that they'd be back in about 20 minutes.

"Please stay until the film is over Mrs D, we'll be in the kitchen in any case."

"If you don't mind I will, it's a good movie. I'll put some plates to warm in the oven in the next commercial break."

"You are a star, Mrs D, thank you so much."

The two boys volunteered to pick up the food. Dragan had already interested Tom in the excellent Indian food available nearby and they both felt like having a peaceful beer while waiting for it.

Lila and Lily walked up past the park, chatting away happily about themselves and their lives. The lighted Christmas tree in the middle, the sparkling frosted grass and the lights of houses round the edge of the park made it look beautiful.

Lily was enchanted.

"Oh, what a lovely place to live."

Then a fox crossed the road, saw them and slid rapidly between the railings into the park.

"Heavens, how marvellous. It's just like the country."

"The foxes are a bloody nuisance," said Lila. "They killed my guinea pigs, then our chickens and I've heard they kill cats too. Yet there are people round here who feed them."

"Perhaps that stops them needing to kill?"

"I doubt that," Lila replied, "it's their instinct, they kill sometimes without bothering to eat their prey."

"Oh," Lily was clearly disappointed that her romantic notions of foxes were being disabused.

They arrived at Lila's home and entered, Lila calling out,

"It's us, Mrs D. Hello Mum!"

The sitting room was in darkness except for the blue light emanating from the TV. Both ladies murmured hello, but their attention was focused on the giant gorilla hanging onto a skyscraper, batting away a small plane.

"King Kong," Lila whispered to Lily. "Come into the kitchen."

As promised the oven was on and the kitchen was warm and welcoming. Mrs D had washed up and cleared and had set the table for four people. She really was a marvel. Lila opened the only bottle of wine which she had, having explained to Lily that the choice was white or water and they sipped it while sitting at the table, still talking. They seemed to have so much to say to each other.

Mrs D appeared in the doorway. "The film has finished Lila, would you like me to help your Mum to bed?"

"No, thank you, Mrs D. I can manage. You have been a wonderful help already, thank you so much."

"A pleasure Lila, me and your Mum we get on just fine. I enjoy her company and she mine. Good night."

She waved vaguely towards Lily, but departed before Lila could introduce her.

Lila was explaining to Lily that she had to put her Mum to bed now and was finding a magazine for Lily read while she did so. Both had their backs to the door. Suddenly Lily looked startled, her mouth opened and gave a quiet

"Oh."

Lila turned. It was one of those rare moments when one sees a parent as they appear to other people, not just as Mum or Dad.

The dark- skinned, grey- haired old lady in a curry- stained twin set and an indestructible Harris tweed skirt (a belated gift from Duncan's parents when they realised she was part of the family), was standing in the doorway with a poker clutched in both hands, raised above her head, about to strike.

Lila defused the situation.

"Hello Mum, how was the film?"

"Oh, my darling, it's you. I thought it was a bungler. The film was very sad. That poor monkey."

Her mother would never have made those mistakes in the past, Lila thought as she shepherded Grace upstairs and into the bathroom, having introduced her to a shaken Lily. The colchicine was helping, but Grace was nowhere near back to her normal IQ. She wondered whether further improvement would happen, slowly, as the deterioration had, or whether this was it. Even if this was Grace's final state it was a lot better than she had been - Grace was continent, tractable and interested herself in things once again - so neither she nor Lila should grumble. Lila's life was pretty good now, although she spent so much of it at work or on what she called domestic trivia, that there was not a lot for herself.

When Grace was settled into bed Lila returned downstairs where Lily asked her if she would mind explaining about dementia and how it affected her mother. Lila told her the story, beginning with how very clever Grace used to be, the initial stages with bank card problems, lost keys and Grace's angry denials of any problem.

"That must have been very hard to cope with."

"Yes, it is all hard to deal with, though the problems change." Lila related the deterioration, how colchicine had taken Grace up a stage once and how it was doing that again.

"Will she go back to how she once was?"

Lila had to say that she had no idea, but thought it unlikely.

Just then Dragan and Tom returned bearing several aromatic-smelling plastic containers. Lila produced the warm plates.

"That smells so good", she said. "Thank you both."

The food was very tasty, obviously freshly cooked. It disappeared fast, all but the okra, which nobody liked because of its soapy texture.

"We can feed that to the fox," joked Lily, to a disapproving frown from Lila.

Once they were full the level of conversation increased, with fairly heated, but friendly discussion on foxes, Brexit, and genetic engineering of foetuses. Dementia, once mentioned, became the focus and Dragan spoke up.

"What do you think of my idea about a newspaper funding your trial?"

"Unlikely to get approval", said Tom. "But what you could do is ask for money for a charity then apply to that for funding."

"Does the hospital have any charities?"

"Yes, I think so. There are some old ones with people's names on them. Not very rich, but sometimes helpful for smaller items."

"Could you find out those names for me?"

"Sure", Tom answered. "Can I have your e – mail?"

Unexpectedly Dragan produced a card with his name and contact details on it.

"OMG", said Tom, "you work for the Daily Chronicle."

"Not you too," Dragan replied, rather hurt, "Lila is always getting at me about it. It is not a bad paper," he said defensively, "and it takes an interest in science and medicine."

"Sure does," Tom laughed, "A cure for cancer is announced, several times a year."

"Have you ever actually read any of the science items?"

"To be honest, no, I haven't. "

"Well before you criticize it please take a look at the website, read some articles and then let me know what is wrong with them."

Tom was chastened. He genuinely liked Dragan and had not meant to upset him.

"You are right, of course. I'll do that."

Mollified, Dragan returned to his charity theme.

"It might be that we could use the Daily Chronicle to obtain money for the trial. I was going to suggest that, but thought it would be anathema to Professor Ferguson, so I substituted the Evening Standard. It is just the kind of slightly off- centre project that Daily Chronicle readers tend to go for. They have had appeals in the past for charities."

He paused, then said

"Would you like me to mention it at an editorial meeting? "

Lila and Tom looked at each other, uncertain what to think or say. She came out with

"I don't want Grace to be mentioned by name."

Tom added, "The name of the drug should not be given either- or there will be loads of people begging their GPs to let them try it"

Dragan looked downcast. "It'd be no good without some details. I don't think our readers would donate to a small hospital charity unless there was a good reason to do so."

"Let's leave it then," Tom decided.

 Soon afterwards Dragan said he had to go home, so did Tom and Lily. Lila dropped, exhausted onto the sofa for a few minutes, trying to raise the energy to go upstairs to bed. Once there she fell asleep fast and slept dreamlessly.

CHAPTER 25.

It was a few days before Christmas. Lila had taken time off work in order to do her Christmas shopping whilst Mrs D was still in London to look after Grace; Marjana was too busy since it was the school holidays. Lila was just about to re- enter the house, bearing numerous bags of food and gifts when Dragan appeared at the gate.

"Hi Dragan, come on in." Lila's voice was muffled as she had her glove in her mouth whilst inserting the door key.

He did and helped relieve her of her burdens, putting the bags into the kitchen and calling hello to Grace on the way. She greeted him warmly and asked Lila to put the kettle on for a cup of tea for them all.

Dragan waited until they were all three settled round the kitchen table in front of steaming mugs, then he said,

"Listen carefully, have I got news for you!"

Both Grace and Lila recognized the reference to the TV show and smiled.

"Is it good news?" asked Lila.

"Yes, it is, very good news."

"Go on then, tell us."

"The proprietor of the DC has heard of your proposed trial and has asked for more details as he wishes to consider funding it."

"What?" Lila was amazed.

I mentioned it at an editorial meeting, giving no personal details, and the Editor liked the sound of it- so he mentioned it to the owner when they next met. He wanted approval for fundraising by the paper, but I think the proprietor wants to do some personal charitable giving, probably to reduce his tax burden and ease his conscience. So he needs to speak to someone in charge."

"That would be EF, "said Lila.

"EF?"

"Edmund Ferguson."

"Oh", said Dragan disappointedly, "I had thought the sexy lady might be involved. I am sure she would get the money."

"You mean Susan Anderson?"

"The one in the shiny dress at the party."

"Susan Anderson." Lila sighed inwardly and wondered again what Susan had that she lacked.

"She is also involved and could talk to him. Perhaps she and EF together would be best."

"How could we organize that?" asked Dragan.

"I think perhaps a request for a meeting or a telephone conference from your proprietor would work. Now is not good- I know Susan has already gone away for Christmas."

"OK, if you give me the contact details of both I'll take them back to my Editor. He's pleased with me, loves a human story."

Lila gave him the correct titles of EF and Susan, plus phone numbers for their secretaries. Dragan left happily, saying,

"See you on Christmas day, 1pm."

For once they were not going to be with Grace's family over Christmas. Lila, having been refused help from them when she needed it, did not feel inclined to take her turn in the rota and have Grace's sisters and her cousins, descend upon them for a few days. She had made the excuse that Grace was not well enough to cope with a house full of people, whom she might regard as strangers. She had also batted away the invitation which followed, to visit them, saying that Grace would prefer to remain quietly at home. However, when Tricia, Dragan's Mum, had found out that Lila and Grace would be in London she had invited them to join her family celebration on December 25th, a Muslim version of Christmas, as she called it. Lila and Grace were both delighted to accept. Lila asked them in return to come to her house for games on Boxing Day. The three children accepted, their parents were already engaged elsewhere. It was enough of an excuse for Lila to buy and decorate a small real tree with lights that still worked, despite a year in the attic.

The day dawned damp and chilly, but without actual rain. Lila gave Grace a padded gilet, knowing that she felt the cold a lot. Grace, to Lila's surprise, offered her a gift.

"Where did you get this?"

"Never you mind. Open it and see if you like them"

Grace was smiling, pleased at her own cleverness.

The present turned out to be a pair of gloves, warm and woolly, but with pads in the fingertips so that a touchscreen could be used whilst wearing them. They were just what Lila needed.

"Perfect, Mum! Thank you. How did you know I needed these?"

"A small bird told me."

Lila suspected that the bird's name might be Dragan.

Marjana and her children appeared, as asked, mid -morning for a celebratory drink and a mince pie. Her husband, who was rather shy, had elected to stay at home, supposedly in charge of Christmas lunch.

Lila had bought a scarf for Marjana and a Tricia Boone book for each child, remembering how much she had loved them when little. The gifts were well received, with Chelsea, the eldest daughter reading hers out loud to her siblings. Grace was delighted with the warm red woolly gloves which Marjana had brought for her and insisted on putting them on inside the house. Lila received a box of chocolates which threatened to disappear rapidly when passed around. Fortunately she remembered that there were chocolate Santas hanging on the tree and gave the girls the task of finding one each. This did not take long, but it gave Lila a chance to say a very sincere thank you to Marjana for her wonderful help with Grace.

"It is a pleasure. I really enjoy spending time with your mum, especially now that she can understand so much more again."

This was music to Lila's ears as it suggested the colchicine was working, Grace's improvement was not just thinkful wishing on her part.

After an hour the girls were getting bored so Marjana took them home and Lila and Grace prepared themselves for the trip to Dragan's house, as they called it.

"Do you think we'll have turkey?" asked Grace on the way. Lila was impressed with this bit of forward thinking, but could not provide an answer.

In the event they had fish, cod to be precise. This was apparently what is eaten in Eastern Europe as a celebration. Both Lila and Grace hid their disappointment as best they could, but on the way home Grace muttered,

Cod- for Christmas, I ask you!"

However that was the only disappointment that day, They were royally treated: given gifts, drinks, delicious puddings, sweets. Grace was allowed to watch the Queen as she always did, Lila meanwhile helped Dragan with the washing up.

During this he asked her,

"Lila would you ever think of having a lodger?"

Lila paused, tea towel in hand, and thought.

"I suppose I might need to sometime in the future, if Grace needs more help and money gets tight."

"What about now? Starting next year?"

"I'm not sure I'd like someone else in our house unless I have to. Why do you ask?"

Dragan looked sad.

"I am going to be thrown out of my home."

"What? Why?"

"My Mum thinks we should take in a refugee. One of her friends knows a lad who is from Eritreia. She met him when she was helping give out clothes to refugees in Calais earlier this month. He is bright and wants to study, but has no family here- my Mum has agreed to sponsor him. She wanted to give him Ferid's room, but Ferid was upset and said he wouldn't feel he had a home any more if he had to share with me when back from Uni. So Mum and I had a talk. She is right – it is about time that I left home again and began to make my own life, separate from theirs. I don't fancy living alone, nor do I want to flat-share, I'm too old for that. Then it struck me that you might think of having me as your lodger- I can pay rent and I can help look after Grace at times."

He looked quizzically at Lila.

"It probably would not be for long- I will watch out for somewhere more permanent. But the lad is coming in early January, all being well, so I am a bit desperate."

"I'll have to ask Mum what she thinks", Lila said, knowing what the answer would be.

"Of course."

"I'll let you know tomorrow. "

"Fantastic, thanks."

Dragan turned back to the washing up,

"I won't interfere with your love life, you know."

Lila laughed,

"What love life? I don't have one. "

Dragan turned to her, surprised.

"What about Tom?"

"Tom?" Before she could stop herself Lila had blurted out, "He's gay."

She had never seen Dragan look so happy. He said nothing, just slowly nodded his head, then walked away.

CHAPTER 26

Grace was delighted at the idea of Dragan as their lodger and welcomed him warmly when he moved in at the end of December. He was given the back bedroom, which had its own small bathroom next to it, so he could be relatively independent. At first he brought only one suitcase, but as the weeks wore on gradually more of his things appeared and the room became decorated with his books, pictures and photographs.

"It feels like my home now", he said to Grace one Saturday morning as she passed by on her way downstairs.

"It is", she said, "and long may it be so."

Lila took longer to adjust to his constant presence in their lives. She was accustomed to living with Grace, their little ways and rituals, and Dragan, without meaning to, interfered with some of these. For example, he liked to watch football on TV – which they never did. He did not care for East Enders, which Lila had followed for years. However, once he realised these things Dragan used his computer to watch matches or listened on the radio in the privacy of his room instead, but came down as soon as they finished to let them know the result and to have a last cuppa before bed.

The rent which he paid into Lila's account was very useful and Dragan himself was certainly so, doing little jobs around the house, cleaning up after himself, washing up after supper- or cooking it for them. He kept his room tidy and was pretty quiet, except when QPR were playing.Lila slowly accepted him. After two months he had to travel for work, back again to the Balkans, and suddenly the house seemed empty without him. She found herself counting the days until his return.

Meanwhile she was kept busy at work preparing for the colchicine study. EF had asked her to take part and to help Tom run the study which had been granted ethical approval. In order to do so she had to obtain CRB clearance so that she could be in Out –Patients and deal with people, rather than mice. It was actually simpler than obtaining a Home Office certificate to work with animals had been. Lila remembered that if an animal was sick and in desperate need a doctor was not allowed to operate; the reverse was not true for vets.

Lila had to produce copies of the patient information sheets and send them out to suitable patients with dementia prior to their next clinic appointment- so that they and their relatives could read about the study, discuss it with their GP if they wanted, and consider whether to give informed consent when they came to the clinic. Tom helped her to find the right subjects from the clinic lists.The business of informed consent was something of a nightmare given concerns about the lack of capacity of potential participants'? They had therefore two consent forms- one for the patient and another for their relative, or friend with power of attorney to the effect that they thought the patient was genuinely willing- both had to be signed before the patient could be enrolled. Some of the subjects were considered unable to give sufficiently informed consent, or could no longer sign anything, so had to be excluded. No- one refused to enter the study, all those afflicted being keen to be cured.

Once included the patient was subject to many tests - those which Grace had gone through. Lila was given the responsibility for seeing that they were all done, in the right order, on that day.This would usually have been the job of a study nurse, but since they did not have one and since Lila was keen to be involved she was allowed to help. Lila also had to check that there had been a previous visit on which the patient had been carefully assessed with objective measurements performed. The PET scan was done last of all - they had a slot once a week on the clinic day. Since there was so much to do only one or at the most, two subjects could be enrolled each week. There was interest and some obvious resentment from other patients and their relatives in the clinic who felt that special treatment was being given to a selected few. EF, Tom and Lila watched for this and, if spotted, they explained the situation carefully, stressing that only a few patients were right for the study but, if it worked, then others would be treated.

"By then it'll be too late for us," said the wife of one man with Alzheimer's disease, echoing the feelings of many.

In the next days, Lila had to enter all the findings into an Excel spreadsheet, having coded the patient from a name to a number, with the coding data held on a separate computer. She had to chase up missing results, such as those from the blood tests. For the PET scan findings, she used a computer system which allowed her to draw round the lighted areas and thus obtain a figure for the degree of involvement of various brain areas. Despite her best efforts not every patient had every test done and recorded. One or two had just gone home halfway through the day, without explaining. She was mortified, but Tom reassured her that this was what happened in real life, unlike mice which rarely escaped from their cages.

After the first three months she had to deal with returning subjects, as well as continuing to recruit new ones. Lila was very disappointed that the first returnee was worse, rather than better. She began to doubt her theory about colchicine. However, on that same day the second returnee and his carer were both enthusiastic about the drug, saying that they both felt there was improvement whilst on it. They asked if the patient could continue to take it. Tom was unsure, but EF said that compassionate use was possible and issued a further prescription for 3 months with another intensive review at the end of it.

By this time Lila was very slick and the processes took her less time to do, so she coped with the returnees plus enrolling the new subjects, though could only enrol one new subject each time. EF saw that the clinic day was overfull and suggested that perhaps Lila and Tom should set up a separate clinic for the returning subjects on a different day. The hospital management was not keen on this idea, so it took a few weeks before they were persuaded to see sense, which they did largely because the deputy Chief Executive had a father who was showing signs of dementia. With more time to spend with the returnees, both Tom and Lila thought that some of them had improved, but not all. The spreadsheet continued to grow.

One or two subjects had not taken the colchicine, for one reason or another. Their data was included in the three month assessment in what is known as the intention to treat analysis, but was also examined separately as control data. Lila decided that mice were much easier to deal with than humans - at least mice could definitively be given a treatment, whereas humans might or might not take it, might do so irregularly and might lie about what actually happened. Also, mice were there in their cages when they were needed, unlike the patients who sometimes failed to turn up, or did so on the wrong day. Her ideas about having missed out by not doing medicine were at least partly reversed.

She explained this to Dragan and Grace one evening. It was Grace who pointed out that people are not robots - they have their own ideas, their own tolerances, and medicine had to allow for this. Lila agreed and was delighted to hear something so thoughtful from her mother, who was continuing to improve. Recently Grace had persuaded Marjana to come to the shops with her and together they had bought food for supper and cooked it. Both Dragan and Lila had welcomed this development and requested that it happen again; Grace was delighted that her cooking was so much appreciated. It was more the fact that she did not have to think about supper and cook it on arriving, tired from work, that pleased Lila. Dragan was simply happy because Lila was in a good mood. He had been careful not to overwhelm Lila with his feelings for her. Sensitive as he was, he had picked up her sadness about Tom and did not want to capitalize on this by catching Lila on the rebound. In his heart he knew that she was the girl for him and that one day he would win her, provided he took things slowly.

Summer arrived with a bang: a heatwave in mid-May. It was initially welcomed by all - the Daily Chronicle carried the predictable headline "Hotter than Benidorm"- but as the hot humid days continued many began to wish for rain, particularly farmers. Lila had switched to riding to work on her bicycle as the tube was unbearably hot. Dragan thought about buying a bicycle and accompanying her - but Lila refused to countenance this, saying that trying to cycle in company was more dangerous than being alone. He continued on the Underground, carrying a bottle of water, as advised. One day when the train was stationary at Lila's work stop he watched as a very reluctant woman was helped, by a deal of cajoling and, eventually, frank pulling, off the train by a young man. He was about to intervene when the lad said,

"I am so sorry. My Mum has dementia. We are going to the hospital."

Dragan understood, he nodded and gave the woman a gentle push in the right direction, then watched as she was grasped firmly by the arm and led towards the exit.

He mentioned the incident to Lila over supper that evening. She asked him for a description of the couple and, when heard, explained that she thought they had been in the clinic. Dragan asked if the woman had entered the trial.

"I can't tell you that. I shouldn't have said anything," came the reply.

"OK," Dragan nodded. "Let's go into the garden when we have finished."

"Good idea."

"I want to watch TV," said Grace.

"OK, Mum. I'll put it on."

"No need," Grace replied firmly, "I know how to do it."

Lila went through the open French doors which led from the kitchen to the garden. The ancient rattan garden furniture was already outside, there being no likelihood of rain for a while, according to the forecast. She sat on the two-seater, protected from its ridges by scarlet cushions. Dragan came to sit beside her. For a while they were quiet, absorbing the peace of their surroundings, smelling the grass, watching the birds. Dragan laughed at an amorous pair of pigeons, the male preening, strutting around the smaller female, touching her with his beak.

"Looks like love to me", he said.

"Whatever love is," quoted Lila. "Poor Prince Charles, he must have wished that he never uttered those words."

Then, after a pause she went on,

"I have a molecular theory of love."

"Do you now? Go on, educate me."

"Well, do you know about molecular bonding?"

"No, that must have passed me by at school."

"OK, basically..."

Dragan laughed, "Whenever you say basically, which is often, I know that I rarely understand what comes next."

"Just try," Lila was getting a little irritated.

"Ba...", she managed to stop herself.

"The initial attraction between two molecules is often what is called ionic."

"Nothing to do with Greek columns, I suppose?" asked Dragan.

"You are winding me up!"

"No, go on, I am interested, really."

"Ionic attraction involves opposite charges: one positive, one negative. This reaction is very powerful because of the electrostatic attraction between the particles. Think of the person you see across a crowded room and immediately fall for them - their eyes, their voice, the way they stand, perhaps their smell - something about them draws you in."

"Like when I first saw you," Dragan said.

Lila blushed and replied quickly,

"And when you first saw Lily."

"Go on."

"Then, when the ionic attraction brings the molecules close together, they may or may not fit into each other. The shapes matter: one molecule may have a side chain which prevents it from docking in the cleft of the other one. Think of a car with wing mirrors which make it too wide for a garage. The molecules will remain close, until another one comes along and parts them by its electrostatic charge. The car will sit outside the garage and is more easily stolen."

Dragan nodded.

Lily continued,

"When molecules are more closely apposed other forces come into play. There is covalent bonding in which molecules share electrons. Covalent bonds are especially important in biology since most carbon molecules interact that way. This allows them to create long chains of compounds, allowing more complexity in life. I think of this as being like having babies, sharing their care and creating a family."

Dragan nodded again, careful not to interrupt as this was obviously important to Lila.

"There are other much weaker forces too, called Van der Waals forces which only act when the molecules are very close together. They are an example of quantum physics: caused by the electron clouds around each molecule. They quickly vanish at longer distances. Most are attractive, occasionally some are repulsive. They form and break repeatedly - but are so numerous that at any one time there are usually enough to hold the molecules together against an opposing force."

She paused to let this sink in, then went on,

"These are like the many links in a relationship: the memories, the mutual interests, the shared language, the shared friends - which would make one think twice about leaving for the next bright young thing."

"Like Lily, you mean?"

"Stop teasing me!"

"Oh, but you react so nicely. "

He dodged as she flung the cushion at him.

"Seriously though, what do you think?"

"Well, basically……."

Dragan ducked as the other cushion came his way.

"Being serious for a moment, I do like your idea. If I have understood it correctly you are saying that initially attraction between two people is one process - forceful and strong, operating at a distance. Like when you fancy someone?"

It was Lila's turn to nod.

"But that's not enough to keep them together. They may not fit – she could be a raging Tory, he a Marxist- so although he loves her face and figure and she his manly beard, they are unlikely to hit it off for long."

"Yes, or it could be more subtle - they just do not have much in common, or one of them has a habit, like smoking, that the other cannot stand."

"OK. However, if they do fit – then it is the goodness of fit that matters, with these other kinds of forces, the vanda whatever that keeps them bonded?"

"Yes, some molecules fit together really well like Lego pieces then the multiple Van der Waals forces can easily happen over their big area of contact to keep them united. Even though the forces form and break continually there are enough at any one time to hold them together. Where there are just small parts of the surfaces of each molecule in apposition they are more liable to be parted because there are fewer opportunities for the forces to occur and to hold them together."

"So, another ionic molecule comes along and pulls one of the pair towards it, breaking them up?"

Yes, that's it. The ionic bit is the passionate part of a relationship, exciting, dramatic. The long term stability is less exciting, but more rewarding in the end, I think. Some people go from one ionic bonding to another and never really become stable – think of film stars like Elizabeth Taylor. "

"I like your ideas. Have you written all this down?"

"Not yet, but I intend to, when it is more clear in my head."

"If you do, please let me read it. I think I understand, but seeing it in writing is always better for me."

"Yes, of course. I'd be glad of your ideas when you've read it. It's starting to get cold, let's go in."

CHAPTER 27

The next weeks passed uneventfully, Dragan was busy ferreting out stories for his newspaper, Lila was recording the findings in treated patients and recruiting the last few into the study. She was also planning another study on mice, involving the bacteria in their mouths, something that Susan had asked her to organize. The weather became warmer still, with dusty, polluted air in central London. Lila took to biking with a mask over her face, even so she was more breathless than usual.

Finally, the day came when the very last subject in the colchicine trial was due to be seen. The results so far were mixed and Lila was afraid that the outcome would be negative, with any improvements just attributable to the placebo effect of being cared for and studied intensively. She waited in the clinic with Tom, mood low, but determined to record all the findings as accurately as possible. The patient was a delightful African-Caribbean gent, accompanied by his wife. Both were smiling broadly. When called into the room the man strode in, took Tom's hand in both of his and shook it up and down several times.

"You done it, man. You done it."

His wife explained that there had been an amazing improvement in her husband. He was able to look after himself again, to take an interest in things and was so much happier and less anxious. Lila and Tom exchanged a smiling glance. The physical examination and the tests bore out what the wife had said: there had been a major change for the better.

They asked for more of the magic new drug and were able to receive some on a compassionate basis. They left the clinic with more handshakes and smiles, Lila was given a hug and a kiss by the wife.

"Phew", said Lila, "I was beginning to think that I had imagined the effects in Mum."

"Me too," said Tom, "but we have a few patients who have really done well on it, though not all."

"I'll put the data all together and work out whether anything is statistically significant, with help from the statistician."

The work took Lila several days, checking the data entered from the paper records into the computer, finding missing values and ensuring that everything was in order. Tom spent time with her, checking too, but finding few errors. Then she informed EF that it had all been done and asked if he would like to do some random checks. He replied that he did.

"Thank you, Lila. Yes, if my name is to go on this paper then I need to be sure that the results are accurate. I will have some time on Friday afternoon, would that be convenient?"

She told him that would be fine and returned to her latest mouse project. Since becoming interested in the possible role of mouth bacteria in dementia she had bought mouthwash for Grace and had also started using it herself.

EF spent all Friday afternoon going through the patient record sheets and the database. Afterwards he congratulated Lila.

"Well done, my dear. I think you have done an excellent job. Now let's lock the database and get the results analysed."

Lila was relieved that he had not found mistakes. She was so eager to get started on the analysis that she decided to come in over the weekend, but then EF spoke again.

"This is so important that I think we need to make entirely sure that there is no bias in the analysis. I suggest it is all done by the statistical department. They have been part of this from the start and are expecting to do the analysis."

Lila nodded sadly. It meant that she would not know anything for days or even weeks - she felt very frustrated, but said nothing.

When EF had gone she rang her contact in the statistics department and, having got his agreement, sent over the anonymised database securely.

However she also copied it onto her own secure USB device and slipped that into her rucksack before leaving for home.

"Is that you darling?" Grace called as Lila entered via the back door. She always kept her bike in the back garden to deter theft. Grace was now able to be left at home alone once Marjana had gone to collect her children. Lila hoped that soon Marjana's services, good though they were, could be dispensed with altogether. That would leave a little extra in the kitty and make life easier, though Dragan's rent had already improved their financial situation somewhat.

"Hi Mum, it's me. How are you?"

"Fine sweetheart. I have made us a salad for supper. Is that OK?"

"Perfect."

They kissed and Lila put on the kettle for a cup of tea.

"Shall we sit in the garden? We could eat at the table outside."

They shared a companionable meal. Dragan was away in Essex, investigating the neo Nazi groups which had sprung up there.

Sitting outside in the low sunlight, Lila was reminded of her conversation with Dragan about love. She decided to explore her parents' relationship, something she had shied away from recently, though when she was young she had asked about her father a lot.

"Mum, please tell me what it was like when you met Dad."

Her mother smiled.

"It seems like yesterday. I remember the first time I saw him. He came to church you know. My father was the preacher. He was a Christian pastor, even though he was from India - a legacy of the Raj, I suppose. As his family, we sat in the front pew, so we could not see what was happening behind us without turning round. That was discouraged by my mother. My sisters and I had to stay there, sitting up straight, looking forward, being quiet and good all through the service. It was a nightmare as far as I was concerned. I always had something to say – so I used hand signals to let Hope and Charity know what I was thinking. We had taught ourselves sign language from a book and used it with our hands in our laps. Our conversation was invisible to the rest of the congregation - but I did not realise one day that the balcony above us, which ran round the three sides of the church, was occupied by your father. I became aware of being watched and when I looked up I saw his face peeping over the railing, smiling down at us. He looked quite strange to me - I had never seen a man with freckles and reddish gold curly hair before. I was embarrassed and stopped my hand signals. All through the rest of the service I was very aware of him, though I didn't look up again.

Afterwards we all trooped out, everyone shaking hands with my father, the pastor, then standing around talking for a while in the sunshine. Your father was the last out, he shook hands and then walked straight up to me. He smiled – oh how I loved his smile. It just melted my heart then and every time afterwards when he smiled, which he did a lot.

He then used his hands to say that he knew some sign language too.

I laughed and said,

"We do it because we can't stay silent for long, even in church."

Your father laughed out loud then and I heard his voice for the first time. Actually that is not true, I had noticed it during the hymns. It was so different from what I was used to. He had deep voice with a rich Scottish accent.

"I thought you couldn't speak!"

I laughed then and told him that I rarely stopped speaking. We just went on from there."

Grace paused, gazing unseeingly into the garden, her mind back to the time she was with Gordon. When she turned back to Lila her eyes were full of tears.

"Oh Mum, I'm so sorry. I didn't mean to upset you."

"Don't be sorry. I like to talk about him. He was taken away far too soon. I don't want him to be forgotten."

Lila ventured further.

"Was it love at first sight?"

Grace thought, then said,

"For him, yes, I think it was. For me, no. I had my own ideas about the man I would marry. He would be tall, dark, handsome and rich. Your father was tall. He was kind of handsome, in his own way. He was certainly not rich. But it didn't take long for me to realise that I needed to keep seeing him. The idea that he would leave for the UK when his elective period was over was awful. At first I just put it to the back of my mind, but as the time grew closer I thought about little else. He was the same - so he spoke to my parents to see if we could get engaged. My father was outraged. He told Gordon that we had known each other for far too short a time and that I was far too young to become engaged to anyone. Gordon was practically banned him from the house. I think my father felt that his hospitality had been abused. It was an awful time. My parents tried to stop me going out to see him- but I was defiant."

"How old were you?"

"I was nineteen, just starting my teacher training."

"What happened in the end?"

"Gordon finished his elective and returned to the UK, but we wrote every day and phoned as often as we could. He did locums while finishing his training and then once he'd done his finals he used the money he'd earned to come back and get me."

"Was you father still opposed?"

"He was not happy – but he could see that Gordon really, really loved me and I him, so in the end he gave us his blessing. I think it helped that Gordon was a doctor by then. We were married from my home, then left to go to the UK for Gordon to do his house jobs."

"Did you work too? "

"I completed my teacher training in the UK, then I got a job in a very tough school in London. It was a relief when I became pregnant with you and could take maternity leave. I never went back to that school, thank goodness."

"When did you realize that you loved Dad?"

Grace looked into the distance, her eyes thoughtful, as though watching a film of her past. Eventually she spoke.

"I think it was the day that he failed to turn up for church. He had gone fishing on a boat with some of the hospital staff. I missed him and worried about him. The idea that I might not see him again was so terrible…"

She broke off, tears again springing to her eyes.

Lila put her arms round Grace and hugged her, rocking gently from side to side. Neither spoke, both remembering the red-haired man they had loved and lost.

CHAPTER 28

Dragan returned the next evening to a warm welcome from both his landladies. Lila offered him supper, but he refused politely saying that he would have liked to share their meal, but that he had arranged to go out.

"Oh, where?" Lila asked.

"To the theatre", he replied.

"What are you going to see?"

"I'm not sure- I was messaged as I was on the train home. Someone dropped out and I am filling the gap."

"Well I hope it is something good. Tell me tomorrow please."

"Sure will- should I do supper then?"

"Great idea."

He disappeared upstairs to his room and descended 10 minutes later, having changed and tidied himself up.

"Looking good," Lila remarked. "Who is she?"

"Tell you later," Dragan replied, giving her a quick peck on the cheek, then departing.

Lila found herself restless that evening. She scanned the Evening Standard, ostensibly for the TV programmes, but also checked the theatre listings. Grace wanted to watch a nature documentary, so she and Lila sat side by side on the sofa in front of the TV. Lila found her attention wandering.

Who was Dragan out with?

Why was she so bothered about it?

In the end she decided to try and do some work so hooked up her USB with the trial results to her computer and began to study them. She thought it would be interesting to try and rank them in order as to the degree of improvement or deterioration in their everyday lives shown during the time of the study. Soon she was engrossed in the details, trying to put a numerical value on attributes such as continence, communication, biddability. After a while she realized that her scoring had subtly altered during the process and she had to write out a scoring sheet, then return to the original ones and re-grade them.

"Good night sweetheart," Grace kissed the top of Lila's head which was bent over her laptop.

"Good night Mum, what time is it?"

"11pm, why don't you stop now and come to bed?"

Lila stretched her arms up into the air, freeing her tensed neck and spine.

"Yes, I think I will. No sign of Dragan yet, is there?"

"No." Grace shook her head as she moved towards the stairs.

"I wouldn't wait up for him."

"Oh, I wasn't going to." Lila rose and went into the kitchen to get her customary glass of water for her bedside.

"No way," she added, unnecessarily as her mother was out of earshot.

Despite that assertion Lila found herself wakeful and realized that she was subconsciously listening for Dragan's footsteps on the front path, hoping to hear his key in the lock.

"Why am I bothered?" she asked herself, but had no clear answer, or at least not one she was prepared to accept.

Finally she slept, only to wake at 4.30 am with thoughts of dementia problems going round in her brain. Quietly she got out of bed and tiptoed to the bathroom, noting that Dragan's door, which had been ajar, was now closed. She used the loo, keeping her feet off the cold floor, then returned to bed and slept again, peacefully, until the alarm woke her at 7am.

Dragan's door was still closed when she passed it going to the bathroom. It was still that way when she returned from her shower to dress. He did not show up at breakfast. Lila wondered whether she should knock on the bedroom door to wake him, but decided against doing so, as he might just have a day off. Having taken Grace her tea and toast in bed, Lila wheeled out her bike and pedalled downhill towards work. As usual she dodged death by inches, riding up inside the queues of cars and buses waiting at traffic lights, then dashing off in front of them when the lights changed, only to be overtaken by them on the next stretch. She enjoyed this game, but always with an undercurrent of fear that one day she would get it wrong and be badly hurt. Finally she arrived and locked her bike in the rack alongside many others.

EF was just parking an electric car as she walked past on her way to the lab. He looked ridiculously tall and bent inside the little machine and Lila had a problem trying not to smile. As he opened the driver's door EF hailed her.

"Good morning Lila, any news yet?"

"No, not yet. I will check with the statistician today and let you know if he has any results."

"Thank you."

EF unwound himself from the clutches of the car, stood upright and stretched. He noticed her half smile.

"It's my wife's car. Mine is being repaired," he explained, looking embarrassed and striding off into the hospital.

True to her promise Lila rang the statistician. He explained that he had not finished his analysis yet, there had not been time to analyse the results of the PET scans, but he would be happy to show her what he had found thus far if she wanted to drop in around noon.

Lila spent the morning with her latest batch of mice, trying to concentrate on what she was doing, but her mind kept wandering - first to Dragan and then to the trial outcome. She was glad when noon arrived and she could make her visit to the Statistics department.

"Hello there, take a seat," said the amiable bespectacled young man. Lila sat down next to him, facing his computer screen.

"What have you found?" she asked.

"Not a lot," came the disappointing reply.

Lila's heart sank. "Is there no difference between pre and post colchicine?"

"There is a difference, small, but just significant at p less than 0.5 in some of the parameters."

"That's good. Which ones?"

He showed her various graphs and explained that some of the patients who received colchicine had done better in areas such as quality of life, word searches, performance on various psychological tests. Lila followed his words carefully, then pointed out something which she had noticed on several of the figures.

 "It could be that there are responders and non-responders.That's was my impression in the clinic."

"What about the patients, any differences?" the statistician asked.

"Loads: age, sex, ethnicity, you name it. They are a cross section of humanity," replied Lila.

"Didn't we see something similar in your mouse study?"

"Of course. Yes, you pointed it out, I had forgotten."

"Was there any difference in the mice?" he asked

"No, they were all the same strain, fed the same, lived in the same room. Though I suppose there could have been something different- maybe I'll check with Terry."

"That would be a good idea- it might help you to find out why some human subjects respond more than others."

"Are the PET scan results variable too?" asked Lila

"I haven't looked at those yet.Prof Ferguson has read them and given me some figures. I am going to make a suggestion - why don't I check them and decide what constitutes a positive response; you go through this data and note the numbers of those who respond positively clinically - then we can see if there is a correlation between the two."

"OK", Lila replied. She gave the young man her USB stick for the graphs and took it away with her to find some lunch.

She spent the afternoon in front of her computer noting the trial numbers of those patients who had really improved, then of those with little or no improvement. Then she e- mailed her statistical colleague with the 20 individual trial numbers in those 2 groups – and asked him to let her know which, if any, of them showed PET scan improvement.

The reply came quickly- those who had improved clinically also had PET scan changes which indicated better function.

"Yes," exclaimed Lila, raising both arms into the air. "Yes, yes, yes!"

Lila was too jumpy and excited to settle to anything. She decided to try to inform EF of the findings- his door was shut so she knocked tentatively on it and waited.

"Come in"

Lila entered, finding EF behind a big desk, dictaphone in hand. He looked up from the notes he was perusing and smiled kindly at Lila.

"I hope it is good news, "he said.

"I think it is."

Lila explained briefly that there seemed to be a subset of those treated with colchicine who had improved- on clinical grounds and that this correlated with PET scan changes.

"I see. That is most interesting. Can you find any variable which would predict a treatment response?"

"I haven't looked yet- but I will."

"Thank you, Lila. I am happy to help if you need it. Please keep me informed."

Lila left, wondering why it had not yet occurred to her to think about looking at how to identify responders - she should have thought of that before seeing EF. She needed to go home now but could perhaps examine the data further there. It was all coded so no patient identification could occur from her computer and her USB stick was also protected, so she was permitted to do this.

On her way out she bumped into Tom.

"Hi Lila, how is it going?"

"Oh Tom, I should have phoned you. It looks as though colchicine helps some, but not all of them."

"That's what we thought, isn't it?"

"Yes, some of the changes in the test results are just statistically significant in the whole group, so we can publish the trial, but, even better, the clinical outcomes are mirrored by those in the PET scans – so we have objective evidence too."

"Lila that is so great. Can I see the data?"

Lila hesitated, she needed to get home as Grace would have been alone for two hours and she was still unsure how safe this was.

"I have to go now. Please could I show you tomorrow?"

"Of course, you realize that you are condemning me to a sleepless night." Then, as her face fell,

"Only joking. Let's meet after the ward round tomorrow in your palatial office."

"Sure, have a nice evening."

"Fat chance, I'm on call."

As she pedalled home Lila thought about Tom and found that she was looking forward to their next meeting for reasons unrelated to science. When she arrived, hot and sweaty, she found that Grace was fine. Dragan had indeed had a day off, having worked overtime in Essex, so had looked after Grace all day, taking her food shopping. During that trip she had let slip her disappointment at the lack of turkey for their Christmas meal (her social skills were still not back to normal). Dragan determined to make this up to her, so they had trailed around trying to buy turkey in the summer. Eventually they had found some, frozen, in Lidl and had borne it home in triumph to make a turkey curry. The kitchen reeked of spices, the back doors were open to the garden to let the smells out and Grace was there setting the table.

"Hi Lila, how was your day?" Dragan asked.

"Good, thanks", said Lila, "how was yours?" She thought how they were getting to be like an old married couple, without any of the benefits.

Dragan told her of the shopping trip, pressed a bottle of cold beer into her hand and said,

"Do you want to shower while I cook the rice?"

She acquiesced and enjoyed the cool shower and the cool beer peacefully upstairs before joining them at the table. Over supper she asked him about the Essex trip.

"How did you get on in darkest Essex? I was worried that you were being used as cannon fodder."

"That crossed my mind too. Headlines such as "Our Chronicle Reporter lynched by locals" went through my mind on the way there, but in fact I was treated surprisingly well. Once I opened my mouth and spoke the Queen's English I was treated as one of them, despite not being snow white. Several people asked where I was born, so I said London, and that was that. It came out that Tricia Boone is my mother - that went down well with those who had teenage children. In the end I felt sorry for them, they feel pushed out of the East End by immigrants, one said

"It ain't like what you see on the TV mate in East Enders, it's all bloody P ****is there now"

They worry about their jobs and about their kids not finding work - with good reason. A lot of the factory jobs are being automated but the ones that they could do, like caring, waiting, cooking, cleaning, they don't want to do. Immigrants are not fussy, so the jobs go to them instead. So, they band together under the Union Jack like the Iceni - a tribe about to become extinct - which is what they are."

"That's so sad."

"It is, and I think there is a lot of manipulation going on by a few troublemakers. There's one who really has a double-barrelled surname, but uses another "man of the people" type name, who organizes actions and demonstrations. I'm not sure what his real motives are but I don't think the welfare of the common citizen is his main concern, though he pretends it is. Anyway, enough of my work. How is yours going?"

Lila explained what had happened in the trial and how the benefit of colchicine seemed limited to certain patients. Dragan was interested.

"Isn't that true of a lot of drugs?"

"I think so, yes. When I did pharmacology as part of my degree we learnt about pharmacogenetics - that your genes can determine how well certain drugs work for you and the risk of certain side effects. There are inherited genetic differences in pathways by which drugs are metabolized and also in drug receptors, enzymes et cetera, which affect individual responses to them, both good actions as well as side effects."

"So now you have to find out who will respond to colchicine?"

"Exactly. But being a cheap drug, the easiest thing might be just to give a trial period of treatment to see. But it would be nice to profile responders so there is no false hope. Also, it might give us another handle on what is happening in dementia."

"Sounds good Lila. What can I tell my boss?"

"Please say nothing specific yet, wait- until the analysis is complete. Apart from a very big thank you, that is, and the fact that we have completed the patient stage and are analysing the results."

"OK."

"Now, tell me about the play you saw. Who took you?"

Dragan hesitated a moment.

"Lily," he said.

"She was let down by her friend at the last minute and so rang me."

Lila's hackles rose. Somehow this did not ring true. She remembered a similar happening with Tom- but that had been real, JJ had been unable to come to the opera. Meanly, she wondered if Lily had learnt of this from her brother. She said nothing so Dragan went on.

"It wasn't a play in the theatre, but it was a live film of the Richard the Third being performed at Stratford. Very good to be able to see the actors up close. Ralph Fiennes was amazing."

Lila had seen this type of thing.

"Yes, it is good – but somehow the feeling of being there, part of it all, is missing. There is a sense of detachment."

She thought for a minute then said,

"I saw Richard the Third at Stratford once, on a school trip. The scene in London where they are trying to "persuade" him to become king was marvellous. Some of the actors came up into the balcony where we were and behaved as though we were all the crowd, inciting him on. They got us to stand up and shout. Of course, we loved it; being teenagers some of us shouted quite inappropriate things, but we were involved and the magic of the theatre washed over us. It was unforgettable, and I think helped us to do well in the exams."

"Maybe we could take your Mum to the theatre this summer in Regent's Park? It is open air so there is some noise from birds, traffic etc, if she spoke out it wouldn't matter too much."

"What a good idea! I think she'd love it. If she doesn't we could always leave at the interval. Let's take a picnic to have beforehand. Dragan, you are so full of good ideas. The curry was great, by the way."

"It wasn't, it was too dry, but never mind. Grace liked it."

"She did and so did I. Now I'll wash up."

Sensibly Lila did not pursue the matter of Lily any further.

CHAPTER 29

Next morning she met Dragan in the hall as he was leaving, early, for work.

"Gosh you are keen!"

"Oh, I have got a lot to do, and I want to get away early tonight."

"Something special?"

"No, not really. I just asked Lily out for supper as a thank you for Richard the Third."

"Oh. " Lila's face fell involuntarily, "Have a lovely time. Where are you going?"

"Cote Brasserie in Charlotte Street, it looks good in the reviews."

"Well, have fun."

Lila turned away to the kitchen to make breakfast.

Later that morning what Lila regarded as the breakthrough signal came. Just as she was going out with her bicycle Grace held out her hand with something white and rectangular in it.

"Darling", she said," please could you post this for me?"

"What is it?"

"It's a letter to Hope. I haven't written to her for ages- so last night when I couldn't sleep I put the time to good use and wrote her a letter."

"Oh, Mum."

Lily was overcome. This was such an advance in Grace's behaviour. Grace had not written anything down for over a year. She took the letter and gave Grace a kiss on the cheek, awkwardly because of the bicycle in between them.

Grace just smiled, please with the approbation.

As she wobbled off with the letter in her pocket Lily wondered whether she was entitled to steam it open and read it, simply in order to check that it was literate enough to send. Not from any other curiosity of course, she assured herself. She considered the matter whilst cycling and the letter was still in her pocket when she arrived at the laboratory.

Having decided, she went to the coffee room, filled and put on the kettle. The envelope was difficult to prise open, even after two steamings. Lila did not want to damage it, so was very careful and gentle. Eventually she had the flap up. Without making her usual coffee she returned fast to her cubby hole to take a look.

The address on the envelope was correct, though written in a fairly childish hand. Inside there was a single sheet of paper in the same childish writing which read,

"Dear Hope,

It is so long since I wrote to you. I am very sorry but I have been unwell. There was something not right in my mind. Now that I feel better I can again put pen to paper and tell you about life here in London.

Lila is very busy with her work. She rides a bicycle to get there and this worries me terribly, but I do not say anything because I know she already senses this and would be angry if I spoke about it. She has been absolutely wonderful during my illness, taking good care of me whilst continuing to work. It is her that I have to thank for the tablets which have helped me to turn the corner back to good health. Now I think that my mind is functioning nearly as well as it ever did - I still forget some words but they usually come back to me later if I spend time not trying to remember, funny that, isn't it?

We have a lodger, a very nice young man whom I call Dragon, though that is not exactly his name it is close enough. He is a journalist and is tidy and clean. What is more he adores Lila, though I am not sure she realizes how much. I have advised him not to pursue her too hard but to give her time to appreciate him. She can never be pushed into anything, but has to follow her own ideas.

Being quite wicked I suggested that he should go out with some other girls – to make Lila realize that he is a good catch. Scheming old busybody, I suspect you are thinking. Well, you know me well enough.

How are you, dearest sisiter? Do you remember that is how I used to refer to you- as my sisiter, before I could pronounce it properly. Please wirte and tell me all your news.

Thinking of you with much love,

Grace XXX."

Apart from the spelling mistake at the end- her mother had probably been getting sleepy – the letter made sense. Not only that, but Grace was aware of what was going on in the household and was even trying to manipulate events. Lila wondered about the evening with Lily at the cinema - had it even been real? Was Dragan really seeing Lily tonight? Her emotions were in turmoil - pleasure at her mother's return of ability, anger that she was being analysed and subtly directed, embarrassment that Dragan apparently cared so much for her when she thought of him more like a brother. Or did she?

The one clear thought was that she needed her coffee, so she headed to the coffee room to make it. When she returned Lila felt calmer and did what was usual to her when troubled: turned to concentrate on her work.

She opened the Excel spreadsheet and began to perform analyses using different variables: patient age, sex, age at onset of disease. Soon she was so caught up in this that the personal matters were temporarily forgotten.

Tom arrived at lunchtime, post ward round.

"Hi Lila, what have you turned up?"

"Well there is a trend for early onset disease to respond better, not quite significant, but the numbers are very small. The same is true of a short history."

"Please can I take a look?"

"Sure," Lila moved out of her seat to let Tom access the computer. As she did so she was once again aware of the smell of him, that heady mix of male perfume and sweat, which acted on her like a pheromone. She was reminded of the pretty box tree moths which fluttered willingly into the capture canister and away from the precious box hedge, drawn by chemical scent alone.

Tom was studying the spreadsheet.

"I have highlighted the good responders", Lila explained, on the basis of their PET scans, that being the most objective value we have. However, the clinical tests correlate pretty well with the PET changes."

"Are they in the order in which we saw them?"

"Yes, I haven't altered that. But I could group them into responders and non – responders if you like."

"No, but I was just thinking of something - you remember our first patient did not do well, but the next ones did."

"Yes."

"Well I just wondered if racial origin might matter, the first was Caucasian, the next two not. In fact, I do not remember a single Caucasian success, can you?"

"No, I don't" said Lila, "let's check."

Ethnicity was something that she had, inadvertently or possibly deliberately following a subconscious impulse, omitted from the final spreadsheet. By going back to the list of patients, held separately, she was able to insert this additional variable.

Tom was right, all the responders were non-white. The result was statistically significant.

"OMG", Lila expostulated, "we have found a racist drug."

"The Daily Chronicle will be delighted," laughed Tom.

They high – fived.

"We must let EF know, he'll still be in his office, I think," Tom reminded her. "Let's go together."

They were warmly received, and the reception improved when EF was made aware of their findings.

"This is extremely important data", EF explained. "Among various explanations it could possibly means that Alzheimer's dementia is not one single disease - that would explain the failure of so many drugs thus far. My congratulations to you both."

Lila and Tom beamed at each other.

"The next vital thing is to get this out there as quickly as possible. It will be accepted by a major journal. Do not speak of it to anyone until it has been accepted for publication."

"What about Professor Armstrong, the Daily Chronicle proprietor, Lila's Mum?" asked Tom.

"No-one" said EF firmly. "You will prejudice acceptance by a journal if the results have been leaked beforehand. So off you go and get this done quickly. Bring what you have written to me tomorrow please."

Their faces fell and they left the office quietly, but once beyond EF's hearing they grumbled to each other about the tight schedule.

"Bloody hell, that was a short time of happiness, "Tom complained.

"Never mind," Lila cajoled him, "we can get something together for him to criticize quite quickly , using the wording for the grant application and putting it into the past tense, then adding the results, mainly as figures."

"True, let's go."

They crammed back into Lila's cubby hole and set to work, taking it in turns to sit at the computer and write.

By the end of the day they had a draft paper, apart from references and figure legends.

"I am shattered," said Lila," I can't think straight anymore."

"Me neither," admitted Tom. "But I can't work on it any more tonight as my parents are in London. Lily and I are having supper with them."

Lila's ears pricked up. Lily could not be having supper with Dragan tonight then. He had been fibbing to her.

"Oh," she said, "I hope you have a lovely time all together."

"It is not purely social, unfortunately. My Mum has just found a lump in her breast - it could be malignant - so she's coming to see a surgeon today. She didn't tell us anything until last night - didn't want to worry Lily and me unnecessarily. It could be a miserable meal."

"Tom, I am so, so sorry. What a worry for you. I hope that the lump turns out to be benign."

"Thanks Lila, much appreciated."

He changed the subject.

"I'll see you in the morning. We can give EF what we have done so far. There's no point in doing the references until we have a final version anyway."

Tom left, his face flushed and close to tears. He had obviously suppressed his worries while they were working, but had to face them that evening. Lila knew the score. She felt helpless. She was still acutely aware of how much her own mother's wellbeing mattered to her and of her enormous relief that Grace's condition had improved.

She picked up her rucksack and went to get her bike for the trip home. Whilst pedalling hard through Regent's Park, which felt cleaner than the polluted main roads, she was wondering whether Dragan would appear, or whether he would pretend to be out with Lily. Her attention was not as focused on the road as usual, so when white van man overtook her at high speed she failed to register it. Therefore she was not prepared when he swerved in to park a short way in front of her and pushed open the driver's door without looking. Lila had nowhere to go - there was something on her outside so she could not swerve round the door. She braked hard, hit the car door, and then had her first and only experience of independent flying.

CHAPTER 30.

Dragan had been saddened by Lily's phone call postponing their dinner date, in part because her Mum was ill, but mainly because he'd been looking forward to it. He really liked Lily- she was beautiful, blonde, uncomplicated and easy. Going somewhere with her was fun and he was aware of the envious looks he received in her company.

He had also thought Grace's advice about Lila - to take someone else out sometimes - was good. They had been sliding into a brother – sister relationship ever since he had moved into the house, and that was not what he wanted. He liked Lily, but he loved Lila, had done ever since he first saw her. Somehow, he had known then that she was the woman for him, otherwise he would never have even considered sending the Metro message. He was unsure of exactly why he had fallen so quickly for Lila. She too was beautiful, but not uncomplicated and not always easy, but he understood her, cared about her, needed her. He had known simply from seeing her that she would be clever, funny and sometimes difficult, almost as though he had known her before in some previous existence. It was as if she was the missing part of the jigsaw puzzle of his life.

He decided to see if Lila would like to join him at Cote – so rang her mobile.

The paramedics had just finished doing what they could and were closing the Ambulance doors when there was the sound of a mobile phone. It was coming from the other side of the road - in fact from a rucksack that might have been thrown there by the impact. One of them went to collect it, pulled out the phone, which was remarkably still functioning, and answered.

****
****

That same day found Susan in Oxford for a meeting at Immunogenomics to review the progress of their putative anti-dementia drug list, with particular reference to IG0047F. It had taken all morning even though the findings from the ongoing study in real patients were not yet available. Susan felt it had been largely unnecessary as she had already contributed what she could at the previous meeting, but it meant a day out from London and she was currently glad of a break in her routine. She felt rather excluded from the excitement of the work on patients at her own hospital and that was almost the only current topic of conversation in her lab.

Although she would not have admitted it to herself, there was a small part of her wanting to see Dermot Banks again, if only to give him a piece of her mind. Lila had not told Susan of the job offer from Dermot, nor of the fact that it would have entailed dropping her current research on colchicine. She had however mentioned it briefly to Shannon who had spoken later to Ann, Susan's secretary and unofficial set of ears. When Ann dropped a hint about possible poaching of Lila by immunogenomics Susan feigned disinterest, but when Ann also said that there was a clause about stopping the work Lila was doing now Susan could not control her anger and disappointment. She returned to her office in high dudgeon and began to dial Dermot's number - but then thought better of it and simply avoided him thereafter, not taking his calls or replying to his e-mails.

Today's invitation was not from Dermot but came from a central organizer – so Susan had decided to attend. She had greeted Dermot coolly when she arrived, just as the meeting was beginning, now that it was ending, she gathered her computer and belongings preparatory to the journey back. Dermot came and stood in front of her.

"Susan, please could I speak to you for a moment?"

Susan looked up.

"Fire away."

"Not here, somewhere more private please. I have some important things to say."

"Where do you suggest?"

"Not at my office. Perhaps I could take you to my house, we could have a quick lunch there if you like. It isn't far."

Then he added,

"Did you come here by car?"

"No, I took the train."

"Then I can drop you at the station afterwards."

She nodded. They left together in Dermot's Porsche, driving to a large house in North Oxford, with little conversation.

It was the garden which took Susan by surprise. She had not thought of Dermot as a garden person and the delightful array of lupins, hollyhocks and cosmos, plus others which Susan could not name made her smile. She had very happy memories of helping her father in the garden as a child.

"Oh, what a lovely garden. Do you do it yourself?"

"You haven't seen anything yet."

Dermot unlocked the front door and shepherded her through the house and into the rear kitchen with its double doors to the seemingly enormous space beyond. It had been cleverly designed so that not all was immediately visible: the eye was led from one curving side to another, colour repetition aiding the process. At the back, a hedge with an archway through it covered in roses, led to somewhere new.

"Heavens, it is magnificent."

"Thank you. It takes up most of my spare time now. Once the kids got older I decided to get rid of the big grass play area and make it into a proper garden."

"Did you design it?"

"Yes, but I had help from a friend down the road. She's a garden designer and put me right when my ideas got too fanciful. Shall we walk round it?"

"Yes please."

They strolled along the York stone path which wound between the planted areas. The smells of lavender and then mint arose as they brushed past overhanging plants. Susan, forgetting her disapproval, asked questions about the names of various plants and where Dermot had obtained them. It turned out that he grew many from seeds and propagated others, as well as buying from catalogues and nurseries. He knew the Latin names of nearly all of them. Susan was both surprised and impressed.

Beyond the hedge was a greenhouse and a small vegetable garden, both neat and productive. Dermot removed a few tomatoes from the vines, picked lettuce, rocket and chicory, together with a handful of parsley.

"Shall we eat outside?" he asked.

The impromptu lunch was light and delicious. Dermot made a salad, added fresh bread and cheese to the table, returned to the kitchen and emerged with a bottle of white wine. Susan recognized it as a Chablis, her favourite.

"Oh no, thank you", said Susan," I have to work this afternoon."

"As you wish, sparkling or still water?"

"Sparkling please."

They sat companionably, eating and making small talk. Susan realized that she needed to leave soon in order to make a further meeting at the university.

"What was it you wanted to say to me?" she asked.

"Sorry," said Dermot, "sorry for being so stupid about your post doc, Lila. I should never have tried to steal her from you."

"It was not just the poaching of a good scientist, Dermot. It was the fact that you tried to stop her research. That is unacceptable."

"But I knew that if it were worthwhile it would be carried on by someone else in your department."

"And how do you think Lila would feel about that?"

"Not good obviously. I had not thought it through. I was trying to do my best for Immunogenomics, but I failed to consider the consequences. Now that I have, I am genuinely sorry."

Susan was not inclined to forgiveness.

"Thank you for apologising. I think that I need to go to the station now please.

"Of course, I'll get the car."

On the journey to the station Dermot tried to return to the subject of Lila and colchicine. Susan was not to be drawn on either. She realized that she was being pumped for possible information about the ongoing trial and wisely kept silent, changing the topic back to the garden.

****
****

Grace was enjoying the afternoon, sitting outside in a deck chair, a cup of tea and a slice of cake on a small table beside her. Mrs D was beside her and they were chatting about local matters - the theft of a car which had been in a neighbouring street having provoked their ideas on the current lawlessness of society. For Grace, being able to recall memories was still a delight - she had spent so long in a state of anxious unknowing that just being able to hold a proper conversation was a source of happiness.

The topic was changed by Mrs D.

"How is that nice young man getting on with Lila?"

Grace grimaced slightly, "Not as well as I hoped. She likes him, no doubt, but I don't think there is that spark there for her. He adores her, anyone can tell. Anyone but Lila, that is."

At that moment the telephone in the house trilled out its imperative notes.

Grace hesitated, hoping that it would stop and that she needn't get up; but it went on ringing so she eased herself up from the chair and went to it.

"6045" she said into the receiver.

"Grace, Grace, is that you?" The male voice sounded desperate

"Yes Dragan, it is me. What's up?"

"It's Lila. She came off her bike. She's in hospital. Grace we need to go there now. I am on my way to get you and take you there. Please get ready."

"Oh Lord. Is she badly hurt?"

"They don't know yet. I rang her mobile and the paramedic had just picked it up. He told me to get hold of the next of kin as soon as possible and ask them to go to the hospital."

Both Dragan and Grace were silent, digesting the implications of what the paramedic had said.

Grace rallied.

"I'll be ready in 5 minutes."

"Great, I'm in an Uber - we'll take that back to the hospital as soon as I pick you up - should be about 10 minutes, I think."

The Uber ride seemed to take forever; Dragan held Grace's hand. She longed to be able to do something, anything, not just sit there in a traffic jam. She was determined not to sob, although something was making her swallow hard and sniffle. At last they arrived at the entrance to A&E in the same university hospital where Lila worked. Grace could not trust herself to speak, so Dragan went up to the desk to enquire after Lila. He came back to the now seated Grace.

"We have to wait here until she is back from the X ray department. Someone will come and speak to us soon."

He stood beside Grace, his left hand resting gently on her shoulder, there being no more free chairs. Like the taxi ride, this wait seemed to take an unconscionably long time. Eventually a young man in theatre scrubs came up to them,

"Are you the relatives of Lila Fraser?"

"Yes", said Grace. "How is she?"

"Come with me and I'll explain."

They followed him to a small room with a couch and lots of equipment, quite a terrifying space for them both. The doctor indicated that they should perch on 2 small stools, while he sat on the couch.

"Lila came off her bike in the park. Apparently a car door was opened immediately in front of her and she had no time to avoid it. She hit it and somersaulted over the handlebars and over the door, landing on her back on the road and sliding along. Her life was probably saved by a quick—thinking taxi driver who was just overtaking her at the time. He managed to avoid hitting her, then protected her by parking his taxi next to her. While he gave first aid his passenger rang 999 for an ambulance and the police."

"Thank the Lord", said Grace, beginning to hope.

"Thank heavens he had first aid training too. He had the sense not to move her and realised that although Lila's heart was beating she was not breathing- so he gave her artificial respiration until the paramedic arrived, fortunately within a few minutes."

"How is she now?" asked Dragan.

"Lila is unconscious and is being ventilated at the moment. She is down in x-ray as we need to check for fractures and see what has happened to her brain and her spinal cord. She also has some burns on her legs from road contact- fortunately she was wearing jeans and a rucksack which took the brunt of that."

"Will she recover?" asked Grace anxiously.

"Impossible to say yet, I'm afraid. I will speak to you again when we have more information."

"Can we see her?"

When she comes back from X- ray she will be put in this cubicle until she is transferred to ITU. If you wait here you can have a few minutes with her."

More waiting. Grace realized that she was hungry but did not want to leave just in case Lila returned and they missed her. Dragan did not think they could bring food into the cubicle- so they waited, stomachs rumbling, scared and uncomfortable.

The squeaking of wheels alerted them to Lila's return. The curtains parted and there she was, pale as death, a tube in her mouth attached to a machine which was making breathing noises. Her face was not scarred (something for which Grace gave thanks, although she knew it was of minor importance now), she looked ethereally beautiful, like Sleeping Beauty. That analogy occurred to both of them – and in response they kissed her cheek gently in turn, speaking quietly into her ear, reassuring her of their presence and their love.

After a few minutes a large nurse entered and explained that Lila was to be moved to ITU now.

"Can we stay and see her there?" asked Dragan.

"You can, in our relatives' room .I'll take you there."

Grace found a comfortable chair and began to doze, Dragan felt the need to pace up and down. After nearly two hours the door opened. Dragan's heart missed a beat. A different nurse put her head round the door, introduced herself and asked if they were Lila's relatives. Dragan nodded, unable to speak.

"She is comfortable now and stable. Nothing is likely to change in the next few hours. You'd do better to go home and get some sleep and come in tomorrow. Please can I check that we have your contact details?"

The nurse took these down and handed Grace a leaflet about ITU with phone numbers and visiting times. She bade them goodnight.

Dragan led Grace out of the cubicle and out of the hospital. Their thoughts were in turmoil. Once in the street Grace remembered all the things she had not asked and suggested they go back in. Dragan steered her away, towards a small café he knew and bought them both a beer and a burger. Grace, somewhat surprisingly, loved beer, having developed a taste for it during her married years. They spoke little whilst enjoying the relief of their hunger and felt better afterwards.

"What do we do now? I feel so impotent." Grace complained.

Dragan took charge.

"We go home, get some sleep and ring up first thing to find out how she is."

Grace found that she was content to be taken in hand and followed Dragan to Euston for the train to Queen's Park.

That night she prayed as hard as she ever had for Lila to survive, and, if God willed it, to survive and be her old healthy self.

CHAPTER 31.

The family supper was going well. Tom had taken them to a restaurant which he knew his mother had wanted to visit for some time. She loved Italian food and the River Café was for her just the perfect place. Tom's father, as Tom well knew, would have preferred an English establishment, but since Caroline was not well her needs took precedence. The food was good, the wine too and soon they were talking over each other, laughing and recalling old holidays, birthdays, the way happy families do. When Tom's mobile rang he was annoyed that he had forgotten to switch it to silent mode and was tempted to ignore it, but curiosity led him to check who had called him. It was Peter, his opposite number on the Neuro team. He felt impelled to answer and, excusing himself, left the table and went outside to do so.

"Hi Peter, what's up? I'm not on call tonight."

"Hi, Tom, I know, you swapped with me, but something has happened that I think you'd want to know about."

His grave tone of voice worried Tom.

"What is it?"

"It's Lila, she's in A&E with a head injury and possibly a spinal one too. She came off her bike."

"Oh no. Poor Lila. How is she?"

Peter gave Tom as much detail as he knew.

"I'm coming in to see her – it'll take me 30-40 minutes to get there. Have you given her any tranexamic acid?"

"What?"

"Tranexamic acid – it helps to stop bleeding, improves the outcome in head injuries. Recent data."

"Do you think I should give it to her?"

"Ask EF – he is the Consultant on call tonight. He has probably read the paper; if not the look it up yourself and discuss with him. I'll be there as soon as I can."

Tom returned to his smiling parents and sister and told them the news. Lily, who of course knew Lila, was most upset. She urged Tom to go to the hospital to see if he could help, his parents, realising that Lila was someone of importance to Tom, seconded that. He kissed them all, paid the bill and hurried out into the night.

Like Dragan and Grace, Tom found the journey took much longer than expected. He had a copy of the Evening Standard to read, but found that he could not take the words in, he kept reading the same paragraph over and over.

Peter texted to let him know that Lila was now in ITU, so Tom went straight there. As soon as he entered the room he could see the tall figure of EF stooping over a bed. Tom joined him.

"How is she, Prof?"

EF looked round.

"Hello Tom. Glad you've come. She is badly hurt, but hard to say just how badly yet. She is unconscious and being ventilated – we'll keep her like that for a few days to allow recovery. Peter asked me about tranexamic acid- told me you had suggested it. I checked the paper, the outcomes are slightly better in those who received it, so I have given her some in addition to routine management with dexamethasone."

Tom looked at the sleeping figure in the bed, tubes emerging from its mouth, its veins. It was hard to associate it with the lively, vivacious girl he knew well. His heart sank.

EF saw his distress and thought of a way to divert him.

"Tom, the best thing that you can do for Lila is to get that paper finished and off to a journal. Go home now and get some sleep, then work on it tomorrow in any spare moments."

"Yes, I'll do that." Tom bent to stroke the hand that was lying on top of the sheet, said

"Goodnight Lila, see you tomorrow" and hurried from the ITU before the tears in his eyes were noted by EF.

The only one who slept well was Lila. Dragan, Grace and Tom all found themselves too upset and anxious to fall into slumber, even EF tossed and turned. Next morning Tom arrived first in the ITU to check on Lila. There was no obvious change apart from the bruising which was becoming apparent. He did as he was bid and went to Lila's cubicle, opened her desktop computer to which she had previously given him the password and began to read through what she had written. Fortunately she had saved the data there as well as on her laptop.

Dragan and Grace met on the upstairs landing, both aiming for the bathroom. Dragan gave way and went downstairs to put the kettle on.

"Should I call the hospital?" he shouted up the stairs.

Grace did not reply. Dragan thought that she had not heard, so tried again, half-way up the stairs.

Grace emerged from the bathroom.

"Please, I am too scared to do it."

Dragan eventually got through to the ward to hear the report that there was no change in Lila's status. They could visit later that morning, after the ward round. He told Grace, then set about making the tea and toast, setting the pattern for many future days.

Lila now looked like a Sleeping Beauty who had done 10 rounds with Mike Tyson. She had remained unconscious and was still on a ventilator with a drip in her arm. Grace and Dragan were told this before they took it in turns to sit beside the bed, as only one visitor at a time was the usual ITU rule.

"I might as well go in to work," said Dragan after half an hour at Lila's bedside.

"Nothing is going to happen soon, I think."

Grace nodded. "Yes, but, if you don't mind, I'll stay a bit longer. I can manage to get home on my own."

"Are you sure?" Dragan was uncertain.

"Yes," said Grace firmly. "I go to Euston and get the Watford train, don't I?"

"Yes, platform 9 usually."

"Thank you, Dragan; and thank you for bringing me here today. "

"Oh Grace, you are most welcome. I just wish Lila hadn't had an accident," he replied wistfully.

"No good wishing, we just have to make the best of it. At least she is still alive, thank God."

Grace's brusque good sense reminded him of Lila and Dragan smiled.

"I'll see you back at home this evening."

"Sure, I'll have some supper waiting, provided nothing happens to Lila."

"Thanks, I'll look forward to it."

As he left Dragan reflected on the amazing improvement in Grace's abilities now that she was on regular colchicine.

"All thanks to Lila," he murmured to himself.

"Oh God, please let her get better too."

EF visited Lila on his ward round later that morning. He greeted Grace like an old friend, asking her to please wait outside until he had checked Lila, after which he would talk to her. Grace found herself in the waiting room, anxiously flipping through old magazines, none of which held any interest for her. She thought briefly of the gap in the market for a magazine that catered to the interests and needs of golden oldies like herself.

Eventually EF came to sit with her, leaving his retinue of junior staff and students outside.

"This must be a terrible time for you. I am so very sorry that it has happened."

Grace nodded. She did not trust herself to speak.

EF then explained that, although she had miraculously not broken any bones, it was still uncertain how badly Lila's brain had been injured even though she had been wearing a helmet.Time would tell whether she would recover completely or whether there would be residual damage. For the next few days she would be kept unconscious and treated to reduce brain swelling, then the sedation would be withdrawn and her condition could be properly assessed.

"Lila has youth and fitness on her side and she is the most remarkable fighter – as we both saw over the colchicine affair." He smiled. "I am optimistic."

He shook Grace's hand and left to return to his round.

Days passed and little changed. Lila's sedation was withdrawn, but she remained unconscious and needing to be ventilated. EF's heart began to sink, only to rise again slightly when she began to fight the ventilator and was weaned off it, still with a tracheostomy tube in place. Each day Lila was fed via a tube into her stomach, turned regularly and given passive physiotherapy. Grace kept vigil all day, except when displaced by the ward round or other medical issues. She talked to Lila, read to her, played her favourite music, all to no avail. Lila slept on, responding to nothing. Sometimes her eyes would open, but her gaze remained unfocused. The word vegetable was in everyone's mind, though never spoken.

When there had been no progress after two weeks EF announced on the ward round that it was time to find out if Lila had any conscious activity in her brain. It was just possible that Lila had Locked in Syndrome and that she could think, but could not make any movements. In vegetative patients about 20 % show brain activity in an MRI scanner. That means that 1 in 5 of them are aware but their doctors do not know this because they have no means of responding.

"How does that happen? "asked Tom.

"When the connection between the upper part of the brain and the lower parts is broken - any insult to the ventral pons can do it. We need to do a functional MRI. I will organise it after this round. Just tell her mother that we are going to do another scan, nothing more."

Tom did as he was asked. The scan was set for the following week, at a time convenient for the Radiology Department and EF. It was a complicated business getting Lila, still ventilated, down to the X-ray unit. Once she was in the scanner EF spoke to her.

"Good morning Lila, I hope you can hear me. If you can please imagine that you are paying a game of tennis."

Tom watched the screen with bated breath, Lila's brain lit up in the frontal regions. Tom breathed out slowly with relief.

"That was good Lila," said EF, "now we can use that for yes. If you want to answer no then please imagine that you are walking round your house. Let's try that now."

The screen showed a different pattern.

"Superb, well done Lila." "Now I am going to ask you some questions."

"Is your mother's name Mary?"

Lila signalled no.

"Is it Grace?"

Lila signalled yes.

In this way EF tested Lila's brain function- it was pretty good. She got one answer wrong, not unexpectedly, and that was the date. Lila thought it was a month earlier- she obviously had retrograde amnesia- loss of memory not only of the accident, but also of time before that.

EF spoke reassuringly to her, explaining about the accident, that she had sustained some brain damage, but that she could slowly and gradually recover.

Yes, she replied, using brain activity.

Lila was returned to the ITU; Tom asked EF what the chances of recovery were.

"Slim, Tom, I'm afraid," he replied. "Her chances of survival are good, about 80%, but only a handful recover fully. Even limited physical recovery enabling patients to return to live with their families improves quality of life though. We need to refer Lila to a rehabilitation service for specialist care and technology. Even something as basic as sniffing can be used to drive a computer, or even a mobility device now."

CHAPTER 32

Everyone was informed that Lila was indeed conscious, although she could not show it. Instructions were given to stimulate her in as many ways as possible, whenever possible. Grace continued her efforts, Dragan popped in each evening and related the news of the day, together with titbits from his own life. Tom spent any spare time with Lila, talking about their paper. Each of them felt somewhat idiotic, speaking into what seemed like a vacuum. But they carried on over weeks and weeks while the specialist referral unit tried to find a bed for her. Then she began to fight the ventilator- a good sign. She was slowly weaned off it – and could breathe on her own, still through the tracheostomy.

Tom was by her bed early one morning when the miracle happened and Lila's eyelids fluttered open and she looked at him.

"Lila, Lila, hello Lila," he said, smiling into her face. Her eyes shut again.

Tom thought EF should be told, having picked up his chief's great concern for her.

On hearing the news, EF hurried to ITU and spoke loudly and clearly.

"Hello Lila, have you come back to us?"

The eyelids opened again and Lila's large brown eyes were looking at him.

"Can you hear me?" EF asked.

Lila blinked once.

"One for yes, two for no, OK?"

Lila blinked again.

EF thought it worth reminding her.

"You had an accident, Lila. You are in hospital, getting better. We are not sure how much you can do right now. Can you grip my fingers?"

EF had taken her right hand in his. Nothing happened.

"No problem. I will let you get used to your surroundings and come back later."

He indicated for Tom to follow him and left the ITU. He turned to Tom, running his fingers backwards through his thinning hair, distractedly.

"Please see how she is in an hour or so. The breathing, and now this, are very good signs."

When he returned Lila was asleep again. He spoke her name and her eyes opened. She smiled, but did not speak.

"Hello Lila, EF has asked me to check you out. Is that OK?

One blink.

Tom performed a full neurological examination, somewhat embarrassed all the while. She was still unable to move any part of her body, except for her eyes. She could breathe, but not speak. Yet by blinking Lila was able to communicate with him in a yes or no fashion, so she was conscious.

"I need to tell EF."

One blink.

"Are you comfortable?"

Two blinks.

Tom was hard put to think how to work out what was wrong but went through a list of possibilities. Finally, it turned out that Lila wanted her mother.

"Grace comes in every day. She will be here soon."

One blink.

"See you later Lila. By the way our paper has been submitted, I had to get on with it. You are first author. I hope you don't mind."

Two blinks.

"Good. Then keep your fingers crossed."

Once he had said it Tom realized how crass this was, but Lila merely blinked once more.

What had been going on in Lila's mind? At first when she briefly surfaced she was unsure whether she was awake, in any case she felt too tired that she simply dozed off. Gradually the wakeful spells became longer. The trip down to Radiology had made her realise that something was badly wrong. Hearing EF's voice through the jungle drums of the machine had been reassuring, being able to communicate through thinking in different ways even more so.

"I am like Morbius in Dr Who," she thought," an isolated brain." For she had no sensation of having a body at all. When awake her mind roved around widely- she tried to remember the words of songs and of poems – and cursed herself for not having learnt many by heart, the way that Grace had. She thought lovingly of Grace and longed to see her. For, as yet, Lila had no vision.

The day that she was finally able to see was wonderful. She recognized Tom and could not at first cope with the effort of looking. She would have expected his examination of her to be an embarrassment but since she could feel nothing it was in fact very scary. She desperately wanted her mother.

Grace had been told that Lila could hear her but could only respond by blinking. She hardly listened, instead raced to Lila's bed and hugged her still daughter, laughing and crying at the same time. The lack of any comeback disconcerted her, she sat down on the only chair by the bed and said nothing, simply stroking Lila's hand while tears flowed down her cheeks. Dragan, who had brought her, saw the problem and going against the rules slipped to the bedside too and began asking Lila yes/ no questions.

"Are you OK?"

Two blinks

"What is the matter? Oh no, that won't do. Are you uncomfortable?"

One blink

"Too hot?"

Two blinks.

"Too cold?"

Two blinks.

"Hungry?"

Two blinks.

"Thirsty?"

One blink.

"I'll get a nurse." Dragan knew that Lila was being fed and watered via a tube into her stomach as she could not swallow.

The nurse obligingly wet Lila's mouth just a little and put some lubricant on her dry lips.

There was a silence while Dragan thought of what else to say.

"You are doing well" was what he finally came out with.

Lila's eyes widened. She blinked several times.

"Oh this is difficult, I want to know what you are thinking."

Silence. Grace stroked Lila's shoulder, oblivious to the fact that Lila felt nothing.

"I know. If I write out the alphabet on a card I can point to each letter in turn and you can blink for the right one. OK?"

One blink.

Dragan went off to the hospital shop to buy the necessary large piece of paper.

Grace leaned over and kissed Lila's forehead, being rewarded with a blink.

Dragan returned and wrote out the alphabet in 4 lines.

"Now Lila, you can talk to us like this. If the letter you want is on the first line please blink once, second line twice et cetera. Then once I know the line, I'll move my finger slowly across it and you blink when I reach the letter you want. OK?"

One blink.

Lila then blinked twice.

Dragan's finger went to the second line, Lila immediately blinked again.

H, said Dragan.

Lila blinked once, the 5th letter, E, was chosen.

L was next- by this time Dragan had guessed.

"Hello? "he asked.

Lila blinked once.

"It works! "Dragan was delighted.

HARD WORK spelled Lila. Then ACCIDENT.

"Yes, you came off your bike. Someone opened their car door and you hit it and went over it and skidded on your back down the road. Your rucksack took the worst of it, but your head had a nasty bang."

OUCH

"Do you hurt anywhere?" Grace asked.

Two blinks.

"Thank goodness" Then Grace thought that perhaps that was not the correct response.

HOW LONG

Dragan realized that he needed to add punctuation to his card and put a question mark after Z.

"You've been here two months. "

OMG

Dragan added an exclamation mark to the sheet.

WHEN HOME?

"We don't know. I think you have to ask EF that question."

COMPUTER?

"It was damaged, I don't know if it can be repaired."

OH DEAR!

"I'll find out for you. See what I can do."

THANKS.

TIRED NOW.

"OK, let's stop."

Grace said,

"I'd like to just sit with you for a while. Is that OK?"

LOVELY MUM.

They sat quietly side by side in a strange reversal of the time that an exhausted Lila had fallen asleep beside Grace's bed on her return from America. Both of them were aware of this, neither commented.

CHAPTER 33

The weeks went by whilst a bed in a rehabilitation unit was being sought. Lila, by now conscious for most of the day and part of the noisy night, was on the Neurology ward, in a small side room. She thought that her life must be like that of a small baby: fed and changed regularly, stimulated when possible, soothed from time to time, but totally unable to look after itself. She grew adept at using the prompt sheet, by now laminated. Kindly staff and visitors would put on the radio and adjust headphones onto her ears and she could specify what she wanted- Radio 4 usually, sometimes 3 or 2.The problem came when she wanted it turned off- with no use of arms or legs it was hard to attract attention – so often she endured unwanted voices in her ears without being able to tune out. Grace sat by her every day, Tom visited daily, as did Dragan. They cheered her up, encouraging her with stories of people who had recovered from being "locked in". Dragan bought and read for her, chapter by chapter, The Diving Bell and the Butterfly, written by journalist Jean Dominique Bauby, describing his life before and after suffering a stroke that left him with locked-in syndrome. Lila cried when she was told that the author died soon after finishing the work. However, she wanted more books, so Dragan gave her his e-reader and helped her to subscribe to audiobooks – these turned out to be a lifeline.

Christmas came and went. It was a parody of a celebration for all of them; but they did their best, giving Lila new books, music and pyjamas. Lila thought longingly of her beautiful green dress. A visit from Susan was horribly embarrassing. Susan, having brought flowers which were disallowed by the nurses, had little to say to Lila other than stuff about work. Once that was finished there was a rather tense silence for a while then Susan announced that she had to leave for a pressing engagement. She was uncertain how to do so, bending forward as if to kiss Lila's forehead she suddenly thought that might be inappropriate and settled for patting the unresponsive right hand. Lila wished that she could sign PHEW!, but there was no-one to help her do so.

After Christmas, Lila began to slip into sadness as there was no sign of any return of sensation in her body. She began to feel that her life was hardly worth living and that she was a burden to her mother and to everyone else. She felt miserable each morning when she awoke to face another of what she termed her "useless days." It was a particularly bad morning in February when Dragan called in on his way to the airport. Lila felt so envious of his ability to travel that she wept.

"What is it? Can I do anything?" Dragan hated to see her sobbing.

"KILL ME" Lila spelt out.

"Oh, my darling I could never do that." His face crumpled and he picked up the hand that he had been holding and kissed it several times.

"I love you so much, Lila"

It was a lightbulb moment for Lila. She realised what an idiot she had been. She blinked rapidly, indicating that she wanted to "speak."

Dragan held up the page with letters. Lila blinked twice.

Dragan's finger moved to the second row and began moving slowly along, watching Lila's eyes. They blinked when he reached L. Two blinks meant second row again, with a blink at I, L again, then last row and a Y.

"Lily? You thought that I loved Lily?"

One blink.

"Oh, no my darling. I like Lily, I am very fond of her. But you are the love of my life."

He looked at Lila's face, she was smiling, so he continued.

"I saw you in the street a couple of times before we bumped into each other at the gate. It was that instant attraction you spoke about, ionic, I think. I just knew that I had to get to meet you. I also already knew what you would be like. It was as if I recognised you from a past life. Your cleverness, diffidence, self-protectiveness and humour were a given. None of it came as a surprise. I realised that there was no instant attraction for you to me, that I would have to play a long game. Helping with Grace was a pleasure, it was also a gift to keep me near you. I hoped that in the end you would learn to love me; but thought I had failed."

He paused, Lila was all attention.

"So, I started seeing Lily. Partly because she is pretty, fun, good company, but also hoping that you would be just a little bit jealous. Perhaps you might decide that I was not simply like a brother to you."

Dragan deliberately omitted Grace's role in this, knowing that it would have antagonized Lila.

She blinked several times, the alphabet paper came out.

Row 2, I

Row 2, L

Row 2 O

Last row, V

Dragan's eyes dilated, his pulse quickened.

E YOU TOO

"You do? Really, really love me?"

Lila blinked once.

Dragan leaned forward, still clutching her hand, bending her arm at the elbow in order to kiss her lips, very gently, then more comprehensively.

He sat back to study Lila's face.

She blinked several times.

"What?"

FELT SOMETHING IN MY SOLAR PLEXUS!

"Is that good?" Dragan had no idea what the solar plexus was.

I THINK SO KISS ME AGAIN PLE

He did not wait for the politeness.

As luck would have it Lily had decided to visit on the same morning as she had no early lectures. She reached the partly open door of Lila's room and peeped round it. Neither occupant noticed her, so she slowly backed away, blinking and hurried from the ward.

She was looking down, trying not to cry and almost bumped into Tom.

"Hi Sis, how are you?"

"Fine, fine. Lovely to see you Tom, but I have got to get to a lecture. Speak later."

Tom, having seen her pale, red - eyed face, watched her rushing down the stairs, wondering what was the matter. He wondered whether to run after her- but decided against it, Lily would explain later, no doubt. He had important news for Lila.

Dragan had just left Lila's bedside by the time Tom arrived.

"Hi Lila. Great news, our paper has been accepted. It will be out online very soon and in the journal in a few weeks. Dragan can tell his editor once the online paper is out. Lila you will be famous!"

THANK YOU. FAME NOT GOOD. PAPER IS.

Life was rapidly improving.

It seemed as though her midbrain had been sleeping and was now gradually waking up again. When the physio came that day Lila felt something, painful, but welcome, when her legs were moved.

She spelt this out to EF on the ward round.

LEGS HURT

EF was very happy.

"That must mean that some impulses are getting through the part of your brain which was not working. Perhaps that means that the problem is not that the fibres are broken, but that they were bruised, so to speak. The fact that you can breathe is unusual- so I am optimistic about further improvement. Keep going Lila, you could get a lot better."

NORMAL?

"I don't know, I wish I could say that; but I really just do not know."

Lila blinked once.

Dragan was away for two days which seemed like an eternity to Lila. She spent the time going over and over the reasons why she had kept him at arm's length for so long and found none of them convincing, except that she had been blinded by her adoration for Tom. Grace came each day as usual. Lila wanted to tell her about Dragan kissing her, but also did not want to, in case it turned out to be all a dream. She also did not want the "I told you so" which Grace was unlikely to express, but which she would certainly be thinking .But Grace noticed the change in Lila's face.

"What's happened sweetheart? You look happier than I have seen you for ages."

FELT SOMETHING

"Oh, how fantastic! Oh child I am so pleased."

Grace leaned sideways and kissed Lila but there was no solar plexus sensation this time.

However, the leg pain returned when they were moved and there was also something uncomfortable in her arms too. When Dragan walked in 48 hours later he was alarmed by a guttural sound from Lila's throat. She was trying to say hello.

Her ability to use her brain to control her body returned remarkably quickly and was practically complete by two months. The request for a rehabilitation place was cancelled and Lila was given intensive physiotherapy every day in the ward and then even outside. She was weak, her muscles having atrophied from disuse, and tired rapidly, needing to lie and rest after a few minutes walking. Her brain also felt scrambled after the effort of moving her and especially after trying to speak. At first she kept her sentences short, but gradually it became easier to get the right words out.

CHAPTER 34

The time came when Lila could cope well enough to return home. Grace got her room ready, Dragan

picked her up, together with all her belongings, in a black cab, thinking that this would be easier for

her to get into. The day coincided with the online publication of her and Tom's paper about the colchicine treatment results. Lila was excited, but felt too exhausted to cope with the volume of

e- mails that she received as a result. Dragan was also thrilled as it meant that his paper could now

release the whole story. He helped Lila into the house, then asked if she minded if he went to work.

"Of course not," she said," Go. I'll be fine."

He kissed her tenderly and left to talk to the Editor about what would go into the Daily Chronicle

story. The proprietor was in on the meeting and was clearly impressed with Dragan's knowledge of

dementia gleaned from Lila.

Next day the headline was

"A CURE FOR ALZHEIMER'S?" in huge letters, with a byline, "Research sponsored by the Daily Chronicle."

Dragan had done a good job in explaining what had happened and had, as requested, left individual

names of researchers out, just mentioning the unit where the work had been done. He made it clear

that further studies were needed to identify which patients would respond. A website run by a

charity was given as the place to go for queries, their staff having been well briefed.

Grace was thrilled by the article as it mentioned that there had been an index patient who

happened to respond to colchicine which was given for other reasons. She did not comment on the

white lie involved as she knew it was necessary to protect Lila. However, Lila's role in identifying the improvement was there, although she was not named. Grace kept the article in a drawer for years.

Dragan was promoted as a result of his efforts in obtaining funding for the research which improved

the image of the paper. He raced home to tell Lila and in the same breath asked her to marry him.

"We don't need to get to know each other, we already do, and I can afford to look after you now."

"But what about Grace?"

"We can stay with her here, if she'll have us, but we can help her pay for things, look after her

when she needs it. You can recover at your own pace."

Lila was both ecstatically happy and very relieved. Once she had allowed the floodgates of her

feelings for Dragan to open she found that she adored him without reservation and longed for his

touch, but they were both too inhibited by Grace's presence to sleep together openly. Once engaged

this could change.

"Yes, yes please," she said.

Grace was predictably delighted by their news and soon began planning an engagement party. Lila

did not have the energy to protest, so a "do" in their house, and possibly the garden too, depending

on the weather, was organized.

It was great fun. Lila's family turned up, as did Dragan's, plus most of their friends and some work colleagues. The Spring day was unusually warm, so they spread out into the garden which was ablaze with daffodils and snowdrops. Champagne was drunk, then a buffet of mixed varieties of ethnic food

provided by both families proved delicious and ample. Some mates of Dragan brought their guitars and played and sang. Tom led the way with the dancing, gyrating onto the lawn, followed by Lily and soon even Grace had joined in. Ferid, who had come down from university was soon dancing with Lily and Tom took the opportunity to speak to Lila who was sitting in a chair watching her guests. He kissed her on the cheek.

"Lila, this is just fantastic. Things have turned out so well. I am really happy for you both."

"Thank you, Tom."

"EF has put in a Medical Research Centre grant application for a big multi-centre study of

colchicine in Alzheimer's with genetic investigations involved. He is quite hopeful that we'll get it,

thanks to you."

She still wanted to run her fingers through his curly hair- why? Then a memory surfaced from her

childhood and she understood. She smiled.

"I hope he does. And that I can be involved again when I am properly better."

"Absolutely. Would you like to dance?"

"No thanks. I don't have a lot of energy yet."

What she meant, but was too polite to say, was that what little energy she had would be spent

dancing with Dragan.

EF and Mercedes arrived late and apologetic - the small car had broken down halfway and they had been forced to abandon it and use the Tube. They remarked upon the beautiful garden and sat

together, sipping champagne and watching the dancers. Lila went to speak to them.

"Hearty congratulations," said EF, "not to you Lila, but to your young man for managing to catch

you. He has done very well for himself."

"Oh, I have done well too," said Lila, defensively.

"Of course you have, my dear. It is, however, not polite to congratulate the lady. It implies she has

been trying to get a husband whereas she is supposed to be a passive element."

"How old-fashioned."

"Yes, it is. However, I can congratulate you on your work and its publication which has created

something of a stir, you know."

"Has it?"

EF nodded and smiled.

"One of the most interesting comments came from Dermot Banks, the Immunogenics boss. He rang

me to congratulate us all, and to let us know that his company now holds all the rights to market

colchicine in the UK."

"Oh no!"

"It means that he will be able to set the price, which is not good news. It will compensate them somewhat however, because their monoclonal drug, on which you did some work, I think, turned out to be a bust in man."

"Poor Duncan, he was banking on that - sorry pun not intended."

"That is great Lila, don't apologize. Puns show that your brain is working well."

"Good, I'd like to return to work please when I feel less tired."

"You are Susan's responsibility, not mine. I would have you back tomorrow. Is she coming today?"

"No."

Lila did not expand further, the truth was that she had invited Susan, but was relieved when the

invitation was turned down. Susan was away for the weekend. In fact, Susan was on a Garden Tour

run by the Royal Horticultural Society as she was thinking of selling her flat and buying somewhere

with a garden to tend.

To change the subject Lila suggested,

"If Dermot Banks tries to charge a fortune for colchicine the Daily Chronicle might step in to help."

"I am sure your clever young man could organize that. He is just over there, why not ask him?"

Lila was happy to be sent in Dragan's direction. Slipping in beside him at the buffet table she took

his hand and raised her face for his kiss. He looked down at her radiant face and his heart felt fit to

burst with joy.

After the last guest had left Lila collapsed into the bed which she was now sharing with Dragan, leaving him downstairs loading the dishwasher. Grace came in to check on her. Lila was sleepy and a

memory returned to her, as sometimes happens when sleep returns.

"I didn't tell you before Mum, because I only remembered recently, that I had a lovely dream about Dad when I was unconscious."

"Did you sweetheart? What happened?"

"I don't remember how it began but he was there, very real, talking to me. It was funny because he

was dressed like Dr Who – you know, a big old-fashioned overcoat, long scarf and a hat. His curly hair was peeping out underneath it. I thought of how I used to love to run my fingers through it when I

was little and he was holding me. He told me that he loved me so much and was very proud of me

because of what I'd done to help you. Then he said that he would always be there for me, but that it

was not my time, I had to go back. He gave me a big hug and I smelled his special lovely smell again.

It was so comforting."

There were tears in her eyes.

Grace was thoughtful.

"Could he have been dressed as Sherlock Holmes?"

"Oh, how stupid I am, of course, that's it, he was Sherlock, nor Dr Who. The hat was a deerstalker."

"That is very interesting."

"Why?"

"Well, we went to a fancy dress party when I was very pregnant with you. I wore a Greek goddess outfit to cover the bulge which was you, he went as Sherlock. There are no photos of us like that, so

why should you see him that way? Did he ever mention it to you?"

"No."

"So perhaps he was sending us a message."

Grace was silent. Lila tried to digest what she was implying.

"You mean that it was not a dream? That somehow I met Dad again?"

"Yes, my darling. That is what I mean."

"Oh, heavens, I mean, wow, I hadn't thought of it like that. That is amazing."

They sat holding hands, tired but happy, thinking of the man they both loved.

THE END.

Printed in Great Britain
by Amazon

75916714R00158